CHECKPOINT

Jean-Christophe Rufin

CHECKPOINT

*Translated from the French
by Alison Anderson*

Europa
editions

Europa Editions
214 West 29th Street
New York, N.Y. 10001
www.europaeditions.com
info@europaeditions.com

Copyright © 2015 by Editions Gallimard, Paris
First Publication 2017 by Europa Editions

Translation by Alison Anderson
Original title: *Check-point*
Translation copyright © 2017 by Europa Editions

Library of Congress Cataloging in Publication Data is available
ISBN 978-1-60945-372-5

Rufin, Jean-Christophe
Checkpoint

Book design by Emanuele Ragnisco
www.mekkanografici.com

Cover photo © Philipp Nemenz/Gallery Stock

Prepress by Grafica Punto Print – Rome

Printed in the USA

CONTENTS

"God created men, Sam Colt made them equal."

CHECKPOINT

PROLOGUE

Central Bosnia, 1995

Marc stopped the truck, with no explanation.

"Give me the binoculars."

Maud took them out of the glove compartment and handed them over. He got out and stood at the edge of the road. She watched as he stared for a long time at the horizon.

Suppressing her pain, she managed to sit up and wipe the condensation from the windshield. From where they had stopped you could see a vast panorama, and if the weather had been better, they might have been able to see all the way to the Adriatic. With the falling snow they could still see most of the high plateau they had crossed. Without binoculars Maud could make out only a white expanse for miles around. Sometimes the road dipped into a hollow, and then it rose up again. They were stopped on a high point. To the south, the ruined towers of a medieval castle stood out against a leaden cloud filled with snow. Marc came back and tossed the binoculars onto the dashboard. More tense than ever, he turned the key in the ignition.

"What did you see?"

"They've been through here."

Maud didn't say anything. She could hear the spite in his voice. She was angry with herself for being injured and unable to drive. If their pursuers were able to take turns driving, Marc on his own would not be able to keep up the pace. He was certainly aware of this and must have been evaluating the consequences of their failure: the inevitable confrontation, the discovery of the cargo, perhaps even death.

Maud tried to move but it was hopeless. As soon as she held out her arms, she felt the pain in her back, so sharp she wanted to cry out.

"How far ahead are we, do you reckon?"

"Barely six hours."

"What can we do?"

He didn't answer and this angered her. As if she didn't matter. He seemed so hostile she could not help but recall what she had thought during the night. When it came to action, he was alone. It was the hidden side of his strength, the rules of the game in his world.

Maud felt like crying, and was annoyed with herself.

They drove in silence for almost an hour. Suddenly Marc stopped the truck again. He gave no explanation and without a word he went back out onto the road. First she saw him squat down in front of the cab and touch the frozen ground. Then he went out of sight, around the back. When he returned, he was covered in snow. It was coming down hard now, and in the space of a few minutes the windshield was covered in a white film.

Marc switched on the wipers and the landscape reappeared. It was then that Maud then saw the narrow track leading off to the left. It was covered in snow and she had not seen it initially. It was surely because of this track that Marc had stopped the truck at that particular place.

"Do you want to go up that way?"

He didn't need to answer. He had already turned the wheels to the left and was heading that way. The track was fairly steep for a few yards and the truck struggled. Then it rose more evenly. It was certainly a dead end, leading to a field or a barn.

"Do you think the snow will cover our tracks? Is that what you went to check?"

He merely nodded.

Then suddenly the track seemed to fade away. They were

surrounded by whiteness and there was no indication of where they should go. Unfortunately they had not gone far enough from the main road to stop. Marc got back out and walked through the snow to try to determine whether it was possible to drive farther up. Maud saw him disappear behind a hedge that the snowflakes were covering in white pom-poms.

She was at her wits' end, filled with a sort of rage, and she did not know whether it stemmed from despair, anger, or shame. She felt as if she had been making the wrong choices for a long time; perhaps she had always been making the wrong choices. She should never have followed this man, should never have made an exception for him to the caution that had always protected her from humiliation and suffering. And now she was here, injured, betrayed, cast adrift. She screamed.

Her long cry, initially shrill, then fading to a deeper note, gave her some relief. She tried again, but it wasn't natural anymore. She felt self-conscious. Her determination was coming back, if not her strength. She would not give in so easily.

Not long thereafter, Marc reappeared. At first he was only a shadow in the white shadow of whirling snow. Then she saw him, covered in snow, and he opened the door.

"Did you find a way through?"

As he did not answer, she ignored the pain that was searing through her back, and slapped him.

I
MISSION

1

This was the time in the truck that Maud liked best. The autumn evening was gently coming on; the cool air did not yet oblige them to roll up the windows. The Bakelite steering wheel was so wide you had to spread your arms to turn it. It transmitted the vibrations from the engine, and when she drove uphill Maud felt as if she were clinging to the neck of an enormous beast.

They had left Lyon ten days earlier. One day had followed another, each one much like the next, despite the variation in the landscapes. After the Mont Blanc tunnel they had driven through the Aosta Valley, then followed the plain of the Po down in its entire length. The late autumn gave a certain luminosity to everything far in the distance and emphasized the little black arrows of cypress trees against a deep blue sky. After Trieste the landscape became more mountainous, the colors drab. When they reached Croatia, Maud hoped they would stop in Zagreb. Before leaving, she had read a guidebook from the 1960s that her parents had bought when they went to Dalmatia on their honeymoon. She wanted to see Saint Mark's Square and the medieval buildings. But they drove around the outside of the city without going into the center and she kept her disappointment to herself. In Italy, Lionel had put her abruptly in her place when she asked to stop off in Bergamo. "We're aid workers, not tourists." He was in charge of the mission and he never missed an opportunity to remind her of the fact. The humanitarian organization in Lyon, La Tête d'Or (which got its name from the park nearby), had put him in charge of the convoy. And there, in Bosnia, the war was waiting for them.

Maud took her turn driving just like the boys. They had stopped joking about her driving already long before. It had been enough for Lionel to scrape the corner of a house in Italy and make a yard-long tear in the tarp for the men to stop talking tough. Maud might drive more slowly, but she was steady and cautious. The fifteen-ton truck did not risk a thing when she was behind the wheel, and the others knew this.

On the bunk behind her Vauthier was asleep. From time to time he gave a snort. The others all used their first names but he preferred to go by his last name. He even referred to himself as "fat Vauthier," no doubt to dispose them favorably to him. He wasn't really fat, and you could see more muscle than flab emerging from his grimy T-shirt. But he had a large square head, framed by ginger sideburns, and a flat nose, which gave him a countrified look that clashed with Maud and Lionel's student allure. He had introduced himself as a Parisian courier, convalescing after a traffic accident. They didn't really believe what he told them. But one thing was sure: he was much older than the others. Lionel thought he must be forty, and Maud, all of twenty-one, thought he was really old.

Lionel was rolling a cigarette in the front seat, not speaking. The cab smelled of fuel and dirty motor oil. Maud considered herself lucky all the same, because she was driving the lead truck and at least they didn't have to inhale the blue exhaust from their other vehicle. They were both secondhand trucks, roughly the same model, which La Tête d'Or had bought on the cheap. They were nearing the end of their useful life, worn out by generations of delivery drivers who had not treated them kindly.

"We're coming to the Serbian zone," said Lionel, handing her the cigarette he had just lit.

Maud took a quick draw on it then handed it back.

"Did you put something in it?" she asked, making a face.

"Tobacco."

Tall and thin, Lionel had a long and slightly crooked nose, and a pale, angular face. It was the sort of face that reminded you of many others, and a witness would find it difficult to give any precise description if called on to provide an Identikit. He must have known as much, and he tried to distinguish himself by wearing a silver loop in his right eyebrow. He and Maud had worked together in Lyon for three months. He had always treated her somewhat condescendingly, because he had more experience, and she was only a recent recruit. He was never very talkative, and when he did talk it was to bark an order. Those who were in the group knew he smoked joints from morning to night. It was not exactly that they minded, but no one smoked as much weed as he did. He was the group's dealer, and he kept his baggies of weed in a round box labeled "condensed milk."

The hilly countryside was increasingly poor as they drew near the Krajina. They went through deserted villages, strings of brick or breeze-block houses along the road. Piles of manure and rusty farm machinery filled the farmyards. From time to time, in the midst of the farms, a white church with a pointed steeple gave a hamlet a passing resemblance to an Austrian village, although drearier. They had not seen any traces of fighting yet, other than the struggle mankind has always waged against nature for survival. And yet they had known since the previous day that they were getting closer to the war zone.

"Shouldn't we be seeing checkpoints soon?" asked Maud, never taking her eyes from the road.

Lionel nodded.

"Yes, it shouldn't be long now."

Up to now they had crossed borders—in other words, the

official limits between states. Checkpoints were something else: unpredictable and shifting separations between ethnic zones that were under the authority of small local warlords. Those among them who had already been to Bosnia talked about them every evening. They didn't use the French term, *"point de contrôle,"* which might have made the thing seem almost normal. The stateless word in English, "checkpoint," used by everyone in the field, was a more apt representation of the improvised, disorderly, unpredictable, and dangerous aspect of these roadblocks. Maud was fairly eager to see what they were like.

The truck was struggling up the switchback road. It was six o'clock in the evening and the shadows were getting longer. It was time to find a place to spend the night. As she was coming out of a long bend, she heard a horn behind her. She looked in her big square rearview mirror, holding it to stop the vibration. An arm was waving from the door of the other vehicle, pointing left toward a big sandy entrance to a large deserted lot. It was plowed with ruts and must have been used as a construction site. An old pile of gravel in one corner had been invaded by wild plants. Maud braked, turned into the lot, and pulled over to the edge. The grass around the parking area was white with dust. Lionel got out to inspect the place.

In the cab, Maud leaned her head back to relax her neck muscles, strained from driving. Because the driver's seat would not go any farther forward, she'd had to put a big cushion behind her back in order to reach the pedals. She had stopped growing at the age of thirteen. Even though she was twenty-one now, she had never become reconciled to the fact that she wasn't taller. Little women are the object of ridiculous solicitude on the part of men, and she hated being treated like a bibelot.

"Okay," said Lionel when he came back, "we'll spend the night here."

Maud turned off the ignition. After several more intense shakes, the vibrations suddenly stopped. She relaxed. For her this was always a moment of complete contentment, an almost physical delight. The return of silence, while her body was still throbbing from the juddering of the diesel, was a true rebirth. The surrounding world was no longer a landscape but a place, with faint sounds and birdsong coming in the open window. The mass of metal cracked and let go, like a horse given free rein at last. It seemed to her she had desired nothing else when she chose this strange life her family failed to understand.

She opened the door and got out. This was the second moment of delight in the evening: stepping onto solid ground, the blood flowing in her legs again as she walked about, the subtle smells of nature as soon as she got away from the engine that stank of fuel. She took off her glasses and wiped them slowly with a corner of her fleece jacket. They were big, tinted glasses with thick frames that covered half her face. She had chosen them on purpose to hide her blue eyes, which had always earned her as many jealous remarks as compliments.

Over the final kilometers the road had climbed considerably and below them lay the plain, covered in thickets, which they had crossed. Around the parking area the grassy moor was scattered with huge white rocks. There were numerous flat spaces where they could pitch their tents.

Vauthier had woken up with a growl, and now he got out in turn, wiping his hand over his bald head. He always looked as if he were in a bad mood, probably because of his thin lips and drooping eyelids. But his little black eyes were in constant movement, searching everywhere, and they were all wary of him. Because it wasn't only his gaze that was searching. He couldn't help nosing around, eavesdropping on conversations, and whenever they stopped in a town he would disappear, then come back with a summary of all the little secrets in the place.

The others were convinced he was going through their belongings, too.

Alex and Marc, the drivers in the second truck, came over slowly, stretching.

It was always an awkward moment when the two teams met up again. Right from the start of the trip, a heavy, hostile atmosphere had reigned in the group. It was a gross understatement to say that the five members of the convoy did not get along. Things did not improve with the passing miles. Clans of convenience were formed. In the lead truck, because they knew one another, Maud and Lionel made one team; Alex and Marc, the two drivers in the other truck, were another. Vauthier did not hide his dislike for them. Every evening their reunion was tense.

"We'll be fine here," said Alex, looking at the area just beyond the parking lot.

Marc was inspecting their surroundings with a wary gaze.

Both of them were former soldiers. They were roughly the same age, no older than thirty, but they were very different. Alex was mixed race, with big, rather slanting eyes and a small nose. No one had asked him where he had gotten his copper skin and frizzy hair. Maud thought he was handsome, but she didn't want him to know. Marc, too, was sporty, but taller than Alex and with a massive build, broad-shouldered with a muscular chest and square jaw. His skin was olive, his hair very dark. He always seemed to be on the lookout, but he affected a calm, virile manner, and this had made Maud feel instantly uncomfortable. Alex had the lively elasticity of a tennis player, whereas you could picture Marc taking part in activities that called for strength, like rugby or boxing. But they shared a deliberate mannerism in their way of walking, of standing very straight and keeping their heads high. No matter how they tried to adopt the casual NGO style, wearing baggy jeans and faded T-shirts, they looked out of place. Military discipline had shaped them on a deeper level. You could still see the soldiers inside them.

The evening ritual had been the same since departure. The camping stove had to come out of the truck Maud was driving, and pots and pans out of the other truck. They had stocked up on canned food in Lyon, and it was stored in crates. They bought fresh produce along the way when they could find it. Since leaving Italy they hadn't found much other than eggs and milk, which the peasants poured out of big metal containers. Not far from Zagreb they had found fresh cheese; it was bitter, but Maud preferred it to canned cassoulet.

Every evening Vauthier would light the camping stove or build a fire, something he seemed to like to do. They took turns with the cooking chores. From the start they had understood it was pointless trying to leave these chores to the only girl in the group. Lionel had tried to joke about it, pointing out to Maud that it wasn't very charitable of her to let four men struggle with saucepans, but she had bluntly put him in his place. In reprisal, when she had difficulty putting up the tents, on the days when it was her turn, he made no attempt to stifle his sniggering.

This was not the first time Maud had had to deal with this sort of behavior. She had an older brother who had not spared her his sarcasm. She hated such stupid remarks, but over time she had come to anticipate them, as a kind of stimulus. The rage they inspired was a driving force. Very early on she had decided to show her defiance. Her truck driver's license had been her first major victory in this respect.

Once dinner was ready, there was a moment of peace that made her forget the tension. The five members of the convoy sat on the ground around the fire. Vauthier always stayed slightly off to one side. Lionel passed a joint. Maud and Alex took a few puffs. Marc never touched it. Vauthier drank. Already during their first stopovers he had finished off the bottles of wine they had packed. Since reaching the Balkans he'd started on beer. It was the easiest thing to find. Every village had a supply.

"Tomorrow morning," announced Lionel, stretched out by the fire and leaning on his elbows, "we'll come to the first checkpoint."

"Croats?"

Vauthier had asked the question with an innocent expression on his face. But he was fiddling with the little gold ring in his right ear, and Maud had noticed this meant he was concentrating.

"No," answered Lionel, "Krajina Serbs."

"Army?"

"Paramilitaries, more like."

"Logically, there should be Croats first," insisted Vauthier. "If we come on Serbs, it means we're not on the main road, the one through Tuzla, right?"

Lionel didn't really like going into details about the route. He kept the road maps to himself, in his truck, and issued instructions one day at a time, as if he wanted to avoid any discussion about the matter.

"That's right," he conceded grudgingly. "We'll head off to the right, through the south of the Krajina."

"What do you mean by the Krajina, actually?" asked Maud.

Lionel felt more comfortable with general questions. This was an opportunity for him to show off his knowledge and act the leader.

"It means edge, border. It's the strip of territory that runs along the border to the west of Bosnia. It's sparsely inhabited. The Serbs have thrown the Croats out of the region and they're in control. But you'll see, they're peasants, with pitchforks and old guns. Nothing like what we'll see farther on."

Lionel had been active in the NGO for three years. He had been on a mission to the Central African Republic, and on a first convoy to Bosnia six months earlier. In between he had worked at the association's headquarters in Lyon. His experience gave him a certain self-assurance when he spoke, even though he was only twenty-four years old.

"Their checkpoints are fairly laid-back. It will be good practice for later."

Vauthier took a long swig of beer from the bottle and wiped his mouth on his sleeve. Visibly he had other questions he wanted to ask. But Lionel did not leave him any time to interrupt.

"Let me remind you how we have to behave, in case we get checked along the way," he said.

He'd almost finished his joint. Before continuing his presentation, he took a long drag on the damp butt, which was turning his fingers yellow.

"All you have to say, if they ask, is that we are going to Kakanj, in central Bosnia. We have a permit from UNPRO-FOR to deliver aid to refugees. Our cargo? Food supplies, winter clothes, and medication. And even if they ask for one: no bribes. Is that clear?"

He was trying to sound like a leader. But the two former soldiers could tell the difference. They'd had experience of true orders. Lionel's curt tone did little to hide a certain lack of confidence.

"And what if they want to search the trucks?" asked Maud.

"We refuse!" said Alex.

Lionel shrugged, and Alex noticed. This only increased his impatience.

"What? You don't agree?"

"Of course not. If they want to search, they will search. How could we stop them?" said Lionel, looking at the sky.

A crescent moon had risen, and wispy clouds drifted over it, driven by high-altitude winds.

"I know these guys," snapped Alex. "They're loudmouths. But if we stand firm, I tell you, they won't touch the trucks."

He and Marc had served for six months as peacekeepers in Bosnia the previous year. Marc was always gloomy and taciturn. Alex, on the other hand, clearly liked to talk about his experience. Maud found him pleasant, as well as attractive. He was sociable, and you could tell he liked to talk. But as soon as he opened his mouth Lionel would look up at him from under his brows, scowling.

Lionel couldn't stand it when Alex went on about his supposed experience in the field. To calm down he would take his plastic tobacco pouch from his pocket and roll another fat joint.

"They won't search us, I tell you," said Lionel. "There is no reason for them to provoke an incident with aid workers. We're too useful to them. To everyone. And if, by chance, we do happen to run into people who don't play by the rules, well, then we'll just let them get on with it, without resisting. Without provoking them, above all. No flexing any muscles. No trying to act clever. We don't do anything that might make them suspect us of anything."

He rubbed his eyes, puffy from the smoke, with the weary air of a man overwhelmed by his responsibilities.

"After all," he concluded, "we have nothing to hide."

When he heard this, Alex glanced over at Marc then sat up straighter.

"Maybe we should inform you—"

It all happened in a flash. Maud noticed the little incident that followed, and she got the impression that Vauthier noticed, too. It was as if Marc was watching his teammate. When he heard what Alex was beginning to say, he gave a start and leapt to his feet. Maud understood that this was to interrupt him. And Alex did fall silent. At some point, of this she was sure, Marc had kicked him lightly in the back.

"Come on, let's get to bed," said Marc.

He went off, taking Alex with him.

Lionel was relieved to see the conversation was over and that the two tough guys had beaten a retreat.

"Goodnight!" he called. "Wake-up call at six."

Vauthier, chewing on some gum, glanced over at the two soldiers with an expression of hatred. He never said a word to them, and he seemed to be nurturing a particularly spiteful grudge against them. He got up in turn and stamped out the fire with his black cowboy boots, the leather old and crazed.

Alex and Marc had vanished into the tent they shared. Lionel went on sitting there for a moment to finish his butt. Then he joined Vauthier in the other tent. As for Maud, she slept in the bunk in the truck.

She climbed into the cab and closed the door. Before getting undressed, she spent a few minutes gazing through the windshield at the landscape. A pale moonlight cast a bluish glow onto the moor. She thought of the nights she used to spend at her parents' chalet in Haute Savoie, when the ground was covered with snow and she would get out of bed, wrapped in her blanket, to daydream on the wooden balcony. It was not nostalgia she felt, but rather an impression that her dreams from that time had taken shape. In all the futures they contained, there was this one, that was called her life. She had not imagined it like this; the toxic atmosphere of the mission was disappointing.

But in spite of everything, she was happy.

2

October mornings were always hard, and now that they had gained in altitude, the damp air was mixed with cold. Those who had slept in tents were frozen, but at least the icy air was not such a shock when they first stuck their noses out. Whereas Maud, when she left the dry, overheated cab, started to shiver all over. She had put on the same clothes as the day before, and which she had hardly changed since their departure: jeans of a moldy green color, a thick wool plaid shirt, a beige fleece jacket, and hiking boots. It was not only for the needs of the mission that she dressed like that. She hated arousing looks of desire in strange men. Several years ago she had decided to cut her blond hair very short and to wear only coarse, shapeless clothes that did nothing for her. Her only exception to this rule was when she went to see her grandmother, who wanted her to look her prettiest, and Maud liked to make her happy. Sometimes, too, she would put on some makeup when she was at home alone, and she would dine with her cat in her maid's room in Vincennes.

That morning as she got dressed in her truck she was a long way from such fantasies. Yet, despite the cold and damp, half asleep as she was, she wished she could wear a light blouse with a short skirt and sandals.

Vauthier, the fire man, had lit the gas stove. It did not burn properly and the saucepan full of water was blackened by the yellow flames licking at its sides. Alex was slicing the thick bread they had bought in a village the previous day. Lionel was sitting on a rock and rolling his first cigarette, his hands shaking.

Only Marc, as was his habit, was shaving, bare-chested above a plastic basin. He had short, coarse black hair, and in the morning his face had the thick shadow of a beard. He had unrolled a khaki toilet kit equipped with a small mirror, which he had hung from a branch. Maud avoided looking at him. She didn't like the tattoos on his arms, images of snakes and weapons.

From time to time Vauthier shot Marc a nasty look. Vauthier never washed, so it was as if he saw the public ablutions of a muscular body as a provocation.

All around, the grass was covered in frost. The night before, they had noticed a low stone house with a thatched roof a hundred yards further along. It looked like a sheepfold that was more or less abandoned. Now they saw it was inhabited when several poorly dressed children emerged in the sooty dawn light and stared at them from the top of a mound of earth.

Without waiting to see the parents, who were not likely to be welcoming, they packed up their supplies and struck their tents. The fly sheets and groundsheets were soaked in cold dew. Before they left, Lionel called to the children and gave them a pot of jam. He was unsmiling, almost ill-tempered. As Maud observed him she wondered if he was acting out of compassion or simply in an effort to reinforce his reputation as an aid worker.

It was always tricky to get the trucks started; they would cough and splutter. To be on the safe side, at night they parked them facing downhill in case they had to push-start them. When the engines finally got going, giving out dull banging sounds, they had to let them warm up for ten minutes or so if they didn't want to stall. While they waited in their cabs, some of them fell asleep again.

Pale sunshine was slanting low across the hills when at last they pulled away. It was Lionel's turn to drive and Maud, on the seat next to him, rolled him a cigarette at his request. She always had trouble with it. She didn't like to see Lionel playing with the irregular cylinder she had fashioned, studying it with an ironic smile before lighting it.

The road was getting worse and worse, full of potholes for a start. Before long it was hardly paved at all, and the rare stretches of asphalt, rather than facilitating their progress, seemed like so many obstacles in addition to the stones and ruts. The trucks were struggling, particularly around the bends. Finally they reached a plateau and the road improved. They had been driving for roughly an hour when they passed the burnt-out carcass of a military vehicle, probably troop transport. The fire had charred the metal, and the chassis was twisted by an explosion. The wreck must have been there for some time already, because it was beginning to rust. Still, it was the first vestige of the fighting they had seen. The sight of the scorched vehicle made them suddenly aware they were entering into another geography, no longer a geography of maps but rather of History, the territory of war.

Lionel, who had studied their itinerary before leaving, announced:

"There's a checkpoint, just over two kilometers from here."

They stopped for a few minutes to allow the other truck, which was falling behind, to catch up. They headed together toward the first roadblock.

They saw it as they came out of a long bend, in an area full of thickets. The trees had already lost most of their leaves. The season was further along, at high altitude, and they could already feel the first signs of winter.

The roadblock was gray and brown, like the countryside. It was a distilled display of misery: two burnt-out Soviet-era cars were tipped on their sides to form an uneven barrier. Shelters had been built on either side with branches and old beams. Torn hay tarps were stretched between metal poles. Four men emerged from their makeshift guard posts. From a distance it was obvious they were hurrying to get dressed and trying to look threatening. Two of them were carrying machine guns while the other two were visibly more at ease with their pitchforks, brandishing them as if they were working in the fields.

The trucks slowed down, and given that their usual speed was already very slow, they were almost at a walking pace. Yet the paramilitaries were agitated, and the two armed men stood in the middle of the road, raising their machine guns. Lionel slowed further still and stopped five yards from the roadblock. He rolled down his window and the cold air entered the cab. One of the militia came to stand on the driver's side while the other, his weapon still pointed at the trucks, was walking around the convoy.

The man who seemed to be in charge placed his head in the window of the truck. He was very young, with a beard, and his dark hair was uncombed. The small patch of skin that emerged from his beard was red, and his eyes were bloodshot. He was breathing noisily through his mouth. The smell of alcohol, mingled with whiffs of tobacco, invaded the cab. Practically leaning inside, he examined the cab. When he noticed Maud, she got the impression his gaze lingered on her. With her short hair and neutral clothing, she must initially have seemed hardly any different from Lionel, who had fine, almost feminine features, if you compared them with the paramilitaries' rough looks. But the man had instantly realized she was a woman. Perhaps because she was overly sensitive, Maud saw an almost animal spark in the way his black eyes stared at her, and she looked away.

"*Pomoć!*" said Lionel placidly.

It was the magic word, one of the only ones they had been made to learn during the two-day training the association had given them in Lyon. It meant "aid" and it was the simplest, most comprehensible way for them to convey that they were relief workers.

To show them his UN permits, Lionel began to reach toward the glove compartment. The paramilitary saw his gesture as threatening, and he kicked the side of the truck and aimed his weapon at Lionel at the same time. Then the man yanked the door open and motioned to everyone to get out. The other man must have done the same thing because once they were outside they found Alex and Marc standing next to their truck.

The paramilitary grouped them together and made them stand to attention while his comrade lifted the tarps at the back of the vehicles and examined their cargo. The trucks were filled to the brim with crates and boxes, so that from outside all you could see was a wall of neatly piled parcels labeled with the name of the NGO, La Tête d'Or.

"Dokument," said the roadblock leader once his colleague had joined him.

In these circumstances, dialogue was limited to exchanging the few words each party had at its disposal to fulfill its mission. Lionel, still watched by the soldier, climbed back into the truck, and this time he reached for the official papers. The paramilitary took the three sheets covered with signatures and stamps and stood looking at them for a long time.

Maud was beginning to understand that this was a sort of theatrical display for two different audiences. The soldier wanted to show his strength to the foreigners under his control. But while he was focusing all his attention on documents he certainly could not read because they were written in English, he was also performing for his companions, to show them that he was indeed the boss. There was something comical about the scene and at the same time, there was only one sure conclusion: in the world they were about to enter, the only true subject, the ultimate motor of all behavior and all thought, was fear. You had to play along, and show you took the matter seriously, and by displaying an obvious fear of the boss, you would help him maintain the respect of his own troops. Lionel excelled at this role. He performed it calmly, and not at all obsequiously. He showed both a deep respect for authority and a total confidence in his own innocence. This was enough to reassure these men who knew nothing but constant threat and suspicion.

As for the two former soldiers, they affected an ironic and laid-back attitude, which made the others wary and aggressive. Without realizing it, or perhaps without even caring, Alex in particular annoyed the paramilitaries. He stared at their rustic weapons with the withering smile of a specialist. As it was taking a while, he began whistling. Firmly planted on his legs, he seemed ready to charge at the slightest alarm. He made it a point of honor to show he was not afraid, and he stared at the little crew at the checkpoint as if they actually were potential adversaries whom he could easily overcome.

Lionel was aware of this and tried to signal to him to calm down. The roadblock commander noticed. However thick he might seem, he was a keen observer, particularly when it came to danger. There was an uneasiness now, and the paramilitaries began talking among themselves. It was obvious that Alex had aroused their suspicions. Standing next to him, Marc had not said anything and even seemed a bit embarrassed by his companion's behavior. But the two of them together, for the same reason that made Lionel immediately aware that they were former soldiers, made for a suspicious pair. Alex's dark skin and frizzy hair only reinforced the paramilitaries' wariness. One of them barked:

"*Passport!*"

This type of request was rare, once they had shown they were an aid convoy. Maud saw it as a confirmation that the

Serbs, initially reassured by Lionel, now sensed there was something not quite right because of the other two.

Fortunately the roadblock was isolated and they clearly had no convenient way of getting in touch with a higher authority, even supposing such an authority existed. The paramilitaries didn't find anything wrong with their passports, so in the end they let the convoy go.

But Lionel was furious.

"Those two jerks are going to get us in trouble," he grumbled as he drove. "We have to split them up."

A few miles farther along he parked the truck in a forest track and got out, in a foul mood. He motioned to the others to gather around him.

"Maud is going to go behind with you, Alex. Marc, you're coming with us."

"Why?"

Marc knew very well what to expect but he wanted to force Lionel to give an explanation. Lionel did not take the bait.

"Because."

The tension between the two men had been palpable from the start. Alex might be the one who talked back, but in fact it was Marc, with his habitual silence and enigmatic gaze, who made Lionel uncomfortable. This instinctive dislike, for no particular reason, had become patently obvious, and one of the two had to yield. No doubt Marc figured this was not the time to provoke a direct confrontation. He did as Lionel asked, but it was clear they hadn't heard the last from him.

"Whatever."

He went to get his backpack out of the cab of the truck he had been driving and tossed it into the other one. It took Maud a little longer to get her things together, then she climbed in next to Alex.

The convoy set off again.

In the lead cab the atmosphere was stifling. Lionel drove

without taking his eyes off the road. Marc, his feet on the dashboard, was swaying back and forth, headphones on, listening to music on his Walkman. Even with the engine noise Johnny Cash was audible, wailing through the headphones.

They drove through dreary countryside still draped in mist. There were not many villages in this part of the Krajina. From time to time they could see a destroyed house, with walls torn open by shells and scorched roof beams. They passed an ancient tractor pulling a hay wagon, going at a snail's pace.

Once he had calmed down, and at a time he chose, Lionel decided to have it out with Marc. Vauthier's silent presence behind them was reassuring.

Vauthier had made no secret of his dislike for the soldiers. He had told Lionel that he had been a conscientious objector. He claimed he'd spent two months in prison in Tarbes, because of some legionnaires on a binge who had tried to hit on the girl he was with. The story, like everything else he told them, could not be proven.

But it was Marc whom the former courier disliked most of all. He never spoke to him, and his close-set little eyes would flash with animosity whenever he looked his way. Lionel could not understand the reason for his dislike but, under the circumstances, it meant Vauthier was a welcome ally who could be useful to him.

"Stop your music for a minute."

"What?"

"I asked you to stop your music," shouted Lionel. "We have to talk."

Marc pulled off his headset.

"Talk about what?"

"Safety."

The other man gave an ironic smile.

"Yeah?"

"You're not in the army anymore. You have to realize that.

If they want to throw us in jail or even make off with everything we've got, there is no way to stop them. So at the checkpoints we keep a low profile. It's absolutely vital, for our safety. You have to tell that to your buddy. You can think what you like about those guys. But they're the ones who have the weapons, and we have to show them respect."

Marc smiled.

"You really believe that?"

"It's part of our mission."

"All right, I'll have a word with Alex. But don't sweat it. We know those guys inside out. The only thing they understand is force. The more you act all quiet and nice, the more trouble they'll make for you. We want to reach our destination just as much as you do. Maybe even more than you do, in fact."

He gave a strange smile as he said it, but Lionel saw only the boastfulness in his smile and didn't take it any further. He would live to regret it bitterly. For now, however, he had decided above all not to lose his temper, just to get his message across.

"We can talk about it when we get back—just come to a meeting at headquarters to share your point of view. But right now we have our instructions and we have to follow them. No fighting back or acting arrogant or provoking them. I'd like us to agree on that."

Behind them, Vauthier yawned noisily. Lionel was grateful to him. By manifesting his presence, he gave a certain weight to Lionel's words, perhaps not the weight of authority, but at least that of the majority.

"We're going to have to go through quite a few checkpoints, and they won't all be as smooth as this one. Not to mention that we can run into patrols at any time. We have to behave like all the other aid workers."

"The other aid workers!" echoed Marc scornfully.

He seemed to have a preconceived and hardly flattering opinion of the profession.

"Whether you like it or not, that's what you are now."

Lionel refrained from adding: Why did you sign up if you have such a poor opinion of us? But he had no desire to question Marc about his commitment or establish any sort of complicity with him.

They had discussed it at headquarters when Alex and Marc volunteered. The directors at La Tête d'Or had devoted an entire meeting to the topic, and Lionel had taken part. To some, the former soldiers' motivations seemed suspicious, and they were of the opinion they ought not to be hired. But convoy drivers were in very short supply, and the human resources people said over and over that they could not afford to be picky. Finally, there was a vote, and the outcome was that if these guys wanted to join up, that was their business, after all. As long as they obeyed the rules, there was no need to go digging into their deeper intentions. This was not the time for Lionel to start acting more Catholic than the Pope.

"All right," concluded Marc, putting his headphones back on. "You're the boss. But sooner or later you'll see that I was right."

They had said what they had to say. Lionel reached up for the joint he had slipped behind his ear, like an old-time grocer with a pencil. He lit it and took a long inhalation. He was not altogether reassured, but for the time being the matter was settled.

3

M aud could understand Lionel's decision, but she was furious at having to change trucks. She had been driving the other one ever since they had left Lyon and she'd gotten used to it. She liked the sound of its engine, she knew its weaknesses and had found little tricks to tame the old beast. For example, when she had to shift from second to third, the gearbox cracked because the synchronization was busted. But she had managed to find the right running speed so that it would go into gear without a problem. She had grown used to her sagging bunk and she knew how to nestle in comfortably. Now everything seemed different in the new cab, poorly laid out, uncomfortable. She didn't like the smell of cheap deodorant that permeated the fabric in the curtains and seats; she even preferred the smell of old motor oil and tobacco that belonged to the other cab.

She knew herself well enough to realize she had a tendency to personalize objects and decors, and to create bonds of antipathy or love with them as if they were alive. But she would rather die than admit to being in love with the truck she had just left behind. She merely went into a silent funk, and scowled at the road as she drove.

Sitting beside her, Alex was tactful enough not to ask any questions and to respect her silence. After they had gone a few miles, she began to be aware of his presence. After all, it wasn't his fault. She felt it was unfair to blame him if she was annoyed.

She turned and gave him a smile. She didn't share Lionel's

dislike. She figured their new cohabitation would at least allow her to become better acquainted with this sturdy kid, who had something elegant about him. She decided to break the silence.

"I'll bet the sparks are flying up front. They must be having a stormy discussion."

Alex smiled back.

"Good thing Vauthier is there to act as referee," she added.

"What exactly is Lionel not happy with, where we're concerned?"

"He thinks you're still acting like soldiers, and you haven't grasped the rules of how an aid worker is supposed to behave."

Alex shook his head. He was still a bit wary. After all, since the departure, no one had said a word to him, except for practical reasons. All the way from Lyon to here, he hadn't had a real conversation on his own with anyone other than Marc.

"That's just a typical civilian reaction. Putting all soldiers in the same bag. Marc is my buddy but we're very different. And when we were in the army, it was even more obvious."

"Were you in the same unit?"

"Yeah, we were peacekeepers in the same battalion of engineers. But that doesn't mean anything. He's a career soldier and I was just drafted in."

Even at headquarters, no one had asked them about their military background. Maud knew nothing at all about that world, but she realized that there, too, like elsewhere, there must be profound differences.

"You didn't have the same rank?"

"He was a sergeant and I was a private. But that's not the most important thing. Rank is just what you see, but then there's all the rest."

"All the rest?"

"Mentality, habits. For a career soldier, a conscript like me is sort of like a civilian in uniform. An intern, in a way. They look down on us."

"It didn't stop you from becoming friends."

"No, because in his way Marc is special. What's more, he didn't like it much in the army."

"Why not?"

"It's hard to explain. He didn't get along with his superiors, and that's why he eventually left. He's fairly generous person, you know. I think all of you have got the wrong idea about him."

Maud was beginning to feel more at ease. She was glad to have a companion who could speak naturally. She was relieved not to have to put up with Lionel's silent spells; increasingly he had his head in the clouds, and he preferred his joints to any other company. And besides, now there were just the two of them, and she could no longer feel Vauthier's indiscreet gaze bearing down on her from behind.

"What were you doing before you were called up?"

"Nothing, hanging out in a technical college."

"Whereabouts?"

"Grenoble."

"Are you from there?"

Maud thought he would tell her about his tropical origins and she was surprised by his answer.

"Yeah, I was born in a little mountain village in the massif of Trièves, can you picture it on the map?"

"It's near Chartreuse, over by Mont Aiguille, around there somewhere?"

She had gone cross-country skiing in the region once with her parents, when she was ten years old.

"Precisely."

She was dying to know how a child of color had ended up in a remote Alpine village. But he seemed to think it was perfectly natural, and she didn't dare ask.

"I suppose you don't really think I look like a mountain dweller, is that it?"

"I didn't say anything."

Alex was smiling. He seemed to think it was funny and, visibly, he was fine with the topic.

"My father is from Guadeloupe. He was orphaned at a very young age and he came to France to live with an uncle in Grenoble. He married my mother, who came from Reunion Island, and he had to start working right away. He was doing one small job after another. One day he found work as a milk quality control inspector in the mountains and he stayed."

"I see."

"He gets up every morning at five, my old man, to go around the farms and collect samples of milk. It's a hard job and doesn't pay well. So my parents wanted me to get an education. Unfortunately, I'm no good at it. I have trouble reading, and they didn't treat it when I was small. I mix up letters, you know what that is?"

"You're dyslexic."

"I'll let you say it, because I've never been able to pronounce the word right."

They both laughed. Maud realized that this was the first time since she'd left France. Yet she loved joking around with her girlfriends, and sometimes at home she could go into a fit of laughter all by herself.

"So I failed my exams and eventually they stopped deferring me. That's when I went off to do my military service."

Alex spoke calmly; Maud liked his voice. From the beginning she'd been stuck with the team on the other truck. She'd misjudged him. So in the end it was a good thing that Lionel had broken down the barrier and mixed up the team.

"Were you the one who wanted to go to Bosnia with the UN?"

"Yes, I volunteered right away after my training. They had posted me to these barracks in Moulins and I was just moping around there. I had passed all my permits—automobile, motorcycle, truck—and that took some time, but afterwards it was routine, just chores. I was wasting my time. I wanted to see the world."

Maud could relate to that. She'd spent two years in law school because her father was a notary. He had encouraged her brother to take over the practice, but it had never occurred to him that *she* might be able to. In the end, her brother had decided he would rather be a math teacher. And she told herself she was up to the challenge: she could take over her father's practice. But she couldn't imagine spending her whole life in the same place. In the end, she'd dropped it all to become an aid worker. The context was different, but her reaction had been the same as Alex's.

"Did they send you here right away?"

"We had special military training for two months. Then they put blue helmets on us and shoved us onto a convoy headed for Kakanj. Central Bosnia, it's a harsh place. Snow everywhere, mountains. It reminded me of where I grew up. I was very happy there."

The lead truck had pulled further ahead, and when they caught up, it was stopped at a checkpoint.

"We're not far from the enclave of Bihać," said Alex. "They're Muslims there. But from what I understood, Lionel doesn't want us to go through there. We're going to make a detour, by the south."

The checkpoint was manned by paramilitaries in full uniform. It was much better organized than the previous one. There was a lot of traffic, given the proximity of the town. They crossed the road leading to the enclave, and saw a number of aid convoys. Ahead of them, a dozen or so semitrailers from the UNHCR were waiting. The paramilitaries were checking papers and summarily inspecting the trucks. It was all more professional, more normal. They didn't have to get out of the cab, and they went through without incident.

"There's a French battalion in Bihać," said Alex.

And they did pass several jeeps transporting peacekeepers with their blue helmets. On their sleeves you could see the UNPROFOR badge, and small French tricolors. Before long they were out in the country again. The road was following a river with gray waters. All the factories along the river had been destroyed. The low sky made the place feel gloomy.

The tension eased and they began talking again. Maud had let Alex take the wheel at the last checkpoint. She found some chewing gum in the glove compartment. The taste of mint in her mouth reminded her that she hadn't brushed her teeth in three days.

"What is Kakanj like, since you've been there?"

"A filthy place. A Croatian enclave surrounded by Muslims, who in turn are surrounded by Serbs. In other places the fighting has drawn fairly homogeneous lines between the zones, but in Kakanj it's impossible. The populations are too mixed up. The atmosphere is really tense."

"What were you doing there?"

"We were protecting the coal mine."

Now that she wasn't driving, Maud could look at Alex while they talked. She got the impression that he had hesitated before answering her last question. He was no longer as natural and relaxed, as if a trap lay hidden in the subject.

"Is it important, this mine?"

"Bosnia has no energy resources other than coal. They have enormous mines. Initially it was an open-pit mine. And you can see it; the hillside is completely caved in. But now they mine underground, so there are miles of tunnels."

He was increasingly animated as he spoke about it, and she couldn't understand why he put so much enthusiasm into his description.

"Are they still mining, even during the war?"

"No. Everything has come to a halt. You should see it: huge factories, all black, completely silent, the conveyor belts have stopped, the ovens are cold. I can imagine that when it was going full blast it must have been a sight to see. But now it's completely dead. A sort of postapocalyptic movie set."

"So why did they send peacekeepers there?"

"For a start, so that the factories would not be destroyed. And then to make sure the pumps kept on working."

"The pumps?"

"The underground tunnels can flood, so there are pumps continually sucking out the water. If they stop working, the tunnels will flood, and that will be it. Once a mine gets flooded, there's no getting it back."

Maud could see that her companion was particularly interested in the topic. But she still couldn't see why. He was talking about important things, but why was he so passionate? Why did he feel so personally involved?

"So, was it your job to keep the pumps going?"

For a moment she feared he might think she was being ironic. But he didn't pause, and continued his train of thought.

"Among other things. Above all, just by being there, we were protecting the site and the people inside."

"And where are the refugees that we're going to help?"

It was odd they had not brought the subject up earlier. Maud had tried to question Lionel, but he either didn't know or wouldn't say. At headquarters, they had simply been told they must take supplies, clothing, and medication to refugees who were in a camp. And the machine had been set in motion. All the talk was of the cargo, the makeup of the team, permits. Now that they were nearing their goal, other questions arose, at least for Maud, questions that had to do with the people they were about to meet and help. Ever since they had begun to see wretched peasants and dirty, shabbily clothed children with runny noses along the roadside, she had begun to care about the people they were going to help, about their lives, their living conditions, their stories.

"The refugees are in the mine," said Alex darkly.

"In the tunnels?"

"No, in the factory."

"But who are they, exactly, these refugees?"

Maud realized that up to now she had made do with the vaguest of notions. She was not the only one. As soon as she joined the association, she was struck by how abstract this humanitarian work seemed. There was talk of geopolitics, the situation of the armies in the field, or what was at stake strategically, but in the end the people they were supposed to be helping remained virtual. The people they called "victims," or when they were talking about aid, "beneficiaries": they were unreal, and nobody seemed to want to put a face on them. The worst of it was that up until now, this had suited her fine. She needed to help someone and it was enough to know that, somewhere, there were people who needed her help. But this feeling was more about her than about them. She told herself it was an almost childlike desire.

"There are roughly five hundred of them. Women, children, old people. The men are elsewhere, probably fighting."

Alex's tone, full of melancholy, showed her that for him, on the contrary, the refugees were made of flesh and blood, they were people he knew, whom he had observed as they went about their lives. Remembering them seemed to stir his emotions, or maybe even something more.

"How did they get there?"

"Most of them are people who lived in the surrounding area. When the war began, the Croats, who were in the majority in the region, burned the houses of anyone belonging to another religion. The Serbs left for the Serbian zone, the Muslims for the Muslim zone. But some of them, particularly those who were of mixed origins, couldn't flee to a safe area. So they took refuge in the mine."

"Hold on, I'm trying to grasp this. There's this mine, and peacekeepers protecting the refugees, and all around there are Croatian paramilitaries—is that it?"

"Exactly. The mine consists of a hill and factories, all surrounded by barbed wire. On one side there are the refugees and on the other, sometimes only a few meters away, are the people who drove them out and who are just waiting for us to leave to finish them off."

"Great atmosphere."

"It's hatred in its purest form. The worst of it is that these people were neighbors before the war. They'd been living together for centuries. And for us, they're exactly the same people. They speak the same language, they look the same, they wear the same clothes—except the refugees have lost everything and they look more wretched."

Maud looked at Alex and was surprised to see how emotional he had become. Up to then she had shared the other aid workers' prejudice regarding soldiers, and she'd thought they were brutes without a conscience. Now at least this one was turning out to be more sensitive and more humane than many of those who made it their job to relieve the sorrows of the world.

"Were you in contact with them? Did you get to know them personally?"

Alex shot her a quick look and seemed to hesitate.

"Very well."

Maud sensed he wanted to say a bit more.

"You made friends among them?"

The young man gave a faint smile. He kept a firm grip on the steering wheel, which vibrated as they drove uphill, and he compensated for the sudden jolts and swerves caused by the ruts in the road. Now he waited a long time before he answered.

"I met a girl there."

"A refugee?"

"Yes."

Maud felt glad and even a bit proud that she had brought this little secret to light. She knew she had touched on something vital, which explained better than anything why Alex had signed up. And at the same time she felt a slight inner twinge of disappointment.

"How old is she?"

"Nineteen."

"What's her name?"

"Bouba. She's in the mine with her two little brothers and her parents. They had to flee after a fire destroyed their house."

"How did it work: could she live with you? Were you able to be together?"

"No. The refugees aren't allowed in the UN camps. I went to see her in her oven."

"In her oven!"

"Yes, she was one of those who had settled in the big coal ovens. Since the plant isn't working, the ovens are empty. They have big cast-iron doors. Inside it's warmer than outside. It's not very comfortable, obviously, but at night there's no wind and they can build a fire for cooking."

He spoke passionately, as if it was a sudden relief to have told his secret, and now he could speak about the woman he loved. But very quickly his face clouded over.

"It would be better if you don't mention this to Marc."

"Does he have a girlfriend there, too?"

"No."

"Okay, I won't say anything. But why would it matter if he knew?"

"He does know. But I would rather he didn't find out we've been talking about it."

He seemed absent once again. Maud remained silent. They didn't talk any more in the hours that followed. But it was first time since leaving France that she'd had something of a personal conversation with a member of the team, and she felt less lonely.

4

It was just past noon when the lead truck suddenly broke down. The convoy was coming out of a long climb, and the engines had overheated. When they reached level ground, the radiator emptied out with a hissing sound. Thick white smoke billowed from under the hood. Vauthier's hour of glory had come.

He was the only one who didn't have a truck driver's license, but he'd been hired for his skill as a mechanic. He was passionate about motorcycles. He boasted that he had won several races on a 250cc. After a bad fall he was no longer fit for competition. Even if he wasn't a specialist in diesel engines, he knew enough to assume the role of mission mechanic.

He lifted the hood and leaned over the engine. The others waited nearby, smoking. Only Marc kept to one side, sitting on the fender of the other truck. When they started out he'd made a few remarks about what poor condition the vehicles were in, and he predicted that the engines would not make it to the end.

Vauthier quickly located what was wrong.

"The radiator hose blew."

He took some wrenches out of a toolbox and a few minutes later held up the defective part. It was a rubber sleeve that must have been black once upon a time, but over the years it had turned gray and was full of cracks. One of the cracks had widened, probably due to the overheating, and the water had leaked out.

"What do we do?" asked Lionel, who could not hide his concern.

They had stopped in the middle of the countryside. A glacial wind from the high plateau was driving a fine rain. Enormous crows had landed in the surrounding fields.

"We could wrap it up with some insulating tape, but it won't hold for long."

"Would it be enough to make it to the next village?"

"I don't know. We can try."

Vauthier fashioned a sleeve with adhesive tape all around the hose, then put it back. He filled the cooling system and the truck started up. They climbed into their cabs and slowly set off. The repair job got them two kilometers along the way, and when they saw the first houses of a village emerge out of the fog they began to regain hope. Unfortunately, there was another long hill to climb. They hadn't gone more than a hundred yards when the hose blew again.

"This time we'll have to change the part," said Vauthier. Since the breakdown he'd been sitting in the front to listen for the engine's reactions.

"Is it easy to find?"

"If they have tractors, they must have radiator hose. Even if it's not quite the same diameter, we can try and finagle something."

They stepped outside again and Vauthier scrambled under the truck.

"I'll try and see if there's another solution, but it would surprise me. In the meanwhile someone should go and check out the village. Maybe there's a garage, or at least some sort of repair shop for farm machinery."

Lionel said he would see to it.

"I'll go with you," said Maud.

She'd been wanting to stretch her legs for several days now. In France she went jogging every morning. She was finding it difficult to stay shut up inside a truck all the livelong day.

"If you want. The rest of you, wait here with Vauthier."

There was nothing nearby other than the village in the distance. But they were still in a war zone. It would be better not to leave the trucks unattended.

Lionel didn't like walking, she could tell. He always held himself slightly stooped, and in spite of his long legs he couldn't keep up with Maud.

"Hey, slow down, there's no rush."

Reluctantly, she slowed her pace. If it were up to her, she would have run. Her Nike shoes were comfortable, the fresh air was a tonic. She liked the cottony silence of the countryside, and the earthy smell of ploughed fields.

"How's it going with Alex?"

"He's nice."

"You think so?"

"All it takes is to speak kindly to him and not treat him like a soldier."

Lionel shrugged. He'd made up his mind, and she wasn't about to make him change it that easily.

"Can I ask you something?" said Maud.

She had become resigned to shuffling along at her companion's pace.

"Go ahead."

"Why are we going to Kakanj, when that's the very place where Marc and Alex served as peacekeepers with the UN? Is it a coincidence?"

"No."

"So what's the connection?"

Lionel took out an old Kleenex and slowed to wipe his forehead. In spite of the cold temperature, walking had warmed him up.

"When your friend Alex came to La Tête d'Or, it was in response to an ad for truck drivers for Sarajevo."

"Yes, that's the one I saw in *Le Dauphiné*."

"Exactly. Except that we were beginning to run into difficulties. You know the mission is funded with European money?"

"Vaguely."

Lionel was always pleased when he could demonstrate he was not a volunteer like the others, but someone in charge, who knew how the system worked. When they had been together at headquarters, Maud had noticed he was always particularly delighted to give her this sort of lesson.

"In Brussels," he continued, looking important, "they decided there was too much aid going to Sarajevo and not enough for the rest of Bosnia. They asked us to come up with another destination."

They had reached the first houses but the actual village was much farther away. They saw it in the hollow of the valley below them. Lionel was disappointed but at least now the road went downhill.

"To make a long story short: it would mean sending a mission to scout for a new site. And that would also mean a waste of time and money."

"I see. So that's when Alex told you about Kakanj."

"You're a smart girl."

Maud had despised others for less. Two or three years ago she would have slapped him. But she had decided not to let it annoy her anymore. She kept silent and clenched her teeth.

"He told us about some refugees who are in the coal mine, and we found out that they were in desperate need."

"Did he tell you about the ovens, too?"

"The ovens? What ovens?"

She gathered he didn't know about Bouba. She decided not to say anything. A little point for her.

"Apparently there are refugees living in the factory's abandoned ovens."

"Oh."

The image, which had made such an impression on her,

meant nothing to Lionel. He didn't care how they lived, the people he was going to help. The only thing that mattered to him, and to the others behind their computers at headquarters, was to find "beneficiaries," thanks to whom the association could get European Union money, and the humanitarian machine could go on turning.

They had reached the entrance to what was a fairly sizeable farming village, smelling of barns and manure. Fences tufted with hen's feathers lined the gardens along the road. In the middle of the village there was a fork in the road, and Lionel didn't seem to know which way to go.

"Have you been here before?"

"No, when I went to Sarajevo, we took another road. I've never set foot here."

There was no one about. They didn't know whether it was because of the war, because it was cold, or simply because people were having lunch. The emptiness created a paradoxical impression of both peace and menace. They turned right in the direction of a big barn. Inside it they saw farm machinery, ancient but apparently still functioning. Next to the barn was a squat house, and the lights were on. They knocked on the door. A tall peasant woman opened it, wearing a flowered apron. She had a handsome, angular face, with blue eyes and short hair. There was a strength to her femininity that Maud liked. And it amused her to see how Lionel seemed to shrink before her, almost pleading.

"*Pomoć. Francuska. Francuski.* Truck kaput!" he muttered, waving his bit of broken hose ridiculously.

Initially the woman gave him a stern look then turned around and called to someone in the house. An old man joined them at the door. He must have been taller and stronger than her once upon a time, but the years had shrunken him and his clothes were too big. He had an enormous gray moustache and bushy eyebrows hid his little eyes, which were gray, too.

Lionel started over with his explanations and the man took hold of the hose. He looked at it attentively then went into the house without closing the door. A moment later he came back out. He had changed his slippers for rubber boots. He walked gingerly across the courtyard, and motioned to the two strangers to follow him.

They went into the barn; it smelled of dry grain and motor oil. All the way at the back the man opened a store-room and rummaged in an open chest that was filled to the brim with spare parts and bits of metal. He couldn't find what he was looking for, came back, out and went over to a workbench splattered with grease spots, where an enormous tail vise was fixed. Under the bench there were some rusty drums that must have dated from the first world war. Lionel looked at Maud and raised his eyebrows. He had lost all hope the old man might find something useful in all that junk.

"In Africa, it's the same thing," he said, sure he would not be understood. "They lead you around the garden for an hour rather than admit they don't have what you're looking for."

With his gnarled hands the man was taking sundry objects out of the drums, holding them up to the sunlight, for he must have had poor eyesight, then lining them up on the work-bench. Before long the countertop looked like a display at a flea market, and Lionel sniggered to himself.

"You wonder why they keep all this crap."

Maud motioned to him to be quiet.

"Maybe he understands . . . "

"Ha! No danger of that."

Suddenly the old peasant became excited. He had his back to them, and Maud could not see what he had found. When he turned around, she saw he was holding a piece of rubber hose, longer than their broken hose but roughly the same diameter.

"Voilà!" he shouted, in French, his face lit up by a broad smile.

Lionel took hold of the part with a stunned look on his face that delighted Maud. Another point for her!

"Do you speak French, Monsieur?" she asked.

The old man cupped his hand around his ear and she repeated her question, more loudly.

"A little, a little," he replied, with a strong accent.

"You've been to France?"

He was as deaf as a post and she had to shout again.

"War," he said, fumbling for words. "Against Nazis. France, friends. Me, soldier."

Their exchange did not go much further. Indignantly, he refused the money Lionel offered him, and Maud thanked him with a big smile.

They headed back to the trucks, holding their precious trophy.

"Good thing he was deaf," she said to Lionel, who was again puffing and laboring up the hill.

When they reached the convoy they found the three men sitting silently around a fire. Vauthier was grilling sausages and the flames turned yellow whenever they licked the fat. Lionel held out his lucky find, and Vauthier seemed pleased.

"A bit wide," he said, "but if we tighten the clamps it should work."

He wiped his hands on an old rag and went straight back to work on the engine.

Less than an hour later the truck was repaired. They had a quick lunch and the two former soldiers packed away the cooking utensils.

Lionel wanted to leave again right away, but Vauthier sat on the embankment by the side of the road and gestured to him to come over.

"Wait for a while," he said firmly. "The hose is repaired but I'm the one who's in need of repair just now. Let's smoke a little joint."

It was not at all like Vauthier to come out with something like that. He was a beer drinker, after all. There must be something wrong.

"We're coming," shouted Lionel to the others, who were already climbing into the cabs. "Warm up the engines."

Maud was in the truck with Alex and she told him about their visit to the village.

As soon as they were sitting side by side, Vauthier, looking as natural as he could, said quietly to Lionel, who was heating up the hash in the flame of his lighter, "Those two are up to something."

"Who are you talking about?"

"The two privates."

"What did they say?"

"Nothing to me. It's just I heard them talking while I was fiddling with the engine. They were some ways away, but sound carries with the cold air. They started arguing and I heard plenty."

"Such as?"

"I don't know exactly what they were talking about. But one of them, the black one, I think—"

"Alex?"

"Yeah, Alex, he said to the other one, 'We have to tell them.' And Marc was losing his temper. He said, 'If you tell them I'll smash your face in.' The other guy didn't agree. He kept on saying, 'I talked to the girl. I'm sure she'd understand.'"

"You have no idea what they were referring to?"

"No, but Alex said, 'If any paramilitaries at a checkpoint find the stuff, Lionel will pin the blame on us and it'll be fucked.' And the other guy wouldn't listen. He said, 'Because you think that if he finds out he'll cover for us?' And then he started insulting us: 'Those guys have no balls. They'll never go along with it.' The black guy got mad and finally he said, 'You're just an asshole. You're going to fuck everything up.'"

"Was that all?"

"Yes."

"What do you think this 'stuff' he referred to could be? What do you make of it?"

"Those fucking soldiers are capable of anything, believe me. They've got some evil trick up their sleeve, I'd stake my life on it. We'll all be up shit creek if we let them go on like this."

Lionel looked at the first truck. Through the reflections in the windshield he could see Marc staring at them. Fortunately the cannabis had relaxed him, because he felt a wave of panic, and Vauthier could see it. Lionel suspected the mechanic had nothing but scorn for aid workers, and for sure he had no respect for him. But he was his ally in this business and feelings had to be set aside.

"What would you do, in my shoes?"

"I'd search the trucks from top to bottom and open all the boxes to see if they haven't stashed weapons or some other crap in the cargo."

Lionel tossed away his butt and stood up.

"We'll see," he said.

This was his way of starting to act the boss again. But he had the creeping suspicion that he wasn't fooling anyone.

5

They set off again, but when the convoy went through
the village where the old man had helped them out,
Lionel stopped the trucks by the barn and went over to
speak to Maud, who was waiting behind the wheel.

"Try and see with the woman whether she has anything to
sell. Eggs, rabbits, whatever. I'll go ask the old man a few questions."

Maud switched off the ignition and went to knock at the
door. The woman opened it and she tried to make herself
understood. The woman was immediately friendlier, even smiling. As Maud couldn't understand what she was saying, the
woman took her by the hand and led her into the kitchen. It
was a huge room, more comfortable than the run-down air of
the house might suggest. She could see that the farmer's wife
had done her best to copy the interior decoration photos in
magazines. Appliances were neatly tucked under the countertops, and wall cupboards painted white flanked an electric
range. Unfortunately all the appliances were made of heavy
materials, inimitably Soviet in their design. At the back of the
kitchen, a door opened onto a pantry with walls of softwood
shelving. Apples were drying on racks. Plump chalky white
cheeses were lined up on several shelves, giving off a faint odor.
The woman displayed her treasures and tried to get Maud to
say the Serbo-Croatian name of each item. Maud mangled the
words and her hostess burst out laughing.

Lionel had found the old man in the barn and they had

come into the main room, which served as both living and dining room, all of it arranged around an enormous television covered with a lace doily. Even though she was not paying him much attention, Maud could hear Lionel shouting to the deaf old man to make himself understood. He had brought a road map with him from the truck and now he spread it on the table. The farmer had put on thick glasses, with a broken lens, and he was leaning over the map. He shared what information he had about the state of the roads and any military roadblocks in the area.

Finally Maud emerged from the pantry carrying a crate filled with all sorts of food. The farmer's wife had her sit down in the kitchen and insisted on serving her some black juice from an enamel coffeepot, probably a concoction made with roasted barley. Maud liked this female complicity: it made her feel safe, she could laugh with her. They had no language to communicate, yet they understood each other on another level. Maud was greatly affected by this type of exchange. She had a deep appreciation for the world of women, and yet because of her lifestyle choices she had found herself constantly fleeing from it.

Lionel called out to her and she remembered she had to pay for her purchases. Unlike the old man, who had refused Lionel's banknote, the woman readily accepted the money Maud held out to her. Maud acknowledged the simplicity, the pragmatism, the absence of pride, and saw it as yet another sign of a female perception of the world which distinguished naturally between various registers of existence. On one level, there was a complicity between them—she might even go so far as to say they were friends—but the value of things and the demands of life meant that a product on sale must be bought at its fair price.

"Did he have anything useful to tell you?" she asked Lionel as they were walking back to the trucks.

"Yes. We'll keep on driving for a while. We have two hours of daylight. I'll brief you at supper."

His martial tone made her smile, but she said nothing and went back to her place next to Alex, at the wheel.

They drove out, blowing their horns to clear the village streets. The sight of the convoy had attracted curious onlookers to the main street, and gangs of children chattered loudly as they ran next to the trucks.

The landscape was much lovelier now that they had left the low-lying valleys. There were gently rolling hills, but clearly the more mountainous terrain resisted human effort at domestication. Fields ended at the foot of rocky slopes, or stopped at the threshold of the pine forests that covered steep escarpments of icy gorges. From time to time they could see high peaks on the horizon. The fog banks that the sunless day had failed to dispel grew thicker with the onset of nightfall.

Lionel pulled the lead truck into the entrance of an old quarry. A vast circular space was strewn with gravel, and all around were the sides of the quarry. It had been excavated in stages, and its yellowish wall was streaked with grooves carved by trickling water. In one corner was a pile of rusty carcasses, not signs of war but rather the abandoned relics of the extracting machinery.

Once again the evening routine obeyed a strict choreography. Vauthier, after his brief hour of glory as the mechanic, was the fire minder, and that day he was also on grub duty.

They had some difficulty driving the tent pegs into the stony ground. Marc twisted several pegs by banging on them with a big stone. When it was pitch dark they lit two storm lamps. Sitting in a circle around the campfire, they ate their dinner in silence. Everyone knew that Lionel had something to say, but he prolonged the waiting to make his speech seem more important.

"Twelve kilometers or so from here we'll be leaving the

Krajina and entering Republika Srpska, the self-proclaimed state of the Bosnian Serbs. They're bound to check us very thoroughly. We have to be well prepared."

Alex, sitting cross-legged, was listening attentively. Marc was tracing arcane signs on the ground with the tip of a stick. Maud was drowsy. Suddenly Lionel raised his voice.

"And that's why I've decided we won't go any farther tomorrow morning."

There was a moment of hesitation in the little group, which Alex then interrupted with a jesting tone.

"So we're staying here? Why not, it's a great place!"

"We won't leave until we've finished taking the inventory of the trucks."

Alex shuddered and Maud noticed that in spite of his usually cocky air, Marc shot him a worried look.

"Inventory. Which means?" he asked, unflinching.

"Which means we unpack everything. There's room here, it's perfect. We open all the crates and we make sure the contents correspond to the freight lists. And then we pack it all up again."

There was a long silence.

"We've just lost a whole day with the breakdown," protested Alex. "You want to waste another one? We'll get there once the war is over at this rate."

His irony fell flat. No one laughed. Marc took advantage of the silence to calmly ask a question.

"Is this usual, this sort of procedure? Or is there a problem?"

"There is a problem."

"Can you tell us what?"

"The old man, this afternoon, told me that the paramilitaries in the region are very jumpy at the moment. I don't want to take the slightest risk. We're going to check the load. That's all."

There was no need for any further explanation; the two former soldiers knew very well what was going on. Lionel's defiance had to be about them. But he didn't want a scene, let alone a fight. He said goodnight, and went off to sleep.

"You can put out the fire," barked Vauthier, following him.

Maud was surprised by Lionel's decision, but she didn't have the courage to question it. She'd slept badly the night before and their walk had tired her out. She said goodnight and headed for her truck.

Alex and Marc sat on alone by the dying embers. Once Maud had drawn the curtains in the truck and the light had gone out in Lionel and Vauthier's tent, pitched at some distance from the fire, they began to whisper.

"You said something," Marc attacked.

"I swear I didn't."

"You told the girl everything. How else would they have found out?"

"Who says they've found out?"

"Why would he be wanting to search the trucks if he hasn't found out?"

"Fuck, will you believe me?"

Alex had raised his voice and Marc looked over at the tent.

"Quiet! Don't make it worse."

"I didn't tell the girl anything," insisted Alex. "It must be something else. Maybe this afternoon. Remember, when we were talking, after we broke down. We weren't paying any attention to Vauthier."

"Could be."

Marc didn't sound convinced. He had not changed his mind, but he had moved on: there was no time left to beat themselves up about the past. Now they had to decide what to do the next day.

"In any case, it's too late now. If you really didn't say anything to him, you'll have to talk to him now."

"Wait, I don't get it. You accuse me of talking to Maud, and now you're asking me to talk."

"The situation has changed, that's all. Before, you weren't supposed to talk to her because she might tell on us. But if you didn't talk to her, that's different. It would be better to explain to her what's going on rather than let them just find the stuff. What would be ideal is if they never open the box. You follow?"

This was the way it always was, between them. Marc inevitably had the upper hand and it was often difficult to know why. Even when Alex was sure he was wrong, he ended up doing what Marc told him to do. It wasn't a question of authority, even less of rank. Initially Alex had faulted himself for being weak, an imbecile. And then he eventually saw something quite beautiful in their relationship, a particular type of friendship. He trusted him, it was as simple as that. He knew Marc well enough to understand that he always did what was best for both of them. And he thought he carried a greater burden of selfishness, cowardice, and conformity than his comrade: consequently, in spite of his reticence, he always ended up falling in with Marc's opinion.

"Okay, I'll talk to her tomorrow morning."

Lying on the cold, uneven ground in his tent, he thought about it at length, and it took him several hours to get to sleep.

In the stony amphitheater of the quarry, the nighttime damp lingered and caused the sides of the tents to stream with condensation. When they got up, they were stiffer than usual. But the sky was clear and the sun was almost warm, a last autumnal sunshine rising in the east above the clusters of trees. The rocky sides of the quarry were glistening with a straw-colored glow, and those bushes that still had leaves turned russet, warm to the gaze. Maud thought to herself that it would have been a good day for traveling. Instead, once they'd had breakfast, they rolled back the tarps on the trucks, took out the lists of items making up their cargo, and got started on their inventory.

Marc displayed unexpected zeal, which meant that thanks to him the first truck was ready to be unloaded before the other one. Lionel started on that one, with Vauthier's help.

Alex and Maud waited their turn, drinking another coffee. They warmed their hands with their tin mugs.

"Do you feel like going for a run?" suggested Alex. "Just a quick lap, to stretch our legs. This will take them a while."

"Good idea."

They emptied their cups and Maud called out to the others: "We're going for a little jog, we'll be right back."

They set off at a trot. The road was still in shadow and it felt damper there. Their breath rose in white scrolls. Alex ran easily, his stride was loose, and despite their steady pace, he didn't get out of breath.

"You know," he began, once they had warmed up, "I have something to tell you. That's why I wanted us to get away."

Maud gave him a sidelong glance. From anyone else, she might have feared a romantic confession, a declaration, a sexual proposition. But she trusted him. Why didn't she feel the least bit wary in his presence?

"Go ahead. I'm listening."

The road came out of a long bend and overlooked some pastureland. Maud raised her face to the sun and blinked with pleasure.

"Do you remember what I told you about the mine in Kakanj?"

"Refugees in the ovens."

The image had stayed with her. Filled her with a sort of horror. At the same time, she couldn't quite picture the scene. She had even dreamt about it. Images of crematoria, which she'd seen in the big book about deportation in her parents' library, had come to mind.

"Yes, but I also mentioned the pumps."

"The pumps that empty the water from the tunnels, you mean."

"And without which the mine would be flooded and could never be used again."

"So?"

"Well, they run on coal."

Maud was disappointed. She had expected a confession about Alex's girlfriend or something in that vein, in other words a human, concrete, emotional issue. Something alive, basically. And she couldn't understand why he was still talking about the pumps.

"And as I told you, they're not extracting coal anymore, since the mine has been shut down."

A flock of blackbirds sat studying them on a nearby rock shaped like a locomotive, and Maud looked at them with a smile.

"So what do they do if they have no more coal?" she said distractedly, to give Alex the impression she was interested in what he was telling her.

"At the beginning of the war, the mine was still running, but they made no more deliveries. For a few days, they built up a supply, and then everything stopped. So to run the pumps, they used coal from the supply."

What an odd boy, honestly! Why was he acting so hesitantly, so awkwardly just to talk about some business with coal? Whatever the case might be, it had given them the opportunity for a little run, and Maud felt good. Never mind if the price to pay was a boring conversation.

"So is it important, this supply?" she went on politely.

"That's just the problem. It's coming to the end."

"Can't the UN send them a convoy of coal?"

"No, it's not allowed. Fuel is considered strategic material. The Serbs have taken that into account, in their war. They have been sabotaging everything that isn't in their own zone. In Sarajevo, for example, right at the beginning they attacked the power plants to deprive the city of electricity."

However fit he might be, Alex was having trouble keeping pace while he was talking so much. He was out of breath and Maud slowed down so he could regain his calm. This conversation was really spoiling her pleasure. She was wondering how to change the subject without annoying him.

"There is only one way the pumps can keep working so that the mine will survive," he insisted.

"Which is?"

"To extract the coal right there. Not a lot, just enough to build up a supply."

"So, what is stopping them? Nothing, I suppose."

"On the contrary."

He really had no intention of talking about anything else. Maud felt a bad mood coming on. She suggested going back to the quarry. Docile, Alex agreed to turn around. But after they had gone a hundred yards, he stopped and changed his tone.

"You have to listen to me, Maud. I'm not just talking to pass the time of day."

She was struck by his serious tone and could hear the real concern in his voice.

"Let's sit down over there," she said, pointing to a mound of stubbly grass dried by the sun.

"I'll get to the point," said Alex. "To extract the coal from a mine like Kakanj, there is no other way than to shatter the coal face in a tunnel. The seam is very hard, and tools are not enough to break it up. Once the face has been cracked, it can be broken by hand or with a drill, and they can mine the coal. But first it has to be shattered."

"And how do you shatter a coal face?" asked Maud, who was beginning to see what might be at stake.

"With explosives."

She turned to Alex. He met her gaze and she understood.

"And getting explosives to the mine is even more difficult than getting coal there, I imagine?"

"It's not even an issue. The Serbs wouldn't want to know."

She was staring at him and suddenly she got the impression that he was a complete stranger, trying to manipulate her.

"However," he hastened to add, "they're not military explosives. They're sticks you drive into a hole and which cause simple cracks to appear in the rock. They can serve no other purpose. You can't blow up just any old thing with them."

"But they are explosives."

"There's no other word for it but in fact they're nothing like military devices. They're used on construction sites."

"And you have stashed some in our trucks, is that it?"

He nodded, like a little kid caught red-handed.

"You put explosives in our cargo!"

She had gotten to her feet and was looking at him, her eyes full of rage.

"You put explosives in our cargo! You are out of your mind! Do you realize the danger you've put us in! You have dragged an entire association into your bullshit plot. And you don't give a damn that three people who are completely innocent will end up in jail?"

She started walking toward the quarry. Alex leapt to his feet, caught up with her, and grabbed her by the arm. She pulled away and spun around. It was always the same thing with men. There was no trusting them, even when they seemed sincere. Maud felt betrayed. She was angry with herself for letting her guard down. Despite his angelic face, Alex was just like the others. Lionel had been right to put him in the same bag as his colleague.

"Calm down. If I'm talking to you, it is precisely because—"

"Because you think you can just turn on the charm and

wind me up inside your stupid plan. You think I can't tell what you're up to?"

Alex looked down.

"I thought you might understand."

There was real disappointment in his voice. Maud went on walking toward the campsite, but she didn't run. He followed her in silence. She was thinking about the situation, and the farther she went, the slower she walked. She felt torn, undecided. Her rage was draining away, and now she could imagine what would happen. The only thing for it was to denounce Alex and provoke an explanation. In spite of everything, this option disgusted her. He had trusted her. Whatever his ulterior motives might be, she was the one he had turned to. She didn't want to behave stupidly, like some apparatchik—like Lionel, in other words. It was at least her duty to hear him out, and to try to understand.

"Why didn't you put your own convoy together to transport it?" she said to herself, not expecting any answer. "After all, there are private individuals who send aid to Bosnia. What was the point dragging a real humanitarian organization into it?"

Alex let her express her disgust, expel the tension that his revelation had caused. Then he collapsed by the side of the road, his head in his hands, and not obviously answering her, he began talking in turn.

6

"Once you've spent some time with these people," said Alex, not addressing anyone in particular, "you no longer see things the same way."

Maud shot him a sharp look. He was going to whine, and talk about his girlfriend, and try to arouse her pity through his emotions. She was prepared to add some pity to her anger. But what would that change?

"In fact they don't give a damn about what we can bring them," he continued. "They're really tough, it's incredible. People like us are lost without our supermarkets and drugstores. But they've never been spoiled."

Maud wondered why she was listening. And yet, he'd struck the right chord, perhaps just by chance. She'd asked herself the same question, in fact. There was this war; there were atrocities being committed. And what was she doing? She was bringing them chocolate and bandages. She had eventually come to accept this state of things as a particular sign of the times. That's just the way it was and, basically, she didn't know what else she could do. But that didn't stop her feeling uneasy, and even ashamed.

"They know the war will end one day," said Alex. "There have been a shitload of wars in this part of the world. They always come to an end."

A cart drawn by a mule was coming down the road. A wrinkled peasant held the reins, slumped on the wooden seat. He didn't even look at them as he went by. It was as if he had come there deliberately, to illustrate Alex's words. You could tell that, since birth, the old man had accepted his fate, a fate that called for both resistance and submission. The very notion of offering him material assistance was ridiculous, completely out of place. Maud joined Alex on the grassy embankment.

"What they want," continued Alex, "is simply to go on living."

The pale sun caressed them. They turned their faces to the light.

"For me, that's what humanitarian work means."

Alex had suddenly regained his energy. He looked at Maud.

"When the war is over, they mustn't be left with a country that is completely devastated, don't you see? People have to be able to go on living. This country has no resources in energy, they have no source of warmth or work, and the most important thing is to preserve what little there is. This industry is their only wealth."

He paused for a moment then delivered his conclusion, his tone full of passion and enthusiasm; there was nothing guilty about it.

"Believe me, the most useful thing in this convoy is those little explosives; they will make it possible for them to save the mine."

Maud didn't like received ideas. She had always deplored the fact that most people could not grasp the complexity of things. She was fascinated by paradoxes. Paradoxes nourished intelligence. The thought that humanitarian work might not be what everyone thought it was—herself included only a few moments earlier—was a troubling discovery, a kind of challenge. She would be angry with herself if she failed to take up that challenge.

"Do you think that aid work should consist in transporting explosives?" she asked, not so much to ridicule Alex's words as to encourage him to go on with the intellectual game he had started playing with her.

"I think that humanitarian aid means a lot of things. And there are also a lot of players in the field. For major organizations like the UN to stick to bringing supplies, that's normal. Those supplies are needed, and the UN can't take any initiative beyond the mandate the member states have given them. But NGOs aren't bound in the same way. They're free. What's the point of their freedom if it doesn't allow them to go one step further and do things that technically are not allowed?"

"Provided it's what they've decided and their people in the field accept the risk. You said nothing. You put your explosives on our trucks and you didn't say a thing."

"Well, we're telling you now."

Maud shrugged.

"That's too easy. We no longer have any choice in the matter."

"Whatever; we're telling you now," said Alex again, looking her straight in the eye. "We're telling you: this is what we intend to bring. And this is why. The only question is, do you think it can help, yes or no?"

She stood up, wiping the dust from the back of her jeans.

It was odd: she felt like laughing. This business with the explosives was the first interesting thing that had happened since they left Lyon. She hadn't wanted to admit as much to herself, but she was bored in the convoy. Other than the excitement to be had driving a truck, there was nothing that thrilled her. The routine of their days and nights was grim, the atmosphere was leaden, the landscape was monotonous. Without realizing, she had had been hoping for an event, anything, provided it was unexpected. And this one exceeded anything she could have imagined.

"What do we risk if we get caught?"

"Not much. They'll take the trucks and put us in jail for a few days. France will send a civil servant, a consul or someone like that, and they'll let us go. Otherwise it would make the lead story on the evening news and the Serbs don't want that."

Maud laughed to herself, imagining her mother weeping by her TV set. What difference would it make? Her mother was already convinced she'd gone off to her death. If her daughter *really* got into trouble, she wouldn't be any more worried than she already was. At least she would have the satisfaction of knowing she was right.

"But I watched you at the checkpoints. You didn't look all that calm . . . "

"Because you guys didn't know about it. That's what I feared more than anything. If we are all on the same page, there's less risk they'll find anything, and if by chance they do, we'll have agreed beforehand about what to say. They're no big deal, these little explosives. Unless we stumble on some specialists, we could even say that they're, I don't know, that they're medical supplies . . . "

"Why? What do they look like?"

"Sticks wrapped in aluminum foil."

"Are there many?"

"Two hundred. But they're spread through several boxes."

"Are you the ones who hid them before we left?"

"Yeah, it was Marc. He managed to get himself locked inside the garage at La Tête d'Or and he opened some of the boxes."

"On both trucks?"

"No, on the one he's driving."

They had been walking fairly slowly but were absorbed in their conversation and before they knew it they were in sight of the quarry.

"So what do we do?" asked Alex.

He was actually asking Maud, because he himself had no choice.

"I don't know," she said, walking faster.

And if she were being completely honest, she really did not know.

The atmosphere was tense. Marc and Lionel were tightening the ropes on the tarp at the back of the first truck. Vauthier was busy at the cooking stove, looking grumpy.

"Where did you get to, the pair of you?" said Lionel. "This is no time for embarking on some romance."

His stupid remark was destined to annoy Maud. Since she was hesitating about which side to choose, all it took was an innocuous detail for the scale to tip to one side. She was vaguely aware, even though she thought it was ridiculous, that Lionel's thoughtless utterance might actually be deciding everything.

"We're going to start on the second truck," said Lionel. "But let's have some lunch first, that way we can take off again right away afterwards."

"It's too early for lunch," said Alex.

"Well, we've been working. We're hungry."

Maud lifted the lid on the casserole that was simmering on the stove. Ratatouille from a can was bubbling underneath the sausages Vauthier had tossed in. They passed around the poorly washed plastic plates, still sticky with smudges of sauce from last night's dinner. Maud served everyone with a tin ladle, and they went to sit on the ground at some distance from each other. Just the thought that this routine would go on, day after day, with this tension in the air, all this unvoiced hostility conveyed in every gesture, she began to hope that suddenly everything would blow sky high, that things would be out in the open, even if it meant a violent reckoning.

She quickly finished eating and wiped her plate with a crust of bread, then took it over to the basin full of dishes.

"Is there any coffee left?"

This was Marc's strong point. Every morning, he made two liters of coffee that he poured into thermoses. The little Maud knew about him was that he was from the north of France and ran all day on coffee.

"The big plastic thermos is empty, but there's still some in the stainless one," he said.

Maud poured a cup. It was a pale liquid, not even black, that looked more like tea than coffee, and took on the taste of the receptacle it was kept in.

The others came over to help themselves as well.

"Did you find anything in the boxes?" she asked.

"Nothing."

"Is there really any point in searching the other vehicle?"

"We're going to finish what we've started," said Lionel firmly.

Drawn by the cooking smells, two crows sat watching them from a distance. Maud noticed that Marc was looking at Alex. She got the impression that Alex was raising his eyebrows, as if to express his bewilderment.

"Okay, shall we get on with it?" grumbled Vauthier.

He was the most determined. For all that he acted high and mighty, Lionel was just following Vauthier. Maud, influenced by the early stages of the journey when she was still in the lead truck, had thought Marc was the most troublesome in the group, with his dark airs and silence. But she was beginning to realize that the constant atmosphere of subdued violence in the group came from Vauthier.

"Let me finish my cigarette and then we'll get started," said Lionel.

"Stay where you are!"

Maud had almost shouted. She surprised even herself with her reaction. They all stared at her.

"Stay where you are, we need to talk."

They hesitated, standing there, coffee in hand. Finally they came closer, and as Maud was sitting on the ground, they also sat down, one after the other.

"There's no point opening the boxes," she started.

Suddenly she was afraid, and wanted to rewind the clock,

not to interfere. But they were all staring at her. A childhood memory came to her. She was at the swimming pool with her brother. They had been diving off the edge, and then at one point her brother challenged her to jump from the big diving board, the thirty-foot one. Children were not allowed to use it. They had climbed up, both of them. From up there the pool seemed tiny. It was an outdoor pool. The sun was playing on the water, sparkling white flashes of light. Her brother had made as if to go forward, but no sooner did he arrive at the end of the diving board than he came back at a run, white with terror. So then Maud walked out to the edge. She was absolutely frozen with panic and wanted to desert her own body. Someone down below had spotted them and sounded the alarm. She heard faraway shouts but inside her there was only a great silence. She had decided: she would not go through with it, she would follow her brother back down the ladder. But just then she saw the people looking at her. Dozens of fearful gazes staring right at her. More than fifteen years had gone by but she was still convinced that it was because of those gazes that she had jumped. For all that she had ended up in the hospital for ten days with a fractured vertebra that could have left her paralyzed, she never remembered that moment without thinking, with a secret pride, that it had determined the course of her entire life.

"Let me tell you what you're going to find in those boxes," she declared.

Vauthier, who had stayed to one side, came nearer. Marc and Alex looked at each other again. Lionel was puffing nervously on his cigarette.

"Some of the boxes contain explosives."

"Bastards, I knew it!" shouted Vauthier.

"Let me finish, will you?"

They were stunned by what Maud had said but even more by her sudden air of authority.

"They're not military explosives. They're small construction explosives, for extracting coal."

Perfectly clearly, without being interrupted, she explained it all: the mine, the pumps, the tunnels that would be flooded. And she finished by giving her opinion, and felt as if she was discovering it for the first time, although it echoed Alex's words:

"It is probably the most useful thing we can give those people. I'm prepared to take the risk."

An ominous silence greeted her closing words. And indeed, once she finished, the storm broke.

"Explosives!" shouted Vauthier. "You want us to transport explosives? I don't believe it!"

He got quickly to his feet.

"I'm going to open these boxes right away, and we're going to leave your crap here."

He was beside himself. You could see he wanted to grab the two soldiers by the scruff of the neck, but he seemed to focus most of his hatred on Marc.

The crows flew away, shrieking, a sudden emphatic contrast to the thick silence that reigned in the quarry.

And then something unexpected happened: Vauthier realized he was alone.

Lionel, even though he had been under his influence, was too sensitive to the balance of power not to realize that he was in the minority. Maud and the two soldiers didn't move. Vauthier's agitation was ineffective in light of the strength they emanated.

"Let's stop and think," said Lionel at last.

Maud knew this meant that she had won this round.

And it was all the more disturbing in that she was not sure she was right. She had jumped off the diving board with no idea what, upon landing, the consequences of her fall into the unknown would be.

As a matter of form, the discussion lasted nearly two more hours. The aim was to dispel any objections, to weigh the risks and distribute the roles. But each of them felt more and more clearly that their decision, in principle, had already been made.

Alex went to get some explosive sticks from his things, a bundle he had kept out on purpose in case he needed to show the others what they looked like. And indeed, you would have to be a specialist to know what they were. They looked like some sort of marzipan wrapped in shiny paper. The interior had the consistency of a candle wax, with a little twisted wick poking out. Alex suggested they should say it was a gift for a church in the region. Lionel regained some of his self-assurance and declared learnedly that, in any case, he had never seen any paramilitaries open boxes at checkpoints. They might, on the other hand, confiscate one or two. So if they left a few boxes open at the back, they might be content just to rummage through those. Marc confirmed that the sticks were well-camouflaged and that they'd really have to go through the load with a fine-tooth comb to find them. Vauthier, off to one side, had begun smoking. No one paid him any attention. The others had vaguely expected him to declare that he wouldn't continue the journey with them and that he'd manage to get home on his own, but he didn't say anything of the sort. Maud wondered if he was really as brave as he made out.

There were a lot of questions about the possibility of accidentally setting off the explosives. At first Alex asserted that there was no danger at all. But Marc protested and said they had to be honest, that there was some risk all the same. It was minimal, but not zero: if they were shot at, a possibility none of them liked to envisage, or if there were a fire, they'd have to be very careful. Oddly enough, his declaration seemed to have a calming effect. For a start, it proved that he was playing fair and square, and this enhanced the feeling of trust. Then, more secretly, the presence of danger, however limited, probably made their transgression all the more exciting.

In the end, when all the questions had been dealt with, a sort of peace seemed to fall over the group. Oddly, the tension had waned, and although the crisis ended with Vauthier going off on his own, it had brought the other team members closer together. Lionel seemed unexpectedly content. He had subscribed more easily than Maud had imagined he would to the humanitarian explanation she had given regarding the explosives.

As it was too late to set off again, they prolonged the conversation until dinner. Lionel talked a lot. What he said gave some indication of the reasons compelling him to take on the risk of transporting forbidden cargo. Basically, like many young aid workers, he suffered from a complex with regard to the pioneers of the movement. Heroic gestures in Biafra, clandestine missions in Kurdistan, the adventures of volunteers crossing snow-covered mountain passes in Soviet-occupied Afghanistan during the Cold War: among the NGOs, these experiences were the stuff of legend, reflecting a heroic era. The youngest aid workers felt a sort of nagging regret—that they had come too late, in an era when missions were less adventurous and more organized. This story of saving coal mines by transporting explosives provided them with a unique opportunity to be part of a grander History, to walk in the footsteps of the movement's founders. Basically, it was because he was an apparatchik of humanitarian aid, deeply imbued with the culture of the association he worked for, that Lionel had so readily agreed to transgress its rules.

Maud prepared the supper, not even aware whether it was her turn that night or not. Marc went to fetch a bottle of white wine from his things. He did not say what he had been saving it for; no one asked, they all drank some. Except Vauthier, who was still brooding, off on his own.

II
COMMITMENT

1

The early morning was still just as difficult, perhaps even more so, because they'd gone to bed late, and were feeling the effects of the wine. But the sun was out again. As soon as they had left the horrible quarry behind, they found themselves amid russet forests and apple-green pastures. They had a feeling the fine weather wouldn't last. Thick clouds lurked in the west and would not leave the sky smiling for long. It hardly mattered: it was now that they were in need of optimism and cheer, and they laid in their store of it.

The barrier between the two former soldiers and the rest of the group had come down. Maud noticed during breakfast that Marc and Lionel were speaking to each other, which was unusual. She supposed that in the lead truck Vauthier must be sulking on his bunk at the back, but between the two drivers the tension had eased. Alex, too, was in a very good mood. He did the first stint of driving. Maud managed to find a station on the truck's old radio. Music coming from who knew where filled the cab with sappy melodies that were in tune with their state of mind, both serene and jovial.

In appearance, nothing had changed. They were driving the same dilapidated vehicles, covered with the same stickers bearing the logo of La Tête d'Or. And yet it was as if suddenly the mission had become their own. They had decided on its aim, and together they were assuming a risk that no one had imposed on them. They did not know any better now than before what to expect, but they sensed that henceforth their experience of events would no longer be purely passive.

Maud in particular was pleased that, thanks to their discussions, she had a more precise vision of the people they were on their way to help. She liked the fact of knowing that the "beneficiaries" were not simply mouths to feed, famished bellies. Their desires were those of conscious beings, they had plans for their future, the will to resist. In short, they were human.

"What does Bouba look like?"

Alex looked at her, surprised. He must be thinking about the people in the place they were headed, too.

"Bouba? She's tall. To be honest, when I first met her, I thought she was a lot older. I thought she was at least twenty-five or twenty-six."

"Is she blond, brunette?"

He reached inside his hip pocket and took out a photo. A poor snapshot with worn edges. A ray of sun veiled an entire segment of the photograph. In the middle was a girl with a long face who bore a resemblance—obviously much younger—to the tall peasant woman who had taken them into her house. She, too, had short hair—chestnut, badly cut—and her clothes were unrefined: a cheap nylon shirt, heavy cotton trousers that were too big. But she'd rolled up the sleeves and left her collar open, and her pose was graceful. She was smiling defiantly, as if to say: none of that matters. On the left-hand side of the snap a thick black metal door with rounded corners was visible.

"Is that the oven?"

"Yes."

"Where did she live before the war?"

"In the town. Her father was an engineer."

"Is she Muslim?"

"According to the Serbs and Croats she is. But she didn't know that before."

"How can that be?"

"People from the cities are often very mixed. Her mother is from Sarajevo. She's the daughter of a Muslim and a Croat. On her father's side there's a bit of everything, even Albanian. Under Tito, no one asked them to choose. They were Yugoslav and that was enough. At the beginning of the war they had a neighbor they'd fallen out with because of some shadowy business about an adjoining barn wall. The neighbor joined the Ustashe, the Croatian nationalists. As soon as the fighting started, he fingered them as mixed race. Their house was one of the first to burn."

"And did the neighbor get the barn?"

"I suppose he did. In any case Bouba's family had to flee in the middle of the night. The only shelter they could find was at the mine. I suppose the others would eventually have killed them if the peacekeepers hadn't arrived."

"Where did you and Bouba used to meet?"

"We would walk around the factory together. Like I said, I wasn't allowed to take her into the military buildings, and around her family we had to behave properly. So we used to go for walks. Even that was dangerous. If we got too close to the barbed wire surrounding the zone, there would be boys on the other side shouting insults at her."

"Did you know any other peacekeepers who got involved the way you did?"

"Not in Kakanj. Most of them are sappers, real yokels, you know, the type of guys who parade on Bastille Day with their leather apron and their sledgehammer over their shoulder. What they're after is whores. They wait till they're on leave then they go find them in Split."

"Marc, too?"

"No, on the contrary. He even stood up for me, when the others were calling me a fag."

Alex gave a long, sad laugh. Silence fell. Maud decided to

speak because she could sense that Alex was in the process of slipping gently into a sorrowful melancholy.

"What do you think you'll do later, with Bouba?"

Alex took his time to answer. There was a big pothole in the road, an enormous cavity full of mud. He steered around it, carefully.

"I want to live there with her," he said, not looking at Maud.

They remained silent after his confession. It was surely the first time that Maud had observed love so close up, the kind of love that made you take risks, cross continents, forget your own self. For a long time she had believed in that sort of love. She eventually concluded it didn't exist.

After lunch, they continued on their way under a lowering gray sky. Once the sun was gone, the cold air returned. The brief interlude of cheer that had followed the crisis from the day before was well and truly over. The thought of danger was once again on their minds, but this time it was an added danger they would all confront together, in full knowledge of the facts.

They caught up with a long UN convoy and followed the brand-new white tractor-trailers. It was slightly after 2 P.M. when the UN vehicles stopped to go through the necessary procedures for entry into Republika Srpska. Serbian soldiers were inspecting the trucks. They were in full uniform and their weapons were in good condition. The checkpoint looked patently more like a border worthy of the name. It was, to be sure, a wartime border, with old Soviet tanks in firing position and the barrels of machine guns peering out of guard posts. But it was all organized and disciplined. It was more serious, but also more reassuring, because there was no need to fear that some jumpy paramilitary, alone with his reactions and prone to irrational behavior, might suddenly lose it.

Most of the procedure was administrative: they had to produce documents that were in order, which theirs were.

The UN convoy was allowed through. Lionel moved his truck up to the barrier. The road was blocked by an actual metal barrier painted red and white, not just an improvised roadblock or even a simple rope stretched across the road, of the sort found at little country checkpoints.

The soldier who had taken their documents went into a house with a burnt roof, where an office had been set up on the ground floor.

While they waited for him to come back out, they chatted, except for Vauthier, who stood off to one side smoking. There was a strange atmosphere. They were in great danger, and they knew it, but the fear was gone. Perhaps this was due to the roadblock itself, which was quiet, or to the soldiers manning the checkpoint and their professional attitude, dolefully carrying out their duties without a hint of aggression. But Maud had another feeling, and she could have sworn that the others shared it: she felt strong. She felt as if she had found her place in this war, and though she might be doing something risky, it was meaningful.

As a child, she had spent almost every July at her grandmother's place in the Berry. She had often gotten her to talk about the demarcation line that cut through the countryside during the war not three kilometers from there. Her grandmother had been roughly her age then and from the photographs she had shown her, they looked alike. The young woman crossed the line almost every day on her bicycle, on her way to her sewing classes in Bourges. The Resistance often entrusted her with messages. She had been decorated for her work at the time of the Liberation. Maud hadn't been interested in details—about the resistance network, or political issues, or the development of the conflict. What she wanted to know was what her grandmother had felt when she rode up to the soldiers and stopped her bike to show them her papers. The old woman found her question awkward. She searched her memories and said, "Nothing." Now Maud understood.

And if someone were to ask her what she felt right at that moment, she would say, "Nothing." For her fear had left her. She had felt it over these last few days, but now that she was looking for it she could not find a trace of it left anywhere inside her. Her mind and body were calm. Her heart was not beating any faster, her palms weren't sweating, she wasn't the least bit impatient or tense. At the most she got the impression that colors were more vivid, even the khaki on the armor plating, or the shiny black of the well-oiled weapons. And sounds seemed to come from farther away, like those birds chirping in the scraggly elm tree that stood a hundred yards or so from there, by the edge of the road. She tested herself, thinking, I am in a war zone, transporting explosives. But the thought did not elicit any sense of panic. Obviously, they weren't high explosives, and in fact the risk was minimal. Still, they'd abandoned the clear conscience of the aid worker, and it was an act that was close to the early stirrings of resistance. She was proud of it.

Before long the soldier came back with their papers duly stamped. They climbed into their cabs and set off again.

That evening at their camp Lionel proved to them that he, too, had changed. He spread out the map which up to now he had jealously kept folded in the door of the truck, and told them what he knew about the next roadblocks. He even went so far as to ask the team for their opinion regarding the route they should take. There could be only one reason for this sudden conversion to democracy: in his opinion, the essence of the convoy had changed. It was no longer the docile instrument of an organization he represented, something that obliged him to take decisions on his own and impose his point of view. Or at least that was what he thought, because it was surely how the leader of his first convoy had behaved, when he, Lionel, was still a simple driver. From now on this expedition, given the particular nature of its cargo, required teamwork, and they had to run it together. Lionel had never felt very comfortable acting the boss. The harsh way he'd gone about his duties was surely the result of his uncertainty. The business with the explosives, even if it was hardly what he would have asked for, provided him with an unhoped-for pretext to share the burden of his responsibilities.

"From now on," he explained, "the situation will change every day. We still have thirty kilometers in the Serbian enclave where they'll leave us alone, but after that we'll come to Croatian and Muslim pockets, and it will change all the time. Central Bosnia is a real patchwork."

"Is there fighting?" asked Maud.

"All the time. But nothing major. The ethnic zones are all mixed up. One day they advance by three houses, they take a field, sometimes an entire village. And then the next day the others take it back."

Marc no longer kept to himself. He had left off his menacing tone now that Lionel had agreed to open discussions, and especially since Vauthier was no longer around.

"Could you show us the complete route you want us to take?"

Lionel spread his hands over the map to smooth the folds, then followed a little gray ribbon with his finger.

"This is our route."

"It's a secondary road," said Maud. "Why didn't we take the main road along the river as far as Tuzla?"

"Good question," said Marc calmly. "To be honest, Lionel, we've been wanting to ask you for a while now. We don't understand why you headed south before Bihać, we don't get it."

"It's the most direct way to Kakanj, isn't it?"

"It is, if you want direct, it's direct! Unfortunately, something is missing on your map."

"What?"

"The relief, for Christ's sake. Why do you think we've hardly run into anyone since we started on this road?"

"We followed the UN convoy a while ago."

"If we had stayed on the main road, it's not just one convoy we would have followed, it's one hundred and fifty."

Lionel was smoking nervously.

"You should have told me sooner if you didn't like the idea."

Marc ignored the bad faith of his reply. They all knew they'd had no say in the matter.

"We figured you had your reasons," he said.

"Actually there's nothing wrong with going this way, there are fewer roadblocks than on the main road," added Alex.

"So you should be grateful, then?" sneered Vauthier.

They all jumped. No one had heard him come over. Everyone thought he was still by the trucks.

Marc turned around quickly and stared at Vauthier. His look was provocative; it expressed defiance, scorn, a desire to fight. Until now, all the hostility had come from Vauthier, and Marc, who had been well aware of it, had been careful not to react. But ever since the mechanic had squealed on them, Marc no longer tried to hide what he thought about Vauthier. Maud was fascinated by how quickly Marc could change his mood. When faced with an adversary, he showed an almost animal strength. His features, his clenched jaw, looked downright cruel. But perhaps because now she knew his other side, she saw a certain charm in his ferocity.

Whatever the case might be, Vauthier's appearance had put an end to the discussion.

"We'll decide tomorrow," said Lionel.

He folded the map and they split up for the night as usual.

The drive through Serbian territory was uneventful, as Marc had predicted. They saw almost no convoys, and in the villages they always found things to buy. There was little destruction in the zone. The countryside went on living as usual, to the rhythm of the farm work. Their last day in the sector fell on a Sunday. The Orthodox churches with their brick walls and onion domes drew crowds of worshippers, who arrived on tractors, in carts, on foot, or on muleback. Cars and trucks seemed to have vanished, no doubt requisitioned for the purposes of the war, unless there had never been any cars and trucks to begin with.

They left Republika Srpska behind them as night was falling, and went through a checkpoint very similar to the one where they had entered, but not as busy with military vehicles. On the other side, after a no-man's-land, they found a tiny agricultural enclave. At first they couldn't figure out what ethnic group it belonged to and then on the way out of the village they saw a minaret. The peasants looked exactly the same as in the Serbian zone. For Maud, this was yet another odd thing about this war, which opposed people who spoke the same language, lived on the same land, and went about their daily lives in the same way.

In the lead truck there was a quick discussion about whether to stop there for the night or keep on going. The shadows were beginning to lengthen. In less than an hour it would be completely dark. Marc suggested they should pitch camp right away.

"Tomorrow, we'll be in the Croatian zone," objected Lionel. "If they suspect we spent the night here, they might search us from top to bottom."

"What difference does that make?"

"They're getting more and more paranoid in this part of the country. And the French have a reputation for supporting the Muslims. They'll never believe we stopped without a reason. They're bound to think we're hiding guys who want to get out of the zone."

"But if we try to go through at night, that will seem even more suspicious."

"Convoys often a cross at night, and if we hurry up, it will still be daylight."

Lionel would not budge. In the end, Marc gave in; they decided to keep going.

According to what a peasant had told them, they had to leave the little valley and cross the pass they could see higher up, where they would reach the Croatian checkpoint. And yet when they reached the summit they didn't see anything that looked like a roadblock. The enclave must be bigger than they thought. Night fell, moonless. The truck's headlights were splattered with mud and lit the road poorly. They had to drive slowly. They began their descent. One hundred yards further along they heard the first shots, fired right at them. Maud had never heard actual gunshots, other then deep in Alpine fir forests during hunting season. She did not immediately make the connection between the cracking sound she heard in the distance and the whistling near the cab. She only realized when they heard a louder detonation, which was the sound of a tire bursting.

But Alex knew exactly what was going on. He opened his door and grabbed her by the arm. She found herself lying on the damp ground, in a ditch.

Once the firing had stopped, she heard Lionel shout, *"Pomoć!"* Marc, who had slightly more vocabulary, said something in a loud voice. There was a long silence, disturbed only by the faint sound of liquid trickling somewhere. Then they heard footsteps on the road and understood that the paramilitaries were coming closer. First they saw their boots under the truck, then they saw them standing above them, guns pointed at them.

They got slowly to their feet and stood in a line in the middle of the road, their hands above their heads. The beam of a flashlight lit their faces one by one. They could still hear a little trickling sound, from somewhere near the trucks.

"The fuel," murmured Alex.

A cylindrical barrel with an extra supply of diesel was fastened to each of the trucks. A bullet must have hit one of the spare tanks. But which one? In the darkness it was impossible to make out whether the leak was under the first truck or under the one carrying the explosives.

The patrol that had stopped them consisted of three men. There might have been others nearby but they couldn't see them. The paramilitaries kept their weapons trained on them, unmoving. They seemed to be waiting for something or someone.

2

T heir eyes were getting used to the dark. The paramilitaries were three fearful young boys, wearing black woolen caps with the edges rolled up. Each one had his finger on the trigger of his weapon, submachine guns that could fire a blast of a dozen shots at the slightest pressure.

The fuel was still dripping and the puddle on the ground must have been fairly big because the trickle of fuel was now a steady flow.

Finally they heard footsteps on the road. Someone was coming, slowly, his hobnailed boots ringing on the asphalt. The paramilitaries moved to one side without lowering their weapons, and the newcomer stood in front of the five foreigners. As they could tell in the dark, he was a very old man. He was bald, with a ring of white hair, and his face was deeply lined. But he held himself very straight and gave an impression of strength and authority. He was probably one of those retired officers whom the Croats, lacking in men and experience, had called back up to train the makeshift army they had thrown together at the beginning of the war. In any case, in this place and at this moment he was the boss. If there was hope to be had, it would come from him.

He asked the boys with the guns something, and one of them said a few words. And then Marc chose to speak. He came out with a long sentence, in a calm voice. Maud recognized the language: she had studied Russian in high school for two years but could not speak it.

The man came forward and stopped in front of Marc. There was a moment of uncertainty. He had a hostile, almost outraged expression on his face. Maud got the impression he was going to hit him. Marc stood there, motionless, staring straight ahead, with no insolence this time.

Finally the man spoke. He asked Marc if he was Russian and when he answered that he was French the man laughed and the tension eased. Most of the officers in the Yugoslav Army, particularly the generation that had fought in the Second World War, had been trained in the Soviet Union. The similarity of the two Slavic languages made it easy for them to learn Russian. Marc and the man began to converse, because Marc also spoke quite fluently.

But he did not relax for all that, and kept his hands obediently above his head.

His explanation seemed to satisfy the officer, because he ordered his men to lower their weapons. He took a cigarette out of his jacket pocket and lit it. He was about to throw the match onto the ground when Marc pointed out that he was standing in diesel. The puddle had spread down the slope of the road until it reached the place where they stood. The old man recoiled. One of the paramilitaries beamed his flashlight onto the puddle and followed it back to the leak. The hole was located fairly high up in the tank, which meant that the flow had slowed now. Marc asked for permission to plug the hole and the officer gave it to him without quibbling.

"Vauthier can fix it for us in no time," said Marc.

Vauthier was furious, but given the circumstances he had no choice but to obey Marc. The old soldier said something in Russian.

"He wants me to go with him to check our papers," Marc translated.

Lionel went to fetch them in the truck, then handed them

to Marc, who followed the officer and disappeared with him into the dark.

In the meantime, still watched over by the paramilitaries, the others got out the spare tire and jack and began changing the tire. The truck had come to a sudden stop, swerving sideways across the road, two wheels halfway into the ditch, and this complicated the lifting maneuver. It would probably take a while. Maud waited, sitting on the embankment. She offered to help with the repair but they replied curtly that they didn't need her. As Marc still hadn't come back, she was beginning to get impatient.

"I'll go see what he's doing," she said to Lionel. "It shouldn't take hours to check papers."

Using sign language, she explained to the soldiers that she wanted to go to see their officer. They spoke among themselves and designated one of them to go with her. They had only one flashlight and they kept it. Maud and her guardian angel walked side by side in the dark. The boy smelled of sweat, and the ditches gave out an odor of vegetal mud. They walked almost all the way up to the little pass. The checkpoint was above all a sort of outpost, camouflaged by the fir trees that covered the ridge. It was a fairly long stone building, probably once a sheepfold. It was completely dark, but just as Maud and the young fighter drew near, a ray of light appeared under the door. The boy knocked three times and a voice shouted to come in.

The interior of the building was lit by an oil lamp. The furnishings were ludicrous. A modern, sixties-style sofa was set opposite an oval glass coffee table. Across from it were two upholstered Louis XV armchairs. Along the stone walls around these rather urban furnishings, no doubt the spoils of a raid on a house in the region, were mangers still full of hay. Marc and the old officer sat chatting comfortably over a bottle of *šljivovica*.

"There you are," said Marc. "Come in. Are they done changing the tire?"

"Not yet."

"Then sit down with us while you wait."

He translated his suggestion. The military man nodded, got up, and showed Maud where to sit, gesticulating with a silent gallantry that merely annoyed her.

"Apparently the day before yesterday there was a major skirmish here during the night. We've just had a close call, because when they saw us coming, they thought it was starting up again. We were lucky their machine gun jammed."

Marc laughed and the officer, who looked considerably tipsy, seemed to feel obliged to do likewise. He was missing a tooth at the front of his mouth.

"Maybe we shouldn't go any further tonight," said Maud gravely.

The old soldier was eyeing her, his expression ribald: she felt uneasy.

"That's just what he was explaining to me. There's a terre-plein in front of the post. He said we can pull in there to sleep."

"I'll go tell the others."

"Wait, he'll be upset if you don't taste his plum brandy."

The Croat handed Maud a chipped glass he had filled almost to overflowing with a straw-colored liquid. She took it and sat down in one of the armchairs. The springs were completely gone and she felt as if she were going to tip over backwards; her knees were almost level with her chin.

The two men had started talking again. The paramilitary who had come with Maud sat smoking on the windowsill. He was a very young boy; she thought he couldn't be older than fifteen. He had pulled off his cap. His curly black hair grew low on his forehead. He was looking up at her from under his eyebrows. The officer, too, did not stop glancing over at her, with a salacious gleam in his eyes she'd noticed the moment she arrived. As for Marc, he seemed very much at ease. He was talking calmly and seemed to have a genuine liking for the paramilitaries.

Maud took a few sips of the alcohol, trying not to cough, because she could see that the soldiers were anticipating her reaction and wanted nothing more than to burst out laughing. When they saw that she managed to swallow their rotgut without letting anything show, they seemed a bit disappointed, and the officer went on conversing in Russian.

She might have swallowed the alcohol, but on her empty stomach it made her head spin. She could pick out words but didn't understand them. Before long she was gazing at the scene in a trance. To avoid looking at the officer, she stared at Marc. He filled her with contradictory feelings. On the one hand his severity, his unflinching self-control, and his restrained violence made him difficult to like. But at the same time, there was something reassuring about him. In the dangerous world they were in now, he was the only one who naturally inspired trust, who gave her hope that they were in with a chance to make it through. He really was an unusual person. Maud remembered what Alex had said about his generosity. This was a quality she ordinarily associated with a certain gentle side, and yet Marc didn't seem to have anything gentle about him. Where did his muscular physique come from, his coarse mannerisms, his Spartan habits? Had he cultivated them, or had life imposed them on him? Why had he become a soldier? Was it out of idealism, obligation, or in spite of himself? She got the impression that for all he was a soldier, with a soldier's habits and appearance and ideas, his soul was not that of a soldier.

These thoughts came into her mind one after the other but she realized she could not control them. The fact that they were speaking a foreign language around her enabled her to focus, rather, on their gestures and facial expressions. She observed Marc and tried to imagine what he'd been like as a child. What he'd inherited from his father, or his mother. She wondered where he got his blue-black hair and his slightly swarthy skin. She projected him into landscapes in North Africa, the Middle East, Greece, Latin America, and she tried to guess which setting would have been the most natural. Before long she was completely raving. Would he have dived with her from a height of thirty feet . . .

Suddenly she gave a start. Someone was shaking her shoulder. And on waking she realized that the alcohol had knocked her out.

Fortunately they went out almost at once to join the others, and she didn't have to put up with the two paramilitaries' ironic smiles for very long.

The tire had been repaired and Vauthier was grumbling as he put the jack back under the chassis. The other two were inspecting the trucks, taking stock of the damage. One bullet had gone through the tarp on the first truck, and the second truck had been shot up front: the bullet had ricocheted on the hood of the engine and fortunately not caused any damage.

And yet the atmosphere had changed. When Marc mentioned it, they had not taken seriously the possibility that their cargo might come under fire. Now they had to face facts: they had the proof that it was not an improbable conjecture. What would have happened if the explosives had been hit? Or if the diesel had caught fire, directly beneath the cargo? No one said anything, but they were all thinking about it. Lightheartedness gave way to fear.

"We're going to spend the night here," said Marc. "There is no point in taking any additional risks tonight."

Lionel shot him a dark look.

"Is there somewhere to pitch our tents?"

"A bit higher up, outside their camp. We'll leave the trucks here; they'll be fine. We may as well avoid backing up in the dark and ending up in the ditch."

"Okay."

The fresh air had sobered Maud up and suddenly she panicked. She grabbed Lionel by the arm and took him over to one side.

"Tell me one thing: do I have to sleep in the cab?"

"What are you afraid of?"

"Didn't you see the expression on those guys' faces, and the way they kept looking at me?"

"Don't worry. We're here."

"Here where? Two hundred meters down the road?"

"If you call us—"

"If I call you once they've each had their turn? Thanks a lot! I'm not at all afraid now."

Marc and Alex had already set off for the camp, with their packs on their backs and their arms full with the tents and sleeping bags. Vauthier was following some distance behind.

"What do you suggest? There's only room for two in the tents."

"I'll sleep with Alex and you stay in the cab."

"You're going to sleep with Alex!"

Lionel's reaction was unexpectedly abrupt. Obviously, he couldn't know that Alex was in love with someone else and thought about no one else. Maud figured she ought to tell him. But she didn't. Alex certainly wouldn't want everyone to know his life story. Besides, it wasn't really the moment to start divulging intimate secrets.

"He won't touch me," she said. "We know each other."

Lionel hesitated. Should he refuse, or suggest rather that she sleep with him? Her gaze was hard, and he was afraid of her reaction, whatever he said.

"Do what you want."

"Thanks."

Maud was afraid, simply afraid, and what mattered to her was to be somewhere safe for the night. She climbed into the cab, found her things in the dark, haphazardly, then headed toward the tents, not turning back.

Lionel sat down on the truck's running board, ran his hand through his hair, and shook his head. There was only one thing to do: roll a big one.

In the tent Maud talked with Alex for a long time, because neither one of them could fall asleep.

He explained to her that in Kakanj Marc used to hang out with the Croatian soldiers who were in control of the enclave.

"You mean the same ones who want to kill Bouba and her family?"

"That's the way things are in this war. It doesn't always make sense."

"And yet the two of you are friends?"

"Marc doesn't have prejudices. He may seem rough and antisocial, but he gets along easily with everyone. I mean, he inspires trust and respect. In Kakanj he was just as comfortable around the refugees as with the people who are keeping them prisoner. And he knows very well that I'm in love with a girl who lives in the ovens."

"And that doesn't bother you?"

Alex thought for a long time before replying.

"You know, he behaves just the way the people in this country used to do before the war. They lived together, intermarried, went to school together."

"Yes, but since then, they've had ethnic cleansing and massacres. You can't pretend nothing has happened. This isn't Care Bear country."

Alex burst out laughing.

"Marc isn't like that at all! On the contrary, he's very committed."

"Committed to whom?"

"You can ask him about it if you want. I think he'll tell you."

Clearly Alex didn't want to say anything more. Maud didn't insist. These scraps of information helped her understand why Marc had been well received by the officer at the post. He must have told him about his Croatian friends, and maybe they even had some shared acquaintances.

Thanks to which, for once they had breakfast indoors, sheltered from the cold. But it was actually worse than usual. The Croatian officer got coffee for them, but he insisted they wash it down with big glassfuls of *šljivovica*. In the daylight, the guardhouse décor had lost some of the romantic allure the oil lamps had given it the night before. It was a sordid, stinking hole. The sofa and armchairs were covered with stains. On the wall, under the mangers full of hay, a portrait of John Paul II hung opposite posters of naked women splattered with fly droppings.

The Croatian officer seemed to enjoy their company. He gave them fairly precise information about the region. Above all, he hinted that an offensive was being prepared in the vicinity of the next checkpoint, and that they would do better to skirt around the zone by taking a forest track that headed off to the right.

Maud courageously refused the second round of brandy, but the others had to comply. Marc and Alex had apparently acquired remarkable resistance to the brew during their previous stay. Above all, they were able to swallow the slices of greasy lard that were offered at the same time. Lionel and Vauthier were sickened by the rancid cold meat, and drank their brandy on an empty stomach. Lionel was looking more and more gloomy. He kept glancing over at Maud and Alex, with a sullen expression on his face. What she had suspected the night before without really believing it was confirmed that morning: he had been mortified by the fact that she went to sleep in Alex's tent. She never dreamed he might be jealous. But she had to accept the fact: he had been deeply hurt.

As for Vauthier, he seemed to be shrinking under the effect of the alcohol. Drunkenness compressed his violence like a gas under pressure. You could sense he was about to explode. The bad energy he had stockpiled was in danger of creating a terrible blast.

When at last they left their hosts behind, each of them was lost in thought, and for several of them those thoughts, visibly, were dark. Everyone sensed that something serious was about to happen but no one knew what form the crisis would take.

3

The track the officer had advised them to take was an old, badly paved, narrow road. It wound its way up the mountain to a pass, which they couldn't see yet. The wheels spun in the hairpin turns because of the mud that had accumulated in the ruts and hadn't dried. The lead truck was struggling. The engine stalled frequently and took a long time to get going again.

The mood in the cab was one of brooding tension. Lionel was still in a foul mood. Vauthier was finding it harder than ever to contain his anger. Marc pretended to ignore the malaise; he was full of energy. He even tried humming, but Lionel shut him up, grumbling that he had a headache.

The spark came, as always, from a few innocuous words. After struggling to get around a steep bend, Marc commented that the engine was overheating, and that he hoped the repaired radiator hose would hold up. Vauthier sprang forward from his bunk.

"If we'd stayed on the proper road, we'd be on the flat and there would have been garages."

Before setting off they had discussed the officer's advice, and Marc had recommended following it. Basically it was his fault now, in a way, if they were on this bad road, which must only be used for farm vehicles and military convoys. But he wasn't about to react to Vauthier's comment; he merely smiled, glancing briefly in the rearview mirror.

"You think it's funny, huh?" said Vauthier.

When he got no answer, he got even more riled up and went on complaining. Nothing was spared: neither the choice of the road nor the gunfire the previous night nor the explosives in the boxes.

"I should have gotten the hell out of here, that's what I should have done."

"Nothing's stopping you."

Marc said it with a smile, his fingers on the radio dial, which he kept turning to no avail, trying to find some music.

Vauthier immediately raised his voice.

"Maybe it's you and your buddy who should be thrown out. With a kick in the ass, while we're at it."

"Be my guest. Why don't you?"

Lionel was holding his head, saying, "Shut the fuck up!"

Vauthier turned to him, trying to draw him into the argument.

"Don't you think so, Lionel? You're the boss, after all, aren't you? You're not gonna let this dumbass decide for you."

"You know what the dumbass has to say?" interrupted Marc.

"You should never let soldiers on convoys like this," insisted Vauthier, shaking his head. "They're swine."

"We used to be soldiers, and we don't hide the fact. So why don't you tell them you're a cop?"

"Who's a cop?"

"You are, old man. You think we haven't figured that out?"

The mechanic registered what he had said then let out a stream of insults. At first, Marc smiled. Then suddenly he lost his cool. Was there one word in particular that set him off? It was on hearing "son of a bitch" that he reacted. Maybe he was just worn out after a sleepless night, made restless by the *šljivovica*-induced nightmares? Regardless, at one point he let go of the wheel and grabbed Vauthier by the collar. The truck swerved to a stop across the road and the truck behind had to slam on the brakes not to run into them. Maud, who was driving, saw the door open and Marc jumped out, dragging Vauthier behind him. The two men fell to the ground, in the mud. Blows were raining down on Vauthier. Initially stunned, he recovered his wits and fought back, stronger than anyone suspected. He also knew how to fight hand-to-hand and dealt Marc several blows to the face that made his lips and temple bleed.

Lionel immediately jumped out and rushed over to them. He tried to grab Marc around the waist to pull them apart. Vauthier seized the opportunity to step back and punch Marc in the stomach. Alex, who had climbed out in turn, grabbed Lionel by the arm.

"Don't get involved. Let him go!"

Lionel turned back to Alex, his face twisted with anger. Maud realized the fight was now in danger of spreading to those two. She began by separating them, then she turned to the men who were still on the ground and screamed at them to stop. Marc had the advantage again, and after one final punch to his opponent's jaw he stood up and stepped back.

Vauthier was a mess. One eye was closed and swollen, and he was holding his right arm and wincing. The blue marks on his neck showed that Marc had nearly strangled him. He got to his knees, as dazed as an ox whacked with a cleaver. His clothes were covered in mud. Maud wondered if he wasn't about to collapse. But he struggled to his feet, one leg after the other, looking around him in a stupor. His gaze came to a halt on Marc, who had taken out a jug of water and was washing his face.

"You," he said, pointing at him, "I'll kill you."

As always, or almost always, whenever they stopped somewhere, there were kids watching from a distance. They had come at a run when the fight began. Who knew whether they wouldn't run for help? Alex was convinced the paramilitaries used them as lookouts.

After the fight, he was the least troubled of them all. He insisted they get the convoy back on the road as quickly as possible. If a patrol came by now and stopped to inspect them, they'd look pretty suspicious. The first truck was still sideways across the road, the doors open. Various items had fallen to the ground when Marc pulled Vauthier from the cab. Lionel was hunting in the mud for his tobacco pouch, which had rolled into the soaking grass by the embankment. The belligerents were standing on either side of the truck, leaning on the slatted sides. Their clothes were streaming with mud, and while Marc had managed to clean his face somewhat, Vauthier still wore a mask of black earth and dried blood.

Maud was upset. She never thought they would go that far. There was one thing about men she didn't understand—or rather, she understood it, but could not accept it: this complete absence of civilization, this innate acceptance of violence. Coming to a territory that was at war she had expected to be confronted with it. But she never expected it to come from the very people who were supposed to incarnate peace and humanity. It was like seeing policemen robbing the very citizens who had come to them for help—just as shocking.

Lionel had found his tobacco. He was inhaling deeply on a hastily rolled cigarette which was splattered with dirt.

Apart from Alex, who was trying to tidy up the battlefield, no one had any energy and they all seemed resigned to inertia. Eventually they got their wits about them when the distant rumbling of an engine reached them on a cold gust of air. It came from higher up, and sounded like a motorcycle. They hurried in disarray toward the cabs. But just as they were climbing on board, the same thought occurred to them: there was no way they could leave Marc and Vauthier in the confined space of a shared cab.

Lionel had to think on his feet. There were only bad solutions. In the end he shouted to Alex to join them in the front truck, and he barked at Marc to go back to Maud's truck.

For once the engines, which had had time to cool down somewhat, started up on the first try. They got in line and by the time the motorcyclist appeared, the convoy looked normal again.

A very young man was riding the motorbike. He wasn't in uniform. Slung across his back on a leather strap was a machine gun. Behind him a large woman all in black was sitting sidesaddle, holding herself in a very dignified position, with a wicker basket on her lap. They went past the convoy without slowing down or responding to the drivers' greetings.

When they reached the pass, the road left the forest behind at last and grew wider. The panorama appeared: below them was a wide valley scattered with dark forests, with metal pylons here and there. The fact that there were quite a few of these pylons suggested there must be a town nearby. And indeed, at the far end of the valley, almost on the horizon, they could see rows of gray apartment buildings.

As the officer had said, there was no checkpoint on the pass. However, on either side of the road they could see clear signs of former trenches and the vestiges of combat. It was a sinister place, with charred trees and wrecks piled in ditches. It was impossible to tell when the fighting had occurred. It would not have surprised them to see corpses on the ground. But it could also have been a long time ago. And there was no one around, nothing anywhere nearby, except the inevitable crows.

It was lunchtime, but given what had just happened, nobody felt like stopping and besides, they weren't hungry. The trucks began their descent.

In the lead cab, Alex was at the wheel and Lionel was

sleeping, dozy from the alcohol at breakfast. Vauthier, behind them, was chewing over his hatred. Alex could hear him rubbing his arm from time to time, stifling a moan.

"Nothing broken, I hope?"

"Mind your own business."

Alex sensed that Vauthier still made no distinction between Marc and him. The conversation would go no further. He concentrated on the road. A rusty road sign riddled with bullet holes read, "Sarajevo 120 km." Ten years earlier, when the city had hosted the Olympic Games, you could come here from the capital for the day to take a walk and have a family picnic.

The sky was heavy with dark, ominous clouds. The weather changed quickly on these late autumn days. The cold had already taken hold in the mountains and the wind, which had veered to the north, was biting. It was dark in the forest. Alex wondered why this atmosphere seemed to him to be war's natural setting. He had often pondered the subject at school, daydreaming during history lessons. Whenever the date of a battle was in the spring or the summer, he pictured it as a pleasant outing in the country, something cheery and not at all serious. He couldn't believe there could be death among the flowers or on tender green fields. When he was a soldier he always felt safe when the fine weather arrived. Only when one of his comrades was hit by a bullet in the middle of June, and he saw him lying beneath a copse of white hawthorns, did he realize how ridiculous his assumption had been.

"Have you been with Maud for long?"

Lionel had emerged from his stupor and was looking at Alex with bloodshot eyes.

"Nice nap?"

"I think I asked you a question?"

"I didn't understand what you meant."

"Of course! You didn't understand . . . "

In the descent, the road was particularly rutted and Alex

had to swing the steering wheel abruptly not to be dragged into the ditch.

"No, I didn't understand. Please explain."

Lionel turned abruptly to face him.

"I asked you when you started sleeping with Maud. That's clear, isn't it?"

"I'm sleeping with Maud? But I'm not sleeping with Maud. Except tonight, and it seems to me you gave me your consent."

"You don't have to lie. I don't give a damn what the two of you are getting up to."

Alex glanced over at him. Against a background of stupor, Lionel's expression was filled with pain. Alex felt like taking his companion by the shoulders and giving him a friendly shake. But given the feeling in the team, he ruled out any display of familiarity.

"Let me tell you something and I hope you will get a better idea of what's going on: I am going to see the woman I love in Kakanj."

"And does Maud know?"

"You want to know exactly what I told her?"

Alex told the whole story, leaving nothing out. Lionel listened and didn't say a word. Alex saw him relax, as surely as if he had smoked another joint. He probably wanted to hide his feelings, and maybe he even thought he'd manage to. But Alex could read him like a book.

"Can I ask you a question now?"

"Go ahead."

"If you want to know how things stand between Maud and me, it must mean that you—"

"Mind your own business," said Lionel.

He bristled. But his bad mood was as transparent as his cheerfulness. And this time, Alex almost felt sorry for him. He let a little time go by, then continued the conversation on a less sensitive topic.

"You know what it reminds me of, our trucks and our adventures as the days go by?"

"No."

"A comic book. But I can't tell which one. I've read so many."

"Oh, you like comics?"

"That's all I ever read. What about you?"

"Which ones are your favorites?"

"I like them all! But especially *Corto Maltese*, *Largo Winch*, all the adventure stuff."

They talked for a good half-hour about their favorite heroes. Alex had won Lionel's trust. The descent was nearly over, and as they went around some of the bends they could make out the first buildings of the town. But Lionel had settled in for a long conversation, comfortably wedged in the corner between the seat and the door.

Lionel was in a joking mood, and when both of them laughed, Alex thought he could hear a vexed sigh coming from Vauthier's bunk. He pictured him shrugging his shoulders, thinking how stupid they were.

"You know, when they gave me the chance to become a peacekeeper, I thought I'd be having a heap of adventures, like Michel Vaillant. Have you read those ones, the *Michel Vaillant* series?"

"Of course! Every one!"

"What about you? Did you go into aid work for the adventure?"

"I might have," said Lionel, shaking his head, "because I read a lot of stuff about the French doctors, and it was fascinating. But that's not the way it happened, because of my parents."

"What do they do for a living?"

"They're in sales. My father was manager at a little Félix Potin supermarket in Écully, and my mother worked with him.

Since they didn't have much time to take care of me, they put me in boarding school in Vénissieux. I hated it, and I started smoking a lot, just to cope. Not the best thing there is for passing exams. I could see disaster looming, so I thought I'd become a truck driver. That's why I got my license. But my father didn't want to know. For him it had to be an office job, some serious thing. He made me take a course so that I could work at a bank."

"And did you?"

"I had no choice."

"To be honest, Lionel, I can't see you as a bank teller."

"But I stuck it out for two years. Little suit, white shirt, and tie. By the time I came home in the evening I was exhausted. I rented a studio in Villeurbanne."

"So why didn't you go on with it?"

"My boss caught me smoking at the office."

"Smoking? You mean—"

"Yeah, exactly. Not that it exactly freaked him out. He would go right ahead and do the same thing on the weekend. But at the bank it was strictly forbidden. And mainly, he was fed up with my mistakes, with my showing up late, all of that. So this was the pretext to give me the shove."

In the distance they could see a major checkpoint looming. Alex slowed down to let the second truck catch up.

"During my month's notice," concluded Lionel, "I saw an ad in the paper. An NGO was looking for administrators. It was at the beginning of the war here. They were hiring left, right, and center. So here I am. Well, that's all very well. Now we're going to say hello to our Serbian friends . . . "

In the cab of the second truck, Maud and Marc were back on the road, after the fight, jaws clenched.

Maud was driving, concentrating on the road. She found it hard to control the steering because of the ruts and the mud.

But it was the sort of difficulty she was determined to deal with by herself, and for nothing on earth would she have asked for help. It was better this way, anyway. The difficult driving distracted her: Marc's massive presence next to her made her ill at ease. It was the first time she had been this close to him. Up to now, unconsciously, she had always kept herself at a distance, as if he were somehow dangerous. And yet she wasn't afraid of him, and since their visit with the Croats her opinion of him had even begun to change. The sight of him rolling around in the mud, giving and receiving blows in that bestial way, had not made him more terrifying. On the contrary. Maud saw the fight again in flashes: there was something revolting about it, as she had felt initially, but with hindsight she was surprised to discover a beauty in the memory that had not been apparent to her at the time. It was like some savage ballet, a brutal, burning pavane, an archaic vision that stemmed from the origins of humankind, its essence. She came to the conclusion that she despised all the unnatural, supposedly civilized forms of male violence; yet in its most primitive expression there was something natural, as in this hand-to-hand combat in the mire; there was even, in a way she could not understand, something desirable.

While she mulled over her silent thoughts, Marc was frenetically trying to erase any trace of the fight. He had taken some clothes out of his backpack and changed first his T-shirt then his trousers, not an easy task in the confined space of the cab. And it probably hurt. Maud did not dare turn her head to see if he was wincing. She supposed that if she'd been in the same circumstances, she would have reacted in the same way: hide your pain, don't let your feelings show, restore your dignity as quickly as possible.

Then Marc took some wipes from the glove compartment that they normally used for the windshield. He cleaned his face and rubbed a few of the cuts he had on his arms and neck to remove any trace of blood and dirt. His most spectacular wound was a long gash on the right-hand side of his upper lip. He rolled a wipe into a ball and began dabbing gently at the wound. It was also a way to hide it. He was more or less presentable by the time they caught up with the lead truck and stopped to go through the checkpoint.

This time, at the entrance to town, a veritable Serbian war station was blocking the road. The soldiers were wearing the regulation uniform of the Yugoslav Army. Their insignia indicated their rank, and the Chetnik badge was in its place on their chests. UN armored vanguard vehicles were parked a little further along, and a group of peacekeepers were talking with the Serbian officers. There was an air of great calm among the soldiers, because the job of checking convoys was like a rest, almost a reward, in comparison to the danger they were exposed to when they were stationed at combat posts. At the same time, an atmosphere of urban warfare pervaded the entire scene with a dull and constant anxiety, and made every gesture seem somehow threatening.

The checkpoint itself was less formidable than the isolated ones they had seen up to now. The regular nature of the army holding the position meant a thorough search was unlikely; equally improbable was any attempt at blackmail or extortion of merchandise. The presence of UNPROFOR was also a reassuring sign. Even if the international forces were reduced to inaction and helplessness, their mere presence made them witnesses, so while they were there, the combatants would refrain from any abuse of power.

And this was the first time they would be going through a major town in the war zone. The urban environment made them uneasy, instilling a fear they had never felt in the countryside.

Marc talked with the soldiers while an officer checked their documents. Maud noticed how quickly he had struck up the conversation. Alex was right: he seemed to be equally at ease with all of them: Serbs, Croats, and company. What could this "commitment" be, then, that Alex had mentioned regarding Marc?

Once they were through the checkpoint without a hitch, they climbed back into the trucks.

"Apparently the town is cut in two. The Serbs have only half of it. The Muslims control the right bank. There are snipers more or less everywhere. For the time being it's quiet, but there are offensives every night."

"Did you tell Lionel?"

"They must have informed him. In any case we're going to UN headquarters and we'll review the situation there."

The convoy drove slowly up a broad avenue with concrete buildings on either side. Several of them had been gutted by shells. The black streaks left by flames were visible on the facades. There were no pedestrians, and most of the handful of cars parked along the street had been torched. Among them they saw a peculiar vehicle, a sort of homemade tank, fashioned with sheets of metal screwed onto the body of a tractor. A huge blast from a mortar had put an end to the poor machine's career. It lay tipped over across a side street.

"At the beginning of the war they built just about anything to defend themselves with. But none of it could stand up to the Serbian army."

He didn't specify who "they" were.

A bit farther along they entered an older neighborhood. The streets were cobbled and tram rails ran along the ground. The buildings on either side of the street were in an Austro-Hungarian style, with stone balconies and caryatids around the windows. Iron shutters indicated that all the shops were closed. It was as if the old buildings, too, had put on a makeshift coat of armor to protect themselves from the war.

Marc opened his window. He was listening out in the

silence for the sharp crack of distant gunfire as it echoed along the facades.

The UNPROFOR detachment was billeted in the main post office building. Sandbags were piled on either side of the front door, which was guarded by a Pakistani peacekeeper. They parked the trucks on a little square planted with trees; in the center stood a decapitated statue.

They climbed out and felt awkward in this open space, in the middle of this ghost town.

"There's a Frenchman in charge of the peacekeepers," said Lionel. "I'll go see if we can stay here today."

"It's only two o'clock," said Alex. "We could drive a bit farther."

Lionel didn't bother to answer him. He was already walking toward the guard, and the others followed.

The sentry glanced distractedly at his papers and let them in.

In the big lobby of the former post office there was a bustle of activity that contrasted sharply with the unearthly quiet on the street. Soldiers moved busily around little desks set throughout the room. There was a high ceiling, heavy with stucco, and lit by massive bronze chandeliers. Hundreds of electric wires zigzagged throughout the hall. They were connected to the chandeliers, to the banisters on the grand staircase, they trailed out through windows that had been hastily walled up with breeze block. It looked like the back lot at some big-budget movie set. The men and women in uniform who were rushing around looked like extras about to walk onto the set.

"Wait for me here," said Lionel. "I'll try and find the section commander."

Since the fight, he had been speaking like the boss again. He disappeared upstairs.

They just stood there, in the middle of the hall. No one paid them any attention. Alex spotted a sofa and some chairs that had been shoved into a corner and they went to sit down. That was when they noticed that Vauthier had disappeared. This was typical of him when they reached a town, so they didn't think much of it.

There were some old magazines on a coffee table. They each took one and began reading. Most of them were military journals like *Terre Magazine, Cols Bleus,* or monographs from the French Army Communications Service. Maud didn't find any of it very interesting but it was nice, all of a sudden, just to be sitting there quietly in an armchair and leafing through printed pages, looking at color illustrations and reading words in her own language.

When he came back down, Lionel found them silent and attentive. Next to him stood a tall jovial man in his fifties with a thick, graying beard. He was wearing fatigues, and clearly visible among his stripes as a lieutenant-colonel and the burgundy border of the medical units was a tricolor badge. He had an accent from the Béarn region and he cultivated his musketeer mannerisms.

"Ah, here are our adventurers!"

"May I introduce Dr. Argelos," said Lionel. "He's in charge of humanitarian work for the sector."

"Zounds, don't exaggerate, young man! There is not much humanitarian work in the sector. If that was all I did, I'd be on vacation. My primary job is to treat our own boys."

They introduced themselves one after the other, shaking the doctor's big solid fist. Lionel suddenly realized they were not all there.

"Where's Vauthier?"

"He must've gone off to file his report," grunted Marc.

"His report?" exclaimed the doctor with a big smile.

"He's joking. He'll be right back."

"Ah, so that's what you lot say when someone goes off to pee. Okay, follow me, I'll show you to your quarters."

They climbed up the grand stairway and started down an endless corridor. All the doors on either side had been removed because the big post office rooms had been divided up by plasterboard partitions. Now there were multiple narrow corridors giving onto the main one. The doctor took the second to the left and opened a door.

"My kingdom here below," he said, leading them into a tiny office piled with documents and computers.

The room was lit by one half of a large picture window. A bullet hole was clearly visible on the glass, with a star against the shattered window all around it. On the wooden partition directly opposite, another hole of the same caliber indicated that the projectile had crossed the entire room.

"A 12.7," said Alex, inspecting the hole.

"Upon my word, his nibs is an expert."

"I served as a peacekeeper in the region for six months."

"So you know the score. On the whole we don't need to worry, but from time to time . . . Bang! Bang! All hell breaks loose and no one is safe."

With a broad smile, the doctor pointed to a mattress underneath the desk.

"Fortunately, I was in bed."

He wasn't trying to frighten them, but rather to communicate his good humor and joie de vivre.

"The colonel told me you're leaving again tomorrow already. It's a pity. I have almost no company around here and there's no lack of work. So where are you headed?"

"Kakanj."

"Kakanj? Kakanj? That's in the mountains between Sarajevo and Zenica, if I'm not mistaken?"

"That's right."

"Sakes alive, you've got a long way to go still! Why are you going there?"

"That's where our association chose to send us," said Lionel hastily; he didn't want the two former soldiers to start going into detail.

"Well, they must have their reasons. I don't always understand the orders I get either, now, do I? Armagnac or beer?"

While they had been talking, he had taken some bottles out of a drawer and was rummaging in the one below for some glasses.

"Beer will be fine," said Alex. "We can drink from the bottle, don't go to any trouble."

"That's just as well, because we're short on glasses here, and anyway they're usually pretty disgusting."

He uncapped the beers with the handle of a fork.

"Right, the young lady can sleep here; I'll go upstairs to the officers' floor. Normally that's where I should sleep but I prefer staying in my office. The rest of you can have the room next door. It belongs to a major from Bangladesh. He's on leave but he gave me his key. Dinner is from seven o'clock on, up in the cafeteria on the fourth floor."

"So what do we do in the meantime?" asked Marc.

He hadn't spoken until now. The doctor turned and went closer to him.

"Let me see you in the light. Gosh, your face is mess. How did you do that?"

"It's nothing, I fell."

The doctor gave a knowing little laugh.

"You fell. And I'm the King of Siam. Right, it's none of my business, but you're going to come with me all the same so I can fix you up. You'll need at least two stitches."

Maud was observing Marc. He looked furious. But to her great surprise he meekly followed the doctor.

"If you want to walk around town while waiting for dinner, go right ahead. But I warn you: this is the only street that is safe."

"I need to call France," said Lionel.

"I know, the colonel told me. You can use this phone. There's an operator. Ask for a line."

"I think I'll go back downstairs to the hall," said Maud, who was stifling in the confined atmosphere of the little room.

Alex followed her and they sat on the sofa.

"Do you think Lionel is going to tell the bosses back at the association about the explosives?"

"I'd be surprised," said Maud.

"And that idiot Vauthier, what's he doing?"

"Why did Marc say he was filing his report?"

"Because he thinks he's a cop. So do I, actually."

"A cop?"

"Some guy they've sent along masquerading as an aid worker so he can check what's going on in the country."

"They do that?"

"Ah, you guys are really naïve, you aid workers! Of course they do that. How else would they get their secret agents into the country?"

"They could put them here, for example, among the peace-keepers."

"They've probably done that, too. But the peacekeepers don't move around, or if they do they're in armored vehicles. The only ones who can go anywhere and talk to everyone are people like you."

"And what makes you think Vauthier is an agent?"

"His history, for a start. Trying to come across as a former left-wing extremist. Yeah, right, a fascist more like. If he was an activist for anarchists, it was surely because he was already acting under orders."

Alex must have sensed that his reasoning had not convinced Maud.

"Moreover, if he's so mad at us, it's probably because he knows we've seen right through him."

Maud was looking askance at him, a sardonic gleam in her eye.

Out of ammunition, Alex added, in a peremptory tone not unlike the one Lionel adopted to impose his decisions:

"And besides, he just smells like a cop, that's all."

Maud shrugged and went on reading.

Alex had found some chewing gum. He offered her some, then said, "Have you known Lionel for long?"

She looked up from her magazine.

"How long have I known Lionel," she echoed, coming to. "Um . . . since I started at La Tête d'Or. I worked three months as an unpaid volunteer before I left with the convoy. Why?"

"Just asking. He's strange guy. He's playing his cards close to his chest. He acts all tough but he's really a softy."

"Could be."

"He's in love with you, isn't he?" added Alex with a laugh.

"In love with me! What makes you say that?"

"He was afraid we would sleep together. He had this whole theory and I had to put his mind at rest."

Maud looked away. It was the sort of topic she hated. She suddenly felt reduced to the status of an object. She didn't want to go there. She put an abrupt end to the conversation.

"That's his problem," she said, immersing herself in her magazine again.

Alex went on chewing his gum. Since she didn't want to speak any more, he stretched out on the armchair and put his head back and stared at the ceiling.

Maud was pretending to read, but she couldn't. She was thinking about what Alex had just told her. Lionel, in love with her? It could be, after all. Deep down she had come to the same conclusion, without formulating it so clearly. Now that she thought about it, it would explain quite a few things. In Lyon she had worked in a tiny office stacked high with files and documents, and she didn't often have any reason to leave it. And yet somehow he was always underfoot. He had "taken her under his wing," as he put it. She didn't mind because in the beginning she didn't know anyone. Particularly since he was very polite. He acted the older brother, without ever letting his feelings show.

He was the one who had insisted she join the convoy. She had seen it as a sign of friendship and trust, and she'd been grateful to him. But maybe he'd had an ulterior motive after all. And when she revealed the business about the explosives, the fact he'd agreed more readily than she expected to take the risk, perhaps that meant he'd done it to please her, so she wouldn't be disappointed, to take up the challenge.

If he really was in love with her, it was not good news. Because she had no intention of playing any sort of game. She would have to be clever, tiptoe around him, perhaps even reject him outright if he confessed to her. It was the sort of thing she hated most. The same old story: guys seeing her as their prey. She had thought she'd be far away from all that on a mission to a war zone, but in the end it was the same wherever you went.

She brooded, increasingly glum. The photographs of tanks and legionnaires in combat that filled the pages of the magazine were hardly likely to distract her from her dark thoughts. She stretched out in turn, and tried to doze off.

From time to time she could hear the muffled sound of a distant explosion. A bit later on, when she woke up, she wondered whether Marc had cried out when the doctor stitched his lip. She hoped he had. And she smiled.

Lionel came back down, and as there was no sign of either Marc or Vauthier, the three of them went on to dinner in the refectory. The huge room was full of soldiers in loungewear. They seemed to be making good use of the exercise benches set up in the long corridor on the third floor. Some of them, in spite of the chilly temperature, were wearing sleeveless T-shirts that emphasized their biceps. At the French tables, men and women mingled, whereas the Pakistanis and Bangladeshis dined among men, and gazed with shining eyes at all the women going in and out.

Just as Maud had thought, Lionel was very proud to announce he had passed on their reassuring news to headquarters, and that everything was going fine. As he said this, he shot her a glance, and she could read something else in it besides defiance. He was particularly talkative during the meal. He had not dared to smoke since they arrived in the UN buildings, and his gaze was sharper. At the same time, he must have been feeling the urge, because he was restless, and seemed to be in a hurry to go out on the town.

"I've been talking to a young kid from the battalion who was in the corridor working out. He told me there's a fairly nice bar just down the street, with good music. D'you feel like going to check it out?"

"Sounds great. I'll come," said Alex.

But Lionel wasn't interested in Alex's opinion. He kept his eyes riveted on Maud, with a predatory smile that didn't suit him at all. Like the orders he gave, his proposal—however confident the delivery—didn't really hide his hesitation and shyness. Maud felt sorry for him, and at first she was tempted to accept. But then she had a fleeting vision of what would ensue. She would rather refuse right away than find herself stuck with him in the promiscuity of a bar and then have to humiliate him.

"Not me, thanks, I'm really tired, I'm going to bed."

She looked away, not to have to read the disappointment Lionel's eyes. She was afraid, more than anything, that she might find them full of hatred. Fortunately, Alex got to his feet and took his companion with him.

"We may as well go now. That way we won't be back too late. There's a curfew at 22:00 hours."

Maud sat on alone at the table. She put her head in her hands, to dim the clatter of plates and the shouts of diners reverberating against the tiles. It was all too much for her. She had never imagined she would find herself in a situation like this. For her, humanitarian work meant Albert Schweitzer, Saint Vincent de Paul, Raoul Follereau, imploring victims and the brave, disinterested people who came to their assistance. But what did she know, in the end. Just that those great forerunners were head and shoulders above their descendants. But there must be something somewhere of their good sides, or so she had thought.

Instead, she had found petty, spineless people who were walled up in their hatred. And this war: a tangled network of criminals who were all alike. Here she was, a woman trying to get away from machismo, and now she felt she had landed in a country where its proponents reigned as absolute masters. If her companions had at least agreed to see her as one of them . . . Instead, it was the old game of attraction and repulsion, and this obligation to handle Lionel tactfully because she didn't fancy him, but he just didn't get it. And he was bound to make her pay for his unrequited love.

Why had she always felt so alone in life? Ever since childhood; for as long as she could remember. What painful experience had left her so demanding, so lucid or perhaps simply so blind and crazy? Her parents were close, so to speak. Her mother had stayed at home—although she'd been a promising jurist, she'd given up her profession in order to raise her children. Her father had taken over an old notarial practice and made it the most prosperous one in town, and now, at the age of fifty, he was bald and potbellied. Her older brother had gotten married the previous year and was already expecting his first child. Why had she always thought so poorly of them? Why did she never have any friends? Why was it so difficult to be a woman—why did she wish she weren't one?

She stared into space, forgetting the noise and the ambient ugliness around her. She was overwhelmed by melancholy.

Tonight she could not banish these painful thoughts, even though she had always stuck to her rule not to think about any of this, but to fight, and to keep busy. But where had all her struggles, rebelliousness, and choices left her?

She lost all sense of time, sitting there transfixed by her dark thoughts. At one point she thought she saw Vauthier at the far end of the huge lobby. He was with some uniformed men. But he had his back to her and she immediately lost interest. Later, the group of people at the next table got up, and she realized the noise level had dropped significantly. Only a few stragglers eating on their own were left in the refectory.

Suddenly, far-off, framed in the double doors of the entrance to the refectory, she saw Marc. He was looking into the room, probably searching for their group. She waved to him to come over. While he was walking toward her, she discreetly wiped her eyes. The bandage Marc was wearing on the right side of his face was very white against his olive skin.

Why, all of a sudden, did she feel so light?

4

W hen the dining room closed, Maud and Marc found themselves out in the corridor with their beer bottles in their hands. A few soldiers in gym clothes were still pumping iron, but most had left for their dorms. The long neon-lit corridor smelled of sweat and supermarket aftershave.

Neither Marc nor Maud felt like sleeping. She followed him past the exercise benches to a door that gave onto the outside. He'd had time to explore the building and visibly knew where he was going. They came out onto a metal fire escape that climbed the entire height of the building's rear façade. From there they looked out on the countryside on the Serbian side of the enclave, and there was no need to fear any snipers along this axis. The moon had risen above the hills. Against the bluish background of sky stood a fringed crest of forest.

The stairway was the refuge of insomniacs, smoking on their own or talking in small clusters, seated on the stairs. Marc and Maud climbed all the way to the top where there was no one and sat down on the last landing. Marc did not smoke very often, but he had an old pack of cigarettes in his pocket. He offered Maud one.

"It wasn't too unpleasant, getting the stitches?" she asked.

"It was okay."

"Oh, I saw Vauthier. I think he was with some soldiers."

"He must have found some other secret agents, to go hang around town."

"Maybe we can leave him behind here?"

"I don't think he'd like that."

"Aren't you afraid he'll cause trouble for you?"

"It's not in his interest. If he's on a mission, the way I think he is, he has to keep a low profile and finish the job."

In the gloom she could see only the white patch of bandage on Marc's face. It made him more human, more vulnerable: as if by puncturing his armor, the wound had laid the man bare. Maud felt less intimidated.

"Why did you decide to become a soldier?"

She could just as easily have said, why did you leave the army? The two things were equally puzzling to her.

"I didn't choose. It's just the way things happened."

There was no reticence in his tone of voice; she figured she could ask him some more questions.

"Well, nobody forced you, did they?

"When I was in uniform, there was this little insignia on it, a little round pin, which meant that others knew immediately what to expect. But it's true I don't wear it anymore. And in any case, it would mean nothing to civilians."

"So what was this insignia?"

"It was the sign that I was a child reared by the army. I've been a soldier since I was five years old."

A little cloud of smoke rose from his mouth into the dark blue moonlit sky. Maud got the impression he was laughing quietly to himself.

"My father was a legionnaire. He was from somewhere around here apparently. I think he was a Hungarian from Vojvodina. That's a province in northern Serbia. He came to France at the age of twenty and joined up."

"And your mother?"

"He met her in Lebanon, when he was serving in the UNFIL."

"Is she Lebanese?"

"Palestinian. She was born in a refugee camp. She was the third of five daughters, and her father was very strict with them. One day, my mother had left the camp, for a man, I suppose, and the family didn't want anything more to do with her."

"Did you know her?"

"Not really. It was a strange story. I never found out exactly what she was doing when she met my father. But he must not have been the only one, if you see what I mean. In any case, by the time I was born he had already left with his unit."

"Were you born in Beirut?"

"In Tyre. But I only stayed there four years."

"So your father came back later to get you?"

"No, he died. In Chad, during an operation."

"So how come the army raised you?"

"It was my mother, you see. She was a very simple woman, but resourceful, the way you have to be when you have nothing and no one to protect you. As soon as she got out of the maternity ward she went to see the UNIFL commander, with me in her arms, and she gave them my father's name. But then when she didn't get an answer, she started showing up at headquarters every day. She threatened to talk to journalists, and to write to the Secretary General of the UN if the father did not recognize his child."

The soldiers who'd been talking on the landing below stood up to go to bed. Now Maud and Marc were alone on the stairs, and the countryside beyond was silent. Dogs were barking to each other in the distance.

"One day, they told her that my father had died. She didn't give up for all that. She said that in that case, it was France that had to recognize me."

"And did she get her way?"

"Apparently she found the right thing to say, and the military were afraid of a scandal. I've also been told she was very close to a French officer at that time. Perhaps he helped her. Whatever the case might be, I was taken on as a war orphan and sent to a military school in the north of France."

As he spoke, Marc stared into space, toward the darkening hilltops. Suddenly he broke off and turned to look at Maud.

"Why'd you get me talking about all this? What do you care?"

"I just like to know, that's all."

She felt embarrassed, as if he'd caught her out, and she choked briefly on her cigarette smoke.

Above all, as she didn't want him to question her in turn. Her normal little family, and the rebelliousness she'd felt during her awkward teenage years: they seemed more ridiculous than ever. But he said nothing, and the silence settled over them.

There was something about Marc that commanded respect, a sort of gravity, and now Maud understood better where it had come from. She thought about the makeshift tank they had seen that morning as they drove down the avenue. Marc was like that: as if he had sheets of metal fastened to him, all around. But all around what? He knew how to fight like a wild animal in the mud, yet at the same time she recalled how distraught he had looked when the bearded doctor took him off to stitch up his cheek.

"Why are you going back there?"

"Back where? Kakanj?"

"Yes."

He thought for a long time. She got the impression he was hesitating.

"To go with Alex," he said at last.

It didn't ring true but she didn't dare come out and say so. She decided to take a more roundabout approach.

"Did you leave the army after you got back, or during the mission?"

"In Kakanj. I resigned."

"Can you tell me why, or would you rather not?"

"It's kind of a long story. We'll talk about it some other time. We've got to get up real early tomorrow morning. You know what they say about soldiers: they're always up at dawn, even if they have nothing to do."

He got slowly to his feet, shaking out the stiffness in his legs. He waited for her to get up too before heading down the stairs. The metal frame of the stairway vibrated to their footsteps. She was slightly above him, so their heads were at the same level. With any other man, she would have kept further away, for fear of some misplaced gesture. But with him, she felt trusting. At one point they started heading into the wrong door and in a moment of confusion bumped into each other. He apologized and didn't try to take advantage. She was grateful to him for that.

And yet when she closed the door behind her and looked around the empty room, she felt terribly lonely.

The next morning, a steady drizzle was falling over the town. A leaden light struggled to pierce the black clouds. The bad weather dampened the snipers' enthusiasm, and all you could hear in the streets was the trickling of the broken gutters. The soldiers who left headquarters were wearing tight-fitting brown raincoats that went down to their ankles. Their huge blue helmets made their heads seem enormous, and they were a comic sight, like some sort of poisonous mushroom.

The convoy was lined up in the street. While they were warming up the engines, Alex and Marc, poorly protected by old hoodless windbreakers, their hair dripping, checked that the rain-slick tarps were properly fastened. Everyone was ready except Vauthier, whom they hadn't seen since the night before.

"Let's leave him, never mind," said Alex.

He had placed his wet hands on the half open window and was talking to Lionel, who was leaning with his arms crossed on the steering wheel.

"If he's decided to stay, let him stay. But we can't leave without letting him know."

"I can't go looking everywhere for him just to plead with him!"

"Not to plead with him. But if you can find him and ask him what he intends to do, that would save time."

Alex let out an oath and headed toward the sandbags at the entrance. At the same moment Vauthier came rushing out and they almost bumped into each other in front of the sentry.

"What were you doing? Everyone is waiting for you."

Vauthier was wearing a fur-lined jacket none of them had ever seen. He was shaven, and his lips looked even thinner than usual. His fight with Marc had left a large bruise on his temple but he'd smeared it with cream and you could hardly see it. When he got in the cab there was a strong smell of menthol. Lionel made a face.

"Any longer and we would have gone off without you," he said.

Alex was wriggling out of his dripping clothes.

"It's not my fault. I only got back an hour ago," said Vauthier calmly, as soon as he was once again installed in his seat at the back.

Lionel waved his hand out the door to motion to Marc, who was at the wheel of the second truck. Then he shifted noisily into first gear.

"Still getting in touch with the locals?" he said mockingly, glancing at Vauthier in the rearview mirror.

"I was with two whores."

He snickered, and seeing that his younger companions were taken aback, he continued in the same tone.

"Frankly, you should try it sometime. Two gorgeous, frisky,

and very young women. I'd go so far as to say they were famished!"

"Shut up," grumbled Alex.

"Believe me, it's way more relaxing than any of your virginal stuff."

"Shut the fuck up!"

This time it was Lionel who had shouted, and he seemed so outraged that Vauthier fell silent and withdrew to the back of his bunk.

In a few words, he had destroyed the mood and the conversation. They drove through the town in silence, and before long they could hear hoarse snoring from the backseat.

The river marked the border between the Serbian and Muslim zones. There used to be two bridges across it, but the one in the center of town had been destroyed the previous year. The only one left was located in one of the suburbs to the east. It was a modern bridge with a steel structure and two concrete piers. Checkpoints had been set up at either end. The bridge itself was in no-man's-land, in permanent danger of machine-gun fire. Only UN and humanitarian convoys were allowed to cross the bridge.

It was still raining and the water was trickling down the Serbian soldiers' side caps and soaking their uniforms, which made them even jumpier. They checked the documents sullenly, then motioned to the trucks to move forward between the security gates, just before the entrance to the bridge itself. Passengers were obliged to cross on foot; only the actual driver could remain in the truck.

During this relatively easy, almost official leg of the journey, they had forgotten to some degree what they were transporting. But now that they were lined up behind the barrier, in the silence of a checkpoint where they had been told there were frequent incidents, among soldiers who were mute, tense, and on the alert, they were all once again fully aware of the danger.

The barrier went up with a groan. Lionel and Marc switched on the ignition. The other three, on foot, were instructed to walk ahead, so that the vehicles could never go faster than walking pace. They were not allowed to wear a hat or anything that hid their faces. The rain came steadily down, even colder on this bridge exposed to the icy wind sweeping along the river. Upon the signal, they moved slowly forward.

Maud felt her hair sticking to her brow. There were raindrops on her eyelashes. Alex pulled his collar tighter and shivered. Only Vauthier with his warm jacket and his shining bald pate, where the rain seemed to bounce off, gave an ironic smile, as if to show he didn't mind the weather at all.

The sidewalks on either side had been stripped of their surface, undoubtedly to get at the thick metal sheets that covered them and which could be used for armor. The pavement was cluttered with debris of all kinds from the fighting. They recognized a dented helmet and some scraps of uniform. Seen from the riverbank the bridge didn't look very long, yet walking across it was interminable.

They could see the gray huddle of the Bosnian checkpoint on the other side more clearly now. They couldn't make out any heads or figures. The defenders must be concealed, observing them.

They had only just reached the middle of the bridge when the first truck stalled. It was too much for its tired gearbox to drive that slowly. They stopped, careful not to turn around. Lionel nervously tried the key in the ignition but the hot engine did not want to start again. The waiting got longer. They thought they could see shadows moving behind the roadblock.

The engine wouldn't start. Alex and Maud looked at each other, worried. At one point, the truck shuddered and seemed to catch, then jerked forward with a splutter, startling them. The fender grazed their legs. They both turned around at the same time. Behind them, from the end of the bridge, they heard the click of a weapon.

Maud had a moment of panic. Her initial reflex was to run, to shout. Alex touched her hand and she regained her self-control. If she wanted to run away, she'd have to do it in a daydream. She focused her gaze on a twisted streetlamp that was hanging in the void above the river, and a memory came to her. She wasn't even six years old when, one summer day in the mountains, during a picnic, she climbed up the side of a cliff. One step, then two, then fifty. She found herself very high up, with no way to get back down. She was terrified by the void. She could see her parents, far below, shouting. She wanted to run to them, to rush into their arms. They'd had to send for help. All night long, despite the fact that she usually never wanted anyone to touch her, she had slept snuggled up against her mother. And now, there was something similar to the diving board. She'd never realized it before. She suddenly wondered if this might be the explanation: danger was the only way she could overcome the obstacles that kept her from love.

Finally the engine coughed, spluttered, and started. They waited until it was running smoothly, then began walking forward again. That was when Maud realized that Vauthier wasn't there anymore. With his hands in the air, slowly, he had walked on his own to the Bosnian checkpoint to explain what was happening. They found him there, handing out cigarettes.

It didn't take long for the Bosnians to check the vehicles and their papers. Clearly in a place like this the paramilitaries were obsessed with the possibility of attack. They carefully inspected the underside of the chassis and the cabs. They seemed reassured when they saw that the load consisted of piles of cardboard boxes. They took out three or four without opening them, just to make sure there was nothing hidden behind them. When they found out it was a French convoy, they called out to someone, and a little man wearing a blue sweatsuit came and joined them. He had an enormous belt around his waist that was studded with rows of copper bullets. Two pistols hung on either side of the belt and their long black barrels reached to the middle of his thighs.

"You're French?"

"'Fraid so, mate," answered Vauthier, "no one's perfect."

"Paris?"

"Lyon," said Lionel.

"Lyon! Congratulations. The Olympique Lyonnais is a fine club. We used to meet every year, and every time, they beat us two-nil."

He was a former professional soccer player. He had played his entire career for Lens, in the Pas-de-Calais. He invited them for some Turkish coffee in a little shelter set up a bit farther away. They sat down on stools under a roof made with a waterproof tarpaulin stretched between old bits of metal.

They couldn't really linger; they still had a long way to go, and the previous day they had not made much headway. But the man felt like talking, and they might get some valuable information from him.

"My wife and kids are still in France. I came back at the beginning of the war to fight. In fact, there were three of us in the club, the three Yugos they used to call us in those days. All from here. The other two got killed."

"What's the situation at the moment?" asked Lionel.

"There has been heavy fighting here right from the start. But then we have the Serbian Army just over on the other side."

"What about central Bosnia, where we're headed?"

"It changes every day. By the looks of it, it should be calm, because the Croats and us, we're supposed to be allies now. Unfortunately the truth of the matter is that this Muslim-Croat Federation is some idea they cooked up in Sarajevo for appearances' sake. There haven't been any major offensives, that's true. But there are raids every day and especially every night."

"Raids between Croats and Muslims?"

"We never know exactly. Particularly as there are also Serbian paramilitaries who've infiltrated everywhere and who commit their massacres to make people believe it was the other side who did it."

"What's in it for them?"

The soccer player shrugged his shoulders. He knew the French well enough to know they didn't understand a thing about this war. You had to explain everything to them as if they were children.

"What's in it for them is that the others can't agree on how to fight the Serbian Army. And for the Serbs, killing people, particularly Muslims, is a duty. And a business, too. They never go away empty-handed."

"Is the road safe, though?" asked Lionel.

"As I said, it depends on when. But in any case, there's not much traffic through here. I haven't seen a civilian convoy cross that bridge in at least two weeks. Last time it was the English, Oxfam. If you have a road map, I'll show you where it might get dicey."

Lionel went over to the truck and came back with a map.

The soccer player showed them the approximate locations of the next checkpoints and the outline of the enclaves they would be going through.

They asked him where they could get supplies.

"Actually this is where you will find the most stuff. Come with me, I'll take you to one of my cousins who has a shop."

Once they'd drunk the Turkish coffee and gone on to a fruit and vegetable depot, by way of a chicken coop set up in garage and a barn where an old peasant was selling milk and white cheese, it was almost eleven o'clock when they were at last able to get under way.

The Muslim side of town was made up of little residential suburbs and industrial zones that had sustained heavy shelling. Before long they were back out in the country. The rain had stopped but the damp was pervasive. Water had collected in ditches and in the furrows of fields. The road looked like a river where little islands of clay had surfaced. For lunch they stopped at the edge of the woods and ate standing up, squelching through the soaking earth that was covered with silvery leaves.

Going uphill they were overtaken by a UN convoy that was moving quickly and sprayed them with mud. They had to stop to clean the windshield.

Many houses, abandoned or disfigured by fire or bullet holes, bore witness to the heavy fighting in the region. Other villages were intact and prosperous. The war had something eerie about it here. There was no sign of any paramilitaries or any military equipment. The destruction they could see in places seemed to have fallen from the sky, like lightning. Misfortune was like some divine decree that had nothing to do with mankind. And yet the destruction was recent, and the absence of fighters did not mean the war was over. It was merely a sign that here, more than anywhere, the danger was hidden, lurking in the dark woods surrounding the villages, nestled in the hollows of valleys or the folds of mountains. At any moment, it could come out and strike.

5

Maud and Marc took turns driving, not speaking. Conversation the previous evening had made them feel awkward. Maud wondered whether her a companion wasn't sorry he had revealed so much. She stole glances at him. His expression was tight again, watchful and tense, as if he were on the lookout. In other words, he was his usual self. Maud figured he probably could not loosen the vise of discipline except on rare occasions like the night before. It was frustrating, because she thought she deserved his trust. At the same time, she would not have liked him to use their brief spell of complicity as a pretext to start taking liberties. So since she could not see clearly through her contradictory feelings, she chose to remain silent and observe the landscape.

Unfortunately, it was disfigured by construction. Ever since they had left Italy behind, two weeks before, their surroundings had been drearily uniform. The natural scenery could be beautiful, when it was unspoiled. But everything human beings had built seemed to bear the stamp of ugliness. Day after day, it was the same dismal sight: brick or breeze-block houses with similar four-sided roofs, the never-ending checkpoints thrown together like slums, the brutish faces—all infinite variations on an identical theme of dirt and mistrust.

In the scorching shower at UN headquarters Maud had experienced a moment of relief as she watched the dirt drain away, then combed her wet hair, its softness restored at last. But now she was not so sure that the miracle could happen again. She had reached the conclusion that all this grayness and mud and violence was clinging to her skin too firmly for her ever to hope she could slough it off. She looked discreetly in the mirror on the back of the sun visor. She thought she looked old and damaged. A natural look was what she preferred; for her it was a necessary expression of honesty. But just now she would have liked to paint her face with color, to make her lips shine red. She was tempted to ask Marc what he thought of her. Then instantly realized it was ridiculous, and she abruptly slammed the mirror back up.

Marc was startled. He glanced over at her and smiled.

"Are you getting bored?"

"No, I'm all right."

"Do you want to drive?"

"Later."

"That's what's so terrible about this country. It's ugly."

She looked at him with surprise. Had he read her thoughts, or were they the same as hers?

"it must be better in summer."

"Not a whole lot. Anyway, in these mountains, the scenery is always sad."

They went through a village. Houses were splattered with gray mud along the bottom of their walls, and hay carts stood drooping in the farmyards.

"The only thing that adds some color to the scenery here is blood."

Maud looked aghast at Marc. He was impassive, unsmiling. How could he say such a thing? What was she supposed to think? Was he saying it to deplore the fact, or was this what drew him to the country?

Blood . . . for a while she had considered training to become a doctor, and it was the thought of blood that had dissuaded her. Blood horrified her. But wasn't it the sight of horror that she, too, had come looking for? Wasn't it blood that they all had in common: soldiers, victims, aid workers? She felt deeply troubled.

No checkpoint had ever seemed so well situated as the one where they had to stop not long thereafter. Maud was relieved to be able to get out of the truck and breathe freely. But as soon as she was outside, she noticed that the icy air smelled of burning wood. She looked all around. Above a thicket of trees she could see the charred roof structure of a house. She thought it was still smoking, and the paramilitaries seemed very nervous.

They were peasants; they all had the same black moustache, and wore the same sheepskin caps. They looked like they might be cousins; perhaps they were, after all.

From a distance Maud could see that Lionel and Alex were negotiating with them. They must be having difficulty making themselves understood. One of the Bosniaks, more wrinkled than the others, wearing a jacket that was too long, was waving his arms and pointing to the road. He didn't look threatening—frightened, more like it. Maud went closer.

"What's going on?"

"We're not really sure," said Alex. "They seem to be saying there's a problem farther along."

"Are they going to let us go on all the same?"

"That's what we don't understand."

"It's all set," Lionel broke in, turning to them. "We can go on."

Now the peasants were talking among themselves. Some of them did not seem to agree with the little old man who had given the convoy permission to go ahead. The old man was delivering a long tirade in his own defense, and to conclude he spat on the ground.

There was no point in waiting for their quarrel to get worse and have them change their mind. Lionel climbed quickly into the truck and waved to the others to get going right away. The village they went through was deserted. In two of the houses, short flames, pink from the rain blowing in from outside, were licking at the window frames. Outside one of them the front door lay on the ground, torn from its frame. This was all only a few dozen yards from the paramilitaries who had stopped them. Now they understood that it wasn't a checkpoint after all. Moreover, there had been no obstacles, no roadblock. They must simply have happened upon a group of armed villagers who had come out of the maquis after an attack. Unless they were the ones who had perpetrated it; there was no telling. In any case, the hamlet was deserted, and they wondered where the inhabitants had gone. Had they managed to find shelter? Were they hiding inside the houses? In the muddy roads, packs of mangy dogs were running every which way, sniffing at doors.

One of the buildings, fairly similar to the others, had a little round tower with a pointed roof and a green metal crescent. It must have been the village mosque. There was a big hole in its façade, and through the wide-open doors they could see that the interior was completely gutted by fire. For a lack of furniture, no doubt, the fire had stopped on its own.

They continued on their way without slowing down and were once again out in the country among pastures and stands of trees. Nature seemed oblivious of human tragedy. But it was a melancholy nature that seemed to convey its own sense of misfortune.

Less than a kilometer farther along, they were stopped once again by soldiers, but this time as they drove closer they saw they were peacekeepers. The UN convoy that had sped past them was parked a few yards beyond the men who were blocking the road. The rear doors of the armored vehicles were open. Inside they could see a few soldiers sitting in a row on the benches, smoking, with their guns between their knees.

They parked the trucks beyond the last APC and got out

without turning off their engines. Among the officers wandering around the white UN vehicles, they recognized a few men they'd seen in the corridors at headquarters and, in particular, a chief warrant officer from the Service Corps. Alex, who had played cards with him at the bar, went up to him.

"Is there a problem here?"

"You could put it that way."

The chief warrant officer had a Parisian accent. As he spoke he raised his visor, the way he would have done with a cap.

"Argelos the medic is over there, if you'd like an explanation."

"Over there" meant the middle of an unplowed field; short straws left behind by the harvest were floating on the liquid surface of black mud. From a distance all they could see was a khaki-colored cluster and a light blue bouquet of helmets. The four of them headed across the field; Vauthier, as usual, went off on his own. He preferred to stay and mingle with the men by the APCs.

There were soldiers coming and going from the road to the place where they had gathered in the field. Some were carrying stretchers, others were unfolding big black plastic bags. No one was talking but suddenly a loud voice started shouting orders. It was the doctor.

"Watch what you're doing, guys! If there are bits, try not to scatter them."

He was crouching on the ground and they only saw him as they wove their way through the soldiers. Maud felt a wave of nausea. On the damp earth there were fifty bodies or more, lying in grotesque positions. Their arms and legs were twisted, their heads lay at a painful angle from their necks, some had their faces in the mud. On the gray mass of bodies, most of which were clothed in dull, drab garments, the only bright color was that of blood.

Scarlet puddles spread across their chests, down their legs

and arms, formed halos around their heads, and against the gray landscape and the lowering sky, their blood was a constellation of gemlike spots.

Maud could not tear her eyes away. The disgust she felt was so powerful that it paralyzed her. At the same time, she was fascinated. On this doleful tableau, the only living thing was the blood oozing from the dead.

The damp air diluted smells, and it was the sight alone that seemed to convey a harsh fustiness of crushed flesh and leaking bodily fluids. Maud felt a sudden need to retch. She just managed to turn to one side and throw up.

Argelos got to his feet, still standing in the middle of the slaughter, and he recognized the aid workers in the front row of the circle of the living.

"Ah, look who's here!"

"We went through the village and saw there had been fighting," said Lionel, relieved to be able to speak to the doctor, to say anything rather than stand there silently gazing at the corpses.

"Fighting! A massacre, indeed. Don't you see there are only women and children?"

Maud had gotten a grip on herself and went back to the others. When she heard the doctor, she found the strength to look once more at the macabre group spread over the ground. And because of what Argelos had said, she saw things differently. Initially she had only noticed a shapeless mass of tortured bodies. Now she could make out individual human beings. She recognized the living creatures they had been. These unnatural remains had been women and children who, not long before, had been breathing, walking, eating. One mother was still clinging to her baby. Maud wondered which of the two had been killed first. The infant's face was nothing but a wound; the bullet that had struck it must have been fired point-blank. But the mother's body seemed intact.

"Who did this?" asked Maud.

"Who knows. The peasants say it was mercenaries working for a Serbian warlord."

"Do you know him?"

Argelos had turned around to give orders to two stretcher bearers who were waiting, not daring to put their brand-new stretcher down in the mud.

"Of course we know him. His name is Arkan. He frequently hangs around town, and I've even seen him coming out of the colonel's office at headquarters, on two occasions."

"So, are you going to arrest him?" said Maud, insistent.

"Arrest him!"

"But if he's massacring women and children . . . "

"What proof do we have? If we accuse him, he will say in all seriousness that it was Arabs in the pay of the Bosnian Muslims who were responsible. And he'll have at least ten people who can testify in his favor."

"His gang," added the Parisian NCO, "have neither lord nor master. Like all the other cutthroats hanging around here, he doesn't belong to any regular army. Officially, no one controls him."

"But still," Maud continued, "there must be a way you can stop him from doing harm. There are so many of you, you could easily overcome him . . . "

"What do you think? That we're at war, too? For a start, someone in New York would have to give the order to bump him off, and that's not really their style. And if we did go after him, don't go thinking he'd let himself get caught all that easily. He's got mortars, and rocket-propelled grenades, everything he needs to make pretty little holes in our windows. You remember my window?"

Marc, who hadn't said a word until then, took Maud by the elbow.

"Come on, let's get going. We're of no use here."

His voice was calm, and Maud, who was trembling with emotion, only seemed to recover her wits when she felt Marc's firm hand around her arm. The others also had difficulty tearing themselves away from the sight.

"Safe travels, kids," shouted Argelos, before returning to his macabre task, "and look after yourselves!"

Once she was back in the truck, Maud began talking. She described the scene, noted the details, commented on things in a way that she herself thought was stupid. But she simply could not stand the silence. She needed to let go of her emotion, to say any old thing, just to talk. She didn't expect an answer. She scarcely noticed how Marc remained silent, jaw clenched, scowling at the road.

"But still," she said at one point, "it was weird we'd had that conversation just before."

Marc glanced over at her and shrugged. His scornful gesture shut her up. She said to herself that he was a soldier, after all, and as such, a man who had killed, too. And she began to despise him.

In the first truck, on the other hand, the mood was one of harmony and forgiveness. As Lionel and Alex were silent, Vauthier began telling them what he had found out while talking with the soldiers. As usual, his companions wanted him to shut up. But what they had just seen filled them with disgust at the thought of violence and hatred. Weren't they too on the path to murder, even if it was on a much smaller scale, if they began to detest this man? Yes, he was unlikable and perhaps even suspect, and they thought he was vulgar and spineless, but was that any reason to respond to him in a violent manner? They remembered the fight with Marc and told themselves that that was how wars began. And after what they had just seen, they wanted to be better, to distance themselves from the savagery that was inside every man—and inside them, too. Of a silent, common accord, Lionel and Alex made an effort to listen to Vauthier and even to answer him.

Used to being snubbed, Vauthier was initially surprised by their sudden attentiveness. When he realized that his companions' attitude had changed for good, without trying too hard to understand the reasons behind the change, he, too, adopted a less provocative tone, leaving off the irony and vulgarity he generally displayed in their presence. And before long, the three of them were able to carry on a normal conversation.

"The guys told me that ten kilometers from here," said Vauthier, "there's an old abandoned holiday camp. We could stop there for the night."

"Is it on the main road or do we have to turn off?"

"Apparently we'll go past a wooden barrier with a thing written in Cyrillic and a drawing of something like two kids holding hands. All we have to do is lift the barrier and go five hundred meters down a little track."

"Is there a guard?"

"No, he was a Serb, and since we're in a Muslim zone, he got the hell out."

"It sounds like a good idea."

The holiday camp was a long, low building in the middle of a clearing surrounded by tall trees. The rooms on the ground floor faced out onto a broad terrace enclosed by a wooden balustrade. The architecture was modern, dreary, and unimaginative. It was easy to picture the party leaders inaugurating the building, spouting hollow sentences extolling the glory of youth, sport, and socialism. Since then, civil war had come to round out that vision, bringing a final touch to the radiant tableau. The picture windows were shattered, all the furnishings had been pillaged. The looters had even decided to spend an evening round the campfire right there in the middle of the main hall, and the walls and ceiling were black with soot.

By the time they arrived the rain had stopped. A hesitant, shifty sunlight was slipping beneath the gray skirt of clouds, swept along by the evening wind. They went in through smashed French doors and visited the rooms, flashlight in hand. The camp was too big for the looters to ravage it from top to bottom; they had merely set an example with the main hall and other rooms in the front, and some of the bedrooms. But there were over a dozen rooms that still had their furniture, and their windowpanes intact. They went to get their sleeping bags in the truck and each of them settled into his or her own room, which was an undreamt-of luxury. Neither the water nor the electricity was working, but they had everything they needed in the way of light and to cook their meal. There was a source of freshwater in a stone fountain by the parking lot. They heated up an entire tub and shared it out for washing in the collective bathrooms. Vauthier confirmed his good disposition by agreeing to do the cooking again.

With night came the cold, damp air, which spread through the drafty rooms. Following the previous occupants' example, they lit a fire in the main hall and ate dinner sitting around it on the floor underneath a cloud of smoke. Then they went to bed, trying not to think about what they had seen that day. And, above all, about the gangs of murderers scouring the region.

6

In the lulling warmth of the sleeping bag, Maud fell asleep almost immediately. She had disturbing nightmares she could not remember, but they woke her up. She looked at the time on the phosphorescent dial of her watch. It was 2:30 in the morning. The metal bed frame creaked as she tossed and turned. Finally, she decided to get up and go out onto the terrace to look at the night sky. A strange glow was coming from outside. When she opened the window, she saw it had snowed. There was a thin white layer over the ground and the trees, and it shone in the moonlight. Maud put a quilted jacket over her fleece and went out. It was the first time since arriving in this country that she had felt such a strong pull toward beauty. Snow, particularly when it was the first of the year, was like one of those fashion accessories that make the most ordinary outfit look elegant. Now, thanks to the snow, the gray woods, scrawny lawn, and concrete parking lot had acquired an unexpected charm.

Maud walked out to the balustrade. The railing was round and the snow did not adhere there, so she leaned on it and gazed at the landscape. She could not help but recall the dead bodies in the field. She wondered what they would look like under the snow, whether the snow could make them look somehow lovely, too. Her mind wandered and she lost all sense of time. How long had she been standing there when she saw a figure emerge from the shelter of the first row of trees and cross the pale lawn? She didn't move, hoping the man hadn't seen her. Because it was a man, with broad shoulders, walking slowly. Who could it be? Should she wake the others and give the alert? Suddenly she heard her name and recognized Marc's voice as he called to her in a whisper.

"Is that you?" she said. "You can't sleep, either?"

He was standing directly below her.

"No, I went for a walk along the road."

"The sky has cleared; it's beautiful."

"From the road, you can see the mountains in the distance. Do you want to go for a walk?"

"Hang on."

She looked for the stairs and found them opposite the parking lot. Marc was dressed fairly lightly. He had his hands rammed into his jeans pockets to keep warm.

"Do you want to go up and get a sweater?"

"No, I'll be fine once we're walking."

They went through the woods and down a path where the snow had not stuck. Before long they came out on the road. They had to walk a little bit farther to get out of the trees and into a clear area. They were walking slowly side by side.

"You didn't sleep?" she asked.

"No."

"Those dead bodies . . . "

"Yes."

She was surprised he would admit to his emotion so frankly.

"But you must have seen this before."

"Precisely."

They had gone beyond the edge of the forest and before them there was rolling countryside as far as the eye could see. The hills sloped gradually to an invisible valley, then suddenly came up against the faraway barrier of snow-covered mountains.

"That's why I left the army."

"Because you couldn't stand the killing?"

"Because I couldn't stand just looking on and not doing anything."

She was astonished. Not for a moment had she ever thought that there was anything anyone could do to *prevent* the horror. At best they could try *afterward* to help the victims. She had been conditioned by the ethos of humanitarian aid work more than she would have thought. Marc had just revealed to her another possibility, something she had not allowed herself to think about until then.

"And what do you want to do?"

He became animated.

"Did you see them? Did you see those UN guys, with their machine guns and their armored vehicles, picking up the bodies, playing nurse or gravedigger? I did that for a while, too. And then I had enough."

"Argelos was categorical: they don't have the means to go after the perpetrators. They'd have to arrest everybody. There are criminals everywhere, in this war."

Marc looked at her, and even in the dark she could tell his gaze was angry and scornful. She was sorry she had contradicted him; she didn't feel like arguing. She just wanted to understand, and above all, understand him.

"Explain, then," she said.

In the wan light of the snowy fields, Marc's face was stripped of its severity, and his features were painted with a shadowy palette. Only his mouth was clearly drawn. Maud had a sudden urge to put her lips there, to feel his breath, the trembling moisture of it, the life in him. She was someone who avoided desire in others, yet now she felt an unexpected dizziness, a whirling inside her, something she had so rarely yielded to. It had taken fear, fatigue, and horror to tunnel deep enough inside her for this sudden flame to catch, from an ember she hadn't known was there.

"There are criminals on all sides," said Marc in a dull voice, "and there are victims on all sides, that much is obvious. But we can't do anything if we leave it at that."

Maud was angry with herself for not being more interested in what he was saying, for being so focused on the troubling sensations he aroused in her. He seemed not to notice her. He continued holding onto his inner rage, staring straight ahead. But she could not take her eyes off his lips as he spoke.

"At some point," he continued, "you have to define what is cause and what is consequence. Among all those who are fighting, there are some who have grabbed power in order to crush the others. A clique in Belgrade has confiscated the former Yugoslav Army, and the entire apparatus of state, and the others can only defend themselves."

Maud had regained some of her self-control and she wanted to show that she was attentive.

"You mean it's the Serbs who are responsible?"

"Not the Serbs as such. They, too, have their share of poor wretches who have been forced to fight, and honest, sensitive people who are victims. But the Serbs who have hijacked the Yugoslav state, the Serbian nationalists who have taken advantage of the country's collapse to embark on their project of hegemony—yes, they're responsible."

It was all very abstract to her. She had always hated politics—the simplifications, the lies. But she liked the idea that there was a moment when things could have direction, and meaning. Whether he was right or wrong, Marc had taken sides, he refused to succumb to helplessness and resignation. That was the one thing she retained from what he had said. She thought again of the murdered women and children, and of the sterile indignation that had overwhelmed her at the sight of those bodies whose deaths would remain unpunished. Any injustice was better than that injustice.

They had stopped and she was standing right in front of

him. Their faces were very close. She could feel his breath. She parted her lips and he took them.

He held her close; she ran her hands impatiently over his woolen shirt; she could feel his muscles. Their kisses were rough, avid, as if in this clinch they had found a way to express all the rebellion and passion, all the rage and despair which only moments before had been silently eating away at them.

"Come," he murmured, standing back and taking her by the hand.

They retraced their own footprints in the snow, but their new footprints mingled because they were walking with their bodies held close together. They climbed the stairs to the terrace, bumping against each other, and then went up to the floor where there were big dormitories. There were no more obstacles to their desire, just the sensual resistance of their clothes: they pulled them off each other with clumsy, feverish gestures. The cold air in the dormitory, the rough cloth on the mattress, and the iron frame of the narrow bed merely enhanced their ardor. Their disorderly embrace was not unlike a struggle, but one where no one conquered or was conquered; the ultimate goal was to be as one body, set against the violence of the world outside.

Maud had never wanted to subject herself to this ordeal, because she regarded it as an unbearable humiliation. In all the boys who had ever approached her she had sensed the same impatience to gain power over her, by inflicting this wound upon her, and she had never felt enough love for any of them to submit to it. She was a virgin out of pride, out of defiance. But here, in this place she could not have given a name to, in the discomfort of a devastated house, she welcomed the intimate pain without fear, because she desired it intensely. And the man who was introducing it to her was like the instrument of a force that surpassed even him, a force with which she wanted to fill herself. She could feel the blood flowing from her, and she could picture how in daylight the gleaming stain would shine in these grim surroundings. They were sharing her blood the way they had shared the blood of the murdered women. But hers was the blood of vengeance and combat, of life and pleasure. She cried out.

They stopped for a moment and listened for any sounds from the floor below. But nothing disturbed the silence, and they returned to their lovemaking.

When at last they had no more strength, they lay entwined, but the cold returned, quickly chilling the sweat on their bodies. Marc covered her with his shirt and silently crept downstairs to get a sleeping bag. He opened it out and they spread it over themselves.

He stroked her wild hair and gazed at her face, where the glow from the snow through the picture window seemed to dust her with a fine bluish powder.

"You're so beautiful," he said.

And she believed him. When it came from others, she always rejected this compliment as an indiscreet judgment, but now, from him, she accepted it, and she wanted to be worthy of it, always.

She kissed him full on the mouth again. With her fingertips she caressed the tattoos on his arms, dreamily, those same tattoos that had initially inspired her disgust but which now, in the semidarkness, looked like the damask surface of a priceless fabric.

At one point he leaned on one elbow and looked at her, his expression grave.

"You have to know."

"Know what?"

For an instant she thought he was going to tell her about some irrevocable commitment that would make their love impossible, and she was afraid. But he had gone back to his obsession, to his struggle.

"In the trucks—"

"Yes?"

"I didn't put explosives for construction."

"No? What did you put, then?"

"Fifteen kilos of military explosives. Real ones, with detonators. Enough materiel to blow up a bridge a hundred meters long."

She didn't want him to speak to her of love. This was their love: shared secrets, danger, combat. He had the grave expression of a serious child as he waited for her response. She looked at him without saying anything. He saw a smile pinned on her face, and he was worried he might not understand the meaning of it.

At that moment, she had a vision of everything. She understood that the most important thing for him was this plan, his mad dreams, the rage that inhabited him, while she did not know where it came from. All the rest, even love, would come after. It was enough to fill a person with despair, and yet she sensed he liked it that way. She slowly reached out one arm and moved a lock of his hair to one side; it was heavy with sweat, falling over his brow.

"I love you," she said.

He kissed her and their desire returned.

They were woken by sooty dawn, filtered through gray trees the wind had stripped of snow. They hurried back to their rooms to lie in their own beds, in their own cold sleeping bags. The others were still asleep and did not notice.

Only Vauthier, lying on his back, parted his lids when Marc walked past the open door of his room. Their eyes met in the gloom.

III
PURSUIT

1

For several days Marc had been thinking of leaving the convoy. He was convinced Vauthier knew more than he let on, and that he was about to act on his desire for revenge. The next evening he suggested to Maud that they should run away.

"Run away? But how?"

"In our truck."

"They'll follow us."

"Not if we make a good plan."

It was a fairly terrifying proposal. Running away would mean severing all ties with the association and subscribing to a logic of theft and war. There would be no going back. But wasn't this the ineluctable consequence of having stowed explosives on the truck? Events were unfolding too quickly for Maud to think things through properly. There had been the massacre, and then this unexpected, intense night, and now, the prospect of flight. It all seemed to be obeying some powerful, implacable mechanism that she could not grasp.

"And what about Alex?"

"He doesn't know. He still thinks I put his construction explosives in the load."

"Are you going to tell him?"

"No."

Maud was fairly tempted by the idea of running away. But she didn't like leaving Alex behind.

"But we could take him with us, couldn't we?"

"It wouldn't be reasonable. We don't know how he'll react. He'll be really angry with me for not letting him in on the plan."

"Why didn't you tell him?"

"We don't see things the same way. He doesn't share my commitment. Worse than that: he doesn't understand it. His plan for the pumps and the coal mine is half-baked at best. It's an issue they can deal with when peace returns. For the time being it's victory they need. Everything has to be devoted to that end, including humanitarian work. He can't grasp that."

"You knew this before leaving."

"With the initial plan, it wasn't a problem. I was supposed to go calmly along to Kakanj with him. He would only have found out about the substitution at the same time he was reunited with his girlfriend, and that would have softened the blow. But things have been so shaky, and now this cop in the convoy . . . Now, we don't have any choice."

"But it's terrible all the same. He's your friend."

Marc pressed his lips. He clearly could not take responsibility for what he was doing without a certain unease. But it was not in his nature to admit as much.

"Besides, on a practical level it's too risky. In this truck we're autonomous. But he belongs to the other team. If we bring him in on it, there is every chance he will fuck it up."

Maud didn't insist. After all, that was between them. And deep down she didn't really mind being alone with Marc on this adventure.

They left the holiday camp all together at dawn, and the convoy drove through the countryside without incident. While they were driving, Marc and Maud went over their plan in detail, to give the others the slip the following night.

The layer of snow was too fine to stick for long to the still-warm earth, and grayish patches began to reappear here and there, making the scenery drab and dirty. They passed a

Norwegian aid convoy going the opposite direction, its load delivered. In the evening, they camped in a pasture where the snow had almost all melted. They had gone back to their original setup for the tents. Marc slept in the tent with Alex, and Maud stayed in the truck. They both knew what they had to do.

Maud had set the alarm on her watch for four o'clock. She got up and moved about silently. She took out her flashlight and the little tool Marc had given her.

The main thing was to avoid making any noise. She had taken careful note of where the tire valve was located at the back of Lionel's truck. Marc had insisted on the importance of letting the air out slowly so the valve would not start whistling. Unfortunately, when Maud pressed on the little metal cylinder, she felt an unexpected resistance. She had to press very hard to overcome it. When the valve finally gave way, it let out a whistle so shrill and intense that she dropped everything. Sound carried in the icy air, and there were no animals on that deserted field, nothing that could make such a noise. She listened to the silence for a long time. Nothing moved in the tents, pitched roughly twenty yards away from the trucks, and Maud was working on the left rear tire, which was farthest away. Her sudden fear subsided.

But when she tried again her hands were trembling. The valve started whistling the moment she put pressure on. The idea was to press very firmly, and not let herself be startled this time, then let the air out with a deeper hiss that was not as likely to wake the others. She thought about Marc, his determination, his tranquil manner, and she tried to act as if he were there next to her. She pressed hard on the valve. There was the same whistling, but more briefly, and then the air escaped with a regular hiss. Maud could feel it on her face, and was careful to maintain the same pressure on the valve so the noise would not start up again. Her fingers were numb with cold and the enormous tire was taking forever to deflate. She winced with pain because a cramp in her hands was threatening to make her drop everything. Finally she saw that the tire was going slack, and this gave her the energy to resist until all the air was out. It had to be completely flat, otherwise their pursuers might be tempted not to repair it right away. When at last she let go, the rim was touching the ground.

Marc joined her silently a bit later. The night before, they had put a sleeping tablet in Alex's water bottle. Marc knew that Alex never went to sleep without his water next to him, and he would wake up two or three times during the night to drink. The dose must have been more than enough, because he didn't budge when they started up their truck. Lionel, on the other hand, sprang out of the tent as soon as he heard the engine turn over. They had been careful, the night before, to park at a fair distance from the first truck, ready to pull straight out. In the rearview mirror Maud saw Lionel running over the muddy ground to try to catch them, but he was barefoot. He slipped, fell, got back to his feet. The truck drove slowly across the field. Lionel began running again. He managed to grab the rear fender but when the track reached the road, it gave a jolt as it drove over a small ridge. Lionel let go. Maud had one last vision of him, sprawled his entire length in the mud and snow. He was still in his undershirt, and the wan moonlight made him look like a corpse.

Never once, since leaving Lyon, had they driven this fast. Marc kept the gas pressed to the floor, and as the road was flat and straight, the old fifteen-tonner sped along. The tired suspension rattled over stones in the road, and they could hear impressive creaking sounds whenever the ruts were deep. Maud clung to the door, her window open, and leaned out from time to time to see if she could see anything behind them.

But Lionel's truck was nowhere to be seen.

The road went slightly uphill, which was in their favor. They knew that their truck was slightly more powerful than the other one. Marc had his jaw clenched, and kept his eyes riveted to the road because of the dim headlights. They only began to relax once the first rays of dawn appeared, which meant that driving fast would be less of a hazard.

"How long will it take them to fix the tire, do you think?"

"We have the pump."

"Can they put on the spare?"

"You know we didn't repair the one with the bullet hole. And we have the other one. On top of it, last night I took the jack."

They looked at each other and burst out laughing.

The clouds were not as thick as the day before. They could even see a patch of clear sky toward the east, turning pink in the dawn.

"Get out the papers, in case we come to a checkpoint."

Before leaving Lyon, Marc and Alex had photocopied all the documents. They had let Lionel proudly show the convoy's papers at every checkpoint, but they had exactly the same ones, hidden in the sun visor on the passenger side. They had made a slit in the padded rectangle, slipped the papers inside, then closed the slit up with a piece of black masking tape. Now Maud took them out of their hiding place and examined them.

"But . . . it says there are two trucks, and five people are listed."

"I know."

"But there's just two of us now. And one truck. The paramilitaries won't like that."

"No, take a look: the freight lists are on two separate sheets. Find ours, and tear up the other one. For the drivers, all we have to do is cross out the three names. We'll say that authorization was requested for five people, to be on the safe side, but that in the end two were enough. In any case, don't worry. You've seen how they check, as a rule . . . "

Maud knew that from time to time they might get fussy civil servant types. But Marc's calm manner reassured her. He seemed to know what he was doing and he certainly had his reasons.

At one point, early in the morning, the sun's rays shone across the tops of the trees, real rays from a real sun, however pale and cold. A little cluster of long-haired donkeys had gathered beneath the branches of an oak tree and were lifting their noses to the light. Streams sparkled their way through the pastures. Maud felt like kissing Marc. But he was wearing his tense, neutral face. It was what Maud thought of as his daytime face, because now she knew that gentle, other face, the one he only revealed at night. She told herself she would wait until evening to approach him. Until the thought gave rise to a doubt.

"Where are we going to spend the night?"

"Here, in the truck," said Marc, patting the seat with the palm of his hand. "While we drive. For at least two days."

"You mean we'll take turns driving during the night, is that it?"

"Precisely."

"Aren't you afraid we'll get lost with these headlights?"

"We'll be careful."

Until now there had been the excitement of the encounter, and the preparation of their flight, which had seemed like little more than a game. Now Maud was abruptly aware of the situation. She was riding in a truck full of dynamite, in the middle of a country that was at war, pursued by people who would not hesitate to identify them as thieves. She had wanted to commit, but she was beginning to realize how the commitment of humanitarian workers was not a commitment. They did have to take risks, and sometimes they found themselves in awkward situations. But the fact remained that they were not involved in the actual fighting. With this business of the construction explosives, she had agreed to a first transgression, but one that was of no great consequence. Even with a load like that, they were still aid workers, and they could have relied on the support of public opinion, if the Serbs arrested them.

With a real explosives it was another matter altogether. They were outlaws. France did not want to be dragged into the war and would disown them. If they were arrested, they would be considered war criminals. They had crossed an invisible line, and now Maud understood its huge symbolic importance. They had become real combatants. They had friends, and enemies. And there was nothing protecting their lives anymore.

Lionel sat in the cold mud next to the deflated tire, completely despondent. Vauthier came over to him at an unhurried pace. He had taken the time to get dressed and put on his shoes before he left his tent. He leaned down to look at the tire.

"It's just an ordinary flat."

"How do you know?" muttered Lionel.

"Because I heard the kid open the valve during the night."

"You heard! And you just stood there?"

"No."

"What, then?"

"I went back to sleep."

Lionel leapt to his feet and grabbed Vauthier by the collar with both hands.

"You went back to sleep! You must be joking. So you were in on it?"

Lionel was tugging on Vauthier with his puny arms but he couldn't make him budge. Vauthier gently pushed his hands aside.

"I'm going to blow up the tire," said Lionel.

"Don't bother. I'm sure they took the pump."

Lionel looked at him, aghast. Vauthier took him by the shoulder.

"Come on. Let's go discuss this calmly."

"Discuss this calmly, while they run off with the truck? Every hour that goes by, they're making headway. And we're sitting here like assholes."

"Don't worry. They won't get far."

Vauthier smiled with his pursed lips. He didn't really look like he was joking, and his hatred for Marc still shone in his shifty little eyes. Lionel let him go and they walked over to the tents. Alex emerged from his, his hair tousled, his eyes puffy.

"I don't know what happened to me. I slept like a—"

"Did you drink any water last night?" asked Vauthier absently.

"Like I do every night."

"I think you'd better empty out your water bottle. Your little friend must have put a good dose in there."

"A dose of what?"

"He put Alex to sleep?" asked Lionel. "So it was premeditated?"

"What are you two talking about? And where's the other truck?"

"Of course it was premeditated," said Vauthier. "Fortunately we, too, have premeditated a few things."

He was the only one who had his wits about him. The other two were not even dressed, and their eyes were frantic, their gestures clumsy.

"Okay, go and get dressed. I'm going to make us some proper breakfast. And we can go over the whole business in detail."

The sun had risen to the top of the trees by the time the three of them gathered around the camp stove, sitting on crates. They cupped their palms around their mugs to keep warm. Lionel had slipped a joint behind his ear and was waiting to finish his coffee to light it.

"So, what's this business about premeditation?"

"Let's backtrack a little," said Vauthier. "At headquarters, where we stopped, remember I ran into some friends?"

"Yes."

"There were a few people in the know."

"Secret police?"

"Let's just say, French agents in UN uniforms."

"What did they tell you?"

"I asked them to look into those two," said Vauthier, looking at Alex.

"Don't say *those two*. You can see damn well that—"

"That he screwed you the way he screwed us? I can see that. But back then, I didn't know."

"So, tell us what they told you," said Lionel.

"I can't give you all the details. There's an investigation under way in France and it's confidential. But I can sum it up as follows."

He sat up straight and gave himself an important air, as if about to adopt a judge or prosecutor's solemn tones.

"Two months ago, explosive weapons were stolen from an arsenal in Orange. They haven't found the culprit yet, but they know for sure that whoever it was had accomplices on the inside and was a former soldier."

"But construction explosives aren't the same as explosive weapons," shouted Alex. "I bought them myself from a civil engineering firm."

"Let him finish! Go on, Vauthier."

"Thanks. I'll get to the crux of it, since you're so eager. Everything would seem to indicate that it is our mutual friend who stole those explosives and hid them in the second truck."

"How do you know?"

"Because the description matches, and my friends had a tip from an informer."

Alex looked stunned. The news had thrown him for a loop. At the same time, this explained some of the things he had constantly wondered about Marc. He had never really understood why he had agreed so enthusiastically to go with him to Kakanj: he didn't have a girlfriend there. If Alex suspected him of anything, it was that he didn't really care whether the pumps at the mine would keep on working or not. Their friendship was real, but not deep enough to explain why Marc was taking so many risks to commit himself to this mission. But if he had his own agenda, that explained a lot. This was why, despite his surprise, Alex was immediately convinced that Vauthier's information had to be the truth.

"And my construction explosives?" he asked. "What did he do with them?"

"I'm sorry to inform you but he used you, my dear Alex. He needed a team to drive his truck and he knew about your hare-brained scheme regarding the mine in Kakanj."

"It's not a hare-brained scheme!"

"No, of course it isn't," said Vauthier suavely. "Whatever the case may be, he put real explosives in the load instead of yours."

"Real explosives? He put real explosives?"

"Yes, my man. He does things properly, your Marc. He doesn't mess around with stories about water pumps."

"I never thought he'd pull such a rotten trick."

"But he did. Unfortunately for him, things haven't gone the way he wanted. You talked too much and Lionel changed the teams around. And he ended up with Maud."

"I don't believe it," moaned Alex, his head in his hands. "I don't believe it."

"But," continued Vauthier, raising a finger, "we're clever, too. We've got more than one trick up our sleeve. We stuck him with Maud; too bad for him! He managed to make her fall in love with him. That can't have been too difficult, with his good looks and smoldering gaze."

"What did you say?" interrupted Lionel. "Maud is in love with him? Okay, stop there. Stop right there. She's never been in love with anyone. That's just her problem."

His tone made it obvious that this was one wound that hadn't healed.

"Stop your whining, please. You have to face facts: she never gave a damn about you. And today even less so."

"Shut up!" shouted Lionel, leaping to his feet.

He had that twisted look on his face; Alex had seen it when Lionel suspected him of sleeping with Maud.

"Why do you want me to shut up? You have to learn to live with the truth in life, otherwise you'll never get ahead. And the truth is that your so-called girlfriend has fallen head over heels in love with Master Marc."

"Shut up."

Lionel echoed his own words like a robot. But he sat back down and stared into space, his anger giving way to despondency.

"At the holiday camp," continued Vauthier without pity, "they spent the night together, on the second floor. I'll spare you the details regarding what they left behind. But the evidence would seem to indicate that the young woman was indeed completely inexperienced. But now she knows life."

His head in his hands, Lionel remained silent. Then he sat up, calm and resigned. Vauthier's authority had a soothing effect on him. He couldn't stand to hear what the man was saying, but oddly, the revelation put an end to a lie that he himself no longer believed. He was almost relieved. All aggression gone, he turned to Vauthier.

"Why did you wait until now to tell us about Marc? Why didn't you tell us when we were at headquarters? We could have locked him up and settled the matter."

"Yeah, sure, I could have had him arrested at headquarters. He would have been put in the clink and then on trial. But he's very clever. He could have denied it, or even implicated us as well and brought us down with him."

"That's true," said Lionel.

"And anyway," said Vauthier, "I didn't want him to go to jail."

"And why not?"

"Because I'd rather deal with him myself."

There was a long silence. The low-angled, straw-colored sunlight made the patches of snow stand out against the muddy black earth. Lionel, leaning over the bluish flame of the camping stove, glanced at Alex and saw that he was dozing again, lying on one elbow, still drowsy from the drug Marc had given him.

"Exactly," said Lionel, shrugging his shoulders, "We'll deal with him ourselves. And what do you propose, can you tell me that?"

"We'll start by fixing the truck, no rush. I'm sure we'll find a farm somewhere nearby where they have a pump or a compressor."

Then he added, more quietly, "For the rest, don't worry: they'll get what they deserve. And it would be better if we're not around when it happens."

"What have you drummed up for them?" asked Lionel.

Vauthier pulled his brand-new fur-lined jacket closer around him. Pointing to Alex with his chin, he gave Lionel a knowing wink, as if to advise caution.

"This is a dangerous region," he continued in a low voice. "You saw, yesterday. The paramilitaries are out of control, there are gangs of killers roaming around. They can do plenty of damage."

"You mean . . . they're going to run into guys like that?" said Lionel with a start. "How do you know?"

"Just an intuition."

Vauthier took a beanie out of his pocket to cover his bald head. Lionel was livid.

"Don't tell me you've taken a contract out on them . . . "

Vauthier didn't answer. He smiled, his expression smug, cruel. He clearly had no intention of saying anything more, and Lionel didn't insist. The prospect of being accessory to a murder frightened him. At the same time, if that was the way things were meant to happen, he couldn't help but feel a real pleasure. Basically, he liked the idea of revenge, provided he didn't have to be responsible. Vauthier did not have such scruples.

At that moment, looking at the big ginger man with his darting little eyes, Lionel almost liked him.

2

They were taking turns driving, and Maud had been at
the wheel for three hours. Now she was back in the passenger seat and was supposed to get some sleep. But
she was too restless to doze off.

"How long will it take us to get to Kakanj?"

"We're not going to Kakanj."

"Oh! Then where are we going?"

"Where they're expecting us."

Coming from anyone else, an answer like this would have
exasperated her. She hated it when people wouldn't give her a
straight answer, as if she were not deserving of serious information. But she was beginning to know Marc. He never ven-
tured anything more than what he'd been asked. It was probably the result of his military upbringing. If you wanted to
know more, you just had to ask him more.

"Who is expecting us, and where?"

He took his left hand off the wheel and rubbed his eyes. It
was the only sign of fatigue he allowed himself. He also made
this gesture when he was about to speak at length. Which
meant he didn't do it often.

"What exactly did Alex tell you about Kakanj?"

Clearly the point of this question was to determine where he
should begin his story, in hopes he could say as little as possible.

"He told me about his girlfriend, Bouba. And he told me
you often went to see the Croats who were surrounding the
camp."

"Is that all?"

"Yes, more or less. I won't hide the fact that I was surprised by what he told me. Apparently they're real bastards. They throw stones at the refugees when they get near the barbed wire."

Marc waited until he'd negotiated a long downhill bend to start speaking again.

"There are bastards on every side. Have you never been to a country at war before?"

"Never."

"That's just what it is, civil war: the triumph of the bastards. You see them coming out of the woodwork. You're even surprised there are so many and that you don't take any more notice of them than usual."

Maud nodded. She had no trouble seeing the bastards. She saw them in every milieu and every circumstance; she could unmask them in spite of their disguise. Basically, she thought, maybe she'd always seen the world as if it were at war.

"But that doesn't matter," said Marc. "Bastards are a product of the war, not the cause. Most of the time those who are really responsible, the ones who unleash the violence and trigger the conflict, are very decent people. Sincere, generous, educated people. Anyway, never mind. That's not the topic."

"It's still not a reason to get all cozy with a bunch of bastards."

"The Croats surrounding Kakanj are not all bastards."

Maud did not seem very convinced.

"Well, that may be, but Alex told me what they did to Bouba's family . . . "

"Of course. As soon as the war started, all the frustrated, jealous neighbors or perverts went berserk. But they're not the only ones fighting."

The clear sky of morning had yielded to thick black clouds, and banks of fog enveloped the road as the valley rose and fell.

Marc did not slow down in the fog but he was more cautious: two or three times they had almost crashed into horse-drawn carts emerging from the mist at the last minute.

"I knew them pretty well, those refugees at the mine, and I have to say I liked them. It wasn't hard, after all. They were defenseless people, women and children, victims. With all due respect to your humanitarian friends, anyone is capable of liking a victim."

Maud could have argued the point. She wondered whether humanitarians—Lionel for example—really did like the victims, or whether it was simply the idea of being able to help victims that they liked, for it gave them a feeling of superiority. But that was a different question.

"In any case," said Marc, "it's another matter altogether, and a lot harder, when it comes to liking combatants—people who are on their feet, who are fighting, not holding out their hands to be fed."

He turned to her for a moment and smiled. It was a serious smile, rather sad, and she got the impression it wasn't really meant for her.

"It's true, I did make a few good friends among the Croats. All sorts of guys. Simple soldiers, in particular, guys who were fighting even when they didn't really want to, and who didn't hate anyone."

"They aren't obliged to fight, in that case."

"You know, when your country collapses, you don't have a choice. You defend your land. You protect your loved ones. That's hard for us to imagine."

"Maybe."

"Those basic soldiers are not the most interesting. In general, they don't really know what's happening. They just know what's going on around them, that's all, and they obey orders. But there are also people who see the bigger picture."

"Real soldiers, is that what you mean?"

Maud smiled as she spoke. But Marc had not grasped her irony.

"Not necessarily. Not at all, even. In fact, it's a makeshift army. Most of the men fighting are not career soldiers. I made friends with a doctor and an architect. They wore stripes so they'd look like real officers. But they were first and foremost civilians."

"What was their role?"

"The doctor was called Filipović. He was a cardiologist from Banja Luka. At the beginning of the war, when the Serbs were bombarding Vukovar, he went there as a doctor. But very quickly he took up arms. After two months he was a colonel. When I met him he was commander for the Kakanj sector."

"And the architect?"

"He's a younger guy, not even thirty-five. His name is Martić. He had just gotten his degree when the war broke out. He was from Mostar. He managed to escape when the Muslims were 'cleansing' his neighborhood. In Kakanj he became head gunner. As he put it, he was now in charge of destroying houses instead of building them. But I still got the impression he knew what he was talking about . . . "

Marc glanced at Maud with a faint smile on his lips. He was not without a sense of humor, she thought. But it was black humor, always focused on death and destruction.

She waited for him to go on with his story but he slammed on the brakes. He fell silent and peered into the fog, leaning forward, looking worried.

"What's that, up ahead?" he said.

They had not seen any checkpoints since they had left the others behind. That might have been normal, because the region was a confused patchwork of enclaves. Perhaps they had crossed an unmanned border, but that was unlikely. In any case, they had to be very careful: in the thickening mist, they might suddenly come upon a checkpoint without warning.

A few hundred yards in front of them there were dark shapes blocking the road. From a distance, however, it didn't look like a checkpoint. It looked rather like a convoy that was stopped, with men moving all around it.

"They don't seem to be moving forward," said Maud. "Do you think they saw us?"

Marc switched off the engine and pulled the handbrake. They were hidden by a curtain of trees, and with the fog, the people on the road had surely not seen them. They just had to hope they had not heard them coming. Marc was thinking fast. It actually looked like some sort of ambush. But who'd set it up? It was unlikely that Lionel and the others could have already alerted the UN. They'd been nowhere near any bases when they'd made their escape. But of course it could always be a coincidence. A UN convoy might have gone by their last camp and reported their flight to all units, thanks to their radio network. Unless it was something else, thought Marc. And in that case, the possibilities were bound to be unpleasant . . .

Just as Vauthier had supposed, they had no difficulty finding a nearby farm. Exceptionally, the farmer had not gone off to fight, because he lived alone. The farm would be lost without him there to look after it. He came himself to reinflate the tire with an electric pump that worked off a battery. Then they took the time to get dressed and put away the tents and the kitchen utensils. Now they were driving down a road that was almost perfectly straight, bordered by bare alder trees. Lionel, at the wheel, was rehashing rap couplets in a muted voice. Vauthier was sitting very calmly on the right-hand side of the front seat. Alex had not yet eliminated all the sedative, and was asleep on the bunk in the back.

"Tell me something, Vauthier. Those agent friends of yours you met in town the other day: are you working for them?"

"You might say that, yes."

"So you didn't volunteer at La Tête d'Or just to go sight-seeing."

"Not at all."

"So you've been spying on us."

"Absolutely not."

There was no reproof in Lionel's tone. He was increasingly grateful to Vauthier for having rescued the situation. What he felt now was curiosity bordering on fascination.

"You weren't spying on us?"

"No."

"I confess I find that hard to understand."

"And yet it's simple. My agent friends, as you call them, needed to be informed about what is happening here: combat zones, opposing armies, front lines. That's why they entrusted me with this mission. In a convoy like this, we're on the move, we go through regions where no one else goes, and we can talk freely with everyone. That's why I came with you. It certainly wasn't to indulge an interest in your pimply little teenage dramas."

Lionel didn't like knowing his convoy was being watched by Intelligence. At the same time, he was rather flattered by the fact that Vauthier trusted him enough to speak openly. In any case, he felt he was on his side now.

"Obviously, when I realized those two former soldiers had infiltrated your mission, I had to inform my superiors as well. And it's a good job I did: that way, they were able to do some cross-checking and find out what that son of a bitch was up to."

Behind them, Alex gave a grunt as he tried to sit up. His hair was disheveled and he was rubbing his eyes. When Vauthier saw he was awake, he fell silent. He played with his earring and his little eyes squinted slightly, as they did whenever he was angry.

3

They were still stopped, and the fog around them was getting thicker. Or perhaps it was simply that night was beginning to fall. In any case, it was getting harder and harder to see. Marc did not switch on the headlights, and before long they were in the dark.

"Do you think they saw us?" asked Maud.

"They would have come over."

"If it's a checkpoint, it's dangerous to hide just next to it, isn't it?"

"I don't think it's a checkpoint."

"Why not?"

Her questions clearly annoyed Marc. He was concentrating, trying to find a solution. The shapes on the road in the distance had not moved. What was more worrying was that they had not turned on their headlights either, even though it was totally dark now. Marc opened his door and stepped out onto the road. It was not wide enough for the truck to turn around without making several maneuvers, particularly as it did not turn on a dime. The ditches on either side were full of brushwood. Marc tested the ditch, cautiously advancing one leg. It was very deep, and if a wheel got stuck in there, there would be no getting back out. He walked a short distance behind them to see whether there was not a way into a field, or a wider stretch of road. But he didn't find anything. He came back to the truck and climbed onto his seat.

"So," said Maud, "what do we do?"

She was afraid now, and Marc's presence had two opposite effects on her. He was the one who had given rise to her alarm. In a way, it was his fear that she was feeling. At the same time, his very presence reassured her. She would leave it up to him to decide what to do.

"You get behind the wheel and I'll push the truck in reverse. The road slopes gently and the ground is fairly even. I should be able to get it rolling. Keep your door open, and try to keep an eye on where you're going. There are ditches on either side. If I see you're starting to veer off, I'll bang on the hood."

Maud slid over to the driver's seat. In the dark she bumped into Marc, who hadn't gotten out yet. She couldn't help herself, she reached up and grabbed him by the neck. She couldn't see his face and she groped to find his lips. They were still pressed hard, the way they were when he had his daytime face. But at the contact of her lips, she felt them part, and they kissed for a long time. In the moonless night, with the creeping cold and danger, their embrace was like a refuge, a denial of the world. Maud did not want it to end, and a deeper, more complete desire came over her. But Marc pushed her away and got out onto the road.

It took her a long time to regain her composure.

"Let's go," he said.

She removed the handbrake, made sure at the gear was in neutral, then, leaning outside with her hands on the wheel, she got ready. The dark pavement was hardly any lighter than the shoulder of the road on either side.

"Whenever you're ready."

She could tell Marc had arched his back and was pushing with all his might, because she heard him grunting. At one point he let go and exhaled noisily. The truck hadn't budged.

"Let's try again," he said.

She gave a new signal. He began pushing. This time, she got

the impression that the truck reversed slightly, but then it rolled forward again.

"I have to clear the wheels. One of them must be stuck in a rut."

She heard him go around the truck and scratch at the ground.

They tried again four times, to no avail. Marc climbed back into the truck. Maud sensed he was thinking hard, and she didn't ask any questions. A moment later, there seemed be an odd quality to the silence. And she realized there were snowflakes on the windshield.

They both had the same thought: if it snowed long enough, it would muffle any sound. It might even cover their tracks. The men up there in the distance must have gotten into their cars for shelter. Any outside noise would not be easy to hear. Maud and Marc waited for a long time. The snow went on falling. The terrain was beginning to take on a pale hue and they could tell the light ground from the dark sky. Marc got out, walked around the truck, and Maud gave him her seat at the wheel. He turned the starter. The diesel started up on the second try.

Not wasting a moment, he put it into reverse and began going back. By braking intermittently, he could use the dim glow from the brake lights as a guide. Slowly, smoothly, he managed to back up about a hundred yards. At that point, the truck would no longer be visible to the men waiting in ambush. Marc switched on the headlights. A very muddy, narrow forest track led off to the left. The snow had collected on the fir trees on either side, but had not yet covered the ground. Marc drove up the track. Thirty or forty yards higher up, the track stopped in a clearing. There were long piles of carefully stacked logs, waiting to be loaded. Marc parked the truck next to one of the stacks. Then he switched off the ignition.

"Are we going to spend the night here?"

"Yes. Tomorrow I'll go and see if the roadblock is still there."

The damp chill had permeated the cab. There was no electric heating in that truck, and no bunk, either.

"What shall we do? Shall we put up the tent?"

"It would be better to stay in the cab. In case anything happens . . . "

Maud took out a second fleece and put it on. She unzipped her sleeping bag and used it as a blanket.

"Lie down on the seat," he said.

The cab was fairly narrow and as she lay down she found her head ended up on Marc's lap.

"What about you? You won't be able to sleep like that."

"Don't worry about me."

He caressed her hair, and for the first time she was sorry she had it so short. She would have liked to cover him with long silky strands, so that he could feel the softness in his fingers, so they would give him a little warmth.

The woods were absolutely silent. Maud could feel the warmth of her body spreading under her sleeping bag. She was determined to stay awake but in a matter of seconds she fell sound asleep.

When Maud woke up, there was pale daylight. She found that Marc had put a backpack under her head to serve as a pillow. He was no longer in the cab. She looked all around. It had stopped snowing, but it must have fallen most of the night because the ground was white and the branches were covered with a thick sparkling sleeve. The clearing was vaster than she remembered, and on one side there were lumberjacks' cabins. Marc was sitting in front of one of them heating water on the stove he had taken from the truck. She put on her shoes and went to join him.

"Did you sleep?"

"Not much. Do you want some coffee?"

He handed her a steaming mug.

"They're gone."

"How do you know?"

"I went to the top of the hill and I watched them through the binoculars."

"Did you figure out who they were, in the end?"

"A bunch of guys in uniform, but with no insignia, paramilitaries by the look of it."

"The cutthroats who were killing the villagers?"

"Could be, or others."

"Were they looking for us?"

"Maybe."

She took little sips of her steaming coffee.

"Maybe we were worried for nothing?"

"Never mind. It was better not to take the risk."

"Do you think Vauthier and the others have managed to raise the alarm?"

"They might have. But in any case, that doesn't matter anymore. Five kilometers further along and we'll be leaving the road."

"Leaving the road? To go where?"

They were already on a very minor road with almost no traffic. She could not imagine driving the truck on an even smaller road, except to drive for a few yards in order to hide.

"We're going to cut through the mountains."

Marc seemed to know what he was doing and she didn't question him further.

They had two slices each of some hard old bread Marc had cut with his pocketknife. Then they packed everything up again and drove off.

They left the woods without difficulty. They were back on the hill they had been going up the night before. The early morning light on the snow gave the pastures and forests of fir trees an Alpine air that Maud knew well. She felt like she was on vacation. She recalled the smell of raclette, her family seated around the table, but this also aroused mixed feelings. She had always felt terribly alone in the joyful, affectionate closeness of those family holidays in the mountains. It was for her the cruelest measure of everything that separated her from others, particularly as they were meant to be close. But during the day she went skiing on her own, off-piste. She got lost in the woods and often ended up walking, carrying her skis. She would get back to the chalet as night was falling, full of dreams and oblivious of her parents reproaching her carelessness. Those memories were the sharpest image she had of happiness.

As Marc had predicted, they found the side road a few kilometers farther along. At first sight, the road leading off to the left looked like it went no farther than a farm. But Marc had taken out a very precise geological survey map, which he kept unfolded on the dashboard. He showed Maud the thin line weaving toward the mountains. No one had been there all night. Behind them on the ground, white with snow, they left two parallel, orphaned tracks.

It had taken Alex an entire day and two nights to fully emerge from the haze of the sleeping tablet.

He came out of the tent where he'd slept alone and stretched. Vauthier and Lionel were still asleep. He seemed to remember they had talked for a long time the night before, but his memories were confused because of the drug. He heated up some coffee and drank it slowly, sitting on a camp stool.

The ground was covered in snow. He thought about Bouba, who must be cold in her gloomy oven. He wanted to be near her. No woman had ever touched him like this before. There were days when he really wondered why she had this power over him.

For Alex, snow meant his childhood. He had loved it when

he was little. All autumn long he would wait eagerly for the first snowflakes. There had to be snow for Christmas. But one year there was none, and he'd been very unhappy. Then he started school, late for his age because his mother had stayed at home to look after him herself. At school the jokes started. They weren't all that mean, just to make fun, and his school-mates were probably simply repeating what they heard at home. The jokes all had something to do with the contrast between his dark skin and the white snow. For the first time, he became aware that he was different. He was not only a black child among white children. He was a black child in the snow. His blackness was only relative, because he was mixed-race, but his skin color stood out more sharply against the absolute whiteness of the snow. And that was when he began, if not to hate the snow, at least to dread it.

It hadn't stopped him from living, or even from being happy and having friends. But he still had a secret wound, the impression that life had set him down in a place where he shouldn't have been. He was aware of an injustice, and though he could find no one to blame, it made him into an exile, some-one who did not feel he belonged in the land where he was born. The girls he went out with could not understand him. They were white girls, mountain girls who lived in surround-ings that suited them. In Grenoble he met a girl from the Antilles, but she had left Martinique at the age of twelve so she had never experienced something like his childhood. And then one day, from under his blue helmet, he saw Bouba. It was snowing that day, too. In her he recognized the same exile. The causes of her exile were different, because it was war, but it was exile all the same, a wrenching feeling. He sensed that he understood her sorrow, and that she would understand his. Thanks to Bouba, he could stop being a victim and become the opposite: a person who would try to save someone who was even worse off. There was a lot of that in his love for Bouba.

And his plan to go and live there with her after the war would be like one experience of exile healing another.

"What are you dreaming about?"

He hadn't heard Lionel come over; he was standing behind him.

"Nothing. You want a coffee?"

"Thanks. With two lumps of sugar."

Alex stirred the powder into the hot water, added the sugar, and handed the mug to Lionel.

"I was really out of it all day yesterday."

"He gave you a mega dose."

Lionel sat down across from him and blew on the hot liquid.

"Listen, maybe I dreamt it, given the state I was in, but weren't you and Vauthier talking about having some paramilitaries do them in?"

"Do them in? That's pretty extreme."

"Well, what was it, then?"

Lionel was a bit embarrassed. He couldn't deny it altogether. But that was no reason to tell Alex everything, because he didn't trust him at all. Above all, he didn't want to take the slightest responsibility.

"The point is just to shake them up a bit, I think."

"Shake them up? With a bunch of murderers? You can't do that!"

Alex suddenly realized how serious the situation had become. Because of his comatose state he had not been in on the decision. Now it might be too late.

"Have you completely lost your minds!? Marc did something stupid, granted. I'm as mad at him as anyone. But to hand him over to a bunch of cutthroats just for that?"

"Listen carefully, Alex. We're in a war zone. We can't control everything. If the paramilitaries bump him off, it won't be our fault. He just shouldn't have gone on ahead by himself."

"You could have handed him over to the UN and had him locked up! But not killed!"

"And didn't he risk getting us all killed, with his explosives?"

Vauthier had gotten up and now he joined in the conversation, shooting Alex a nasty look.

"What's going on?"

"He's worried about what's going to happen to his buddy."

"I always knew those two were hand in glove. They're not soldiers for nothing."

"That's not the point," shouted Alex. "Soldier or not, you have no reason to have him killed."

Suddenly, something else occurred to him.

"And Maud? Are you going to do away with her, too?"

"You might have missed an episode, given what you consumed. But may I remind you that they are sleeping together. She's an accomplice."

"Sleeping together!" echoed Alex, stunned.

He looked at Lionel, who had a crooked smile on his face. Then he suddenly stood up.

"So that's a reason to let her die? You're mad at her for rejecting you and falling in love with Marc. You're just jealous. You're pathetic!"

"Will you shut up?"

"Drop it," said Vauthier, "we get it, now. And besides, we've known it all along: he'll never abandon his buddy. We should have let the three of them go off together, at this moment in time . . . "

"What about you? You're a cop, and all you know is hatred . . . "

"Our friend is sharing his deepest thoughts," said Vauthier calmly, narrowing his eyes. "In my opinion, next time we meet up with the UN, we should just hand him over to the authorities and have him repatriated."

"You won't need to. I'm the one who's going to leave. You disgust me, both of you."

With that, Alex walked away and started brusquely folding up his tent.

Vauthier motioned to Lionel to calm him down.

"Let him say what he likes. We don't care. Besides, it'll be done by now."

They calmly finished breakfast and put away their camping gear. Then they climbed back onto the truck.

Alex sat in back, silent and sullen. Lionel was driving without saying a word, and Vauthier was humming, to show he was in a good mood and not at all affected by the insults.

The fog from the previous day had dissolved. The sky was still leaden, but luminous, and the snowy landscape was soft and sensual, hiding all trace of war.

At around ten o'clock they saw a group of men in the distance walking toward them along the road. Most of them were on foot, but they were followed by two jeeps.

"Well, well," said Vauthier, "looks like our paramilitary friends."

Alex, on the backseat, sat up straight.

They drove a bit farther and before long they were only a few yards from the paramilitaries.

"It's them, all right. I recognize Arkan, the tall one with the black cap."

The paramilitaries surrounded the truck, waving their weapons. Vauthier jumped out and went over to Arkan. From the truck Alex and Lionel couldn't hear what they were saying but they could see that the conversation was animated. They were a fierce-looking bunch, much scarier than any of the men they had encountered up to now. At the checkpoints they usually had to deal with disciplined soldiers glumly carrying out their tasks, or peasants who were more or less able-bodied but good for little else. But these were hardened fighters of the most dangerous kind: killers. And they had the cold gaze of men who knew neither fear nor pity.

The more the rebel leader said, the gloomier Vauthier seemed to become. He came back over to the truck and Lionel opened his window to talk to him.

"What did they say?"

"They didn't find them."

"You're joking."

"Do I look like it?"

"I don't believe it."

"Arkan was categorical. They went all the way back up the road and they did not see the truck."

Alex felt relieved but he was careful not to show it.

"That's incredible. Where could they have gotten to?"

"They must have gone into hiding. Apparently there was a lot of fog last night. Unless . . . "

"Unless what?"

"Show me the map."

4

Where does this track end up?"

Maud was studying the map but it wasn't very clear. The narrow passage they were taking branched out just as it crossed the mountains. Apparently there were several possibilities.

"We'll see which is the best way through," said Marc.

"But to get where?"

Marc changed hands on the steering wheel and as he was driving he stabbed one finger onto the map spread across Maud's lap.

"Over here. To the east of Zenica. It's still the Kakanj enclave, but we won't go into the town. We'll stay farther west."

"Is that where they're waiting for us?"

"Yes."

"Who is it? Your two friends, the doctor and the architect?"

"Among others."

It was tiring, in the end, to have to worm the information out of him. Maud folded the map with a sharp snap.

"Don't you think you could tell me straight out what we're going to do? I'm in this thing with you. I'm taking the same risks. It seems to me I have a right to know."

Marc said nothing. He took a tissue from his pocket and wiped his nose. She wondered if she had annoyed him. If so, well then, the hell with it. When he had that face, she felt distant from him. Why should she put up with behavior from him that she would not have tolerated from anyone else?

"I wanted to tell you everything yesterday. But we got interrupted."

That was true, and he was speaking calmly. She was sorry she had been so short with him.

"The two men I told you about, and who have become my friends, have a lot of foresight. They realized it was in their best interests to join forces with the Muslims against the Bosnian Serbs."

"Which doesn't stop them from threatening the refugees who are in the mine."

"That is some sick game the local kids are playing. But on a higher level, among the leaders, things are different: they're cooperating. Yes, I know, it must be hard to understand."

"I think I can manage."

He smiled at her and held out his arm to put his hand on her knee. She quivered, not so much because of his gesture but from the physical emotion he aroused in her.

"Go on."

"With the Muslims in the neighboring zone, my two friends have come up with a plan. It's sort of outside their usual remit, but that's another feature of this war: there are a lot of local initiatives. Armies are not very centralized."

"So what is the plan?"

"The concept is simple, even if the situation is complicated. The Bosnian Serbs can only continue surrounding the other groups and shelling them if they can be sure of their supplies of weapons and ammunition from Serbia. To cut them off from their supplies, we have to stop them from using the roads that lead to Belgrade."

Maud had opened the map again and was trying to picture what he meant.

"To supply central Bosnia, that's the road they use. Do you see it?"

It was easy enough to find, the road symbolized by a wide red ribbon.

"As they have neither aviation nor artillery worthy of the name, the only way—"

"—is to blow up this bridge."

Maud had her finger on the spot where the red ribbon crossed a vertical blue line indicating the river Drina. She got the impression he had let her finish as if she were a child whom one is prompting for the answer. But she reproached herself for being on her guard, and she forced a smile.

"All they're waiting for is our explosives," said Marc.

Maud felt a sudden dizziness. The weapons they were transporting—for they had to call them by their name, they were weapons—were no longer just a forbidden freight which they had to smuggle in. They were an instrument of a military action, a decisive action that might change the face of the conflict. An action that, in the long run, might save lives, but that would take other lives first. In a word, they were going to kill.

The road was very narrow, scarcely larger than the truck in places. The virgin snow made it look easy, but it actually hid an irregular surface. The ground had not frozen enough to solidify the mud, and frequently the wheels skidded and spun. At one point the horizon opened up ahead of them and they could see summits and passes at high altitude. The spectacle would have been beautiful had those lofty regions not constituted the obstacle they were going to have to overcome. She asked Marc for his binoculars and she studied the distance. Most of the slopes were covered in forests and she could not see any houses or roads. It all looked deserted and inhospitable.

"Are you sure we can get through at this time of year?"

"That's what we're going to find out."

As the morning progressed, the sky grew lighter. The clouds no longer formed a gray ceiling, but fragmented into round bundles that floated against a pale blue background.

The outside temperature had risen and the snow melted on the track, which was warmer than the fields. It was now a black ribbon winding across the white carpet of countryside. They went past several farms and stopped outside one of them. A farmer's wife, her head covered with a flowered kerchief, agreed to sell them some eggs and milk, and a big loaf of bread she herself had baked in her oven.

Early in the afternoon they saw two fighter jets appear in the sky above the mountains, which were now very near. The planes were flying low. The pilots must have spotted them because they banked tightly and flew a second time directly above the truck. As the UN had banned the Serbs from flying over, and the others had no air force, they were probably fighters belonging to one of the countries in the international coalition.

"What are they looking for?"

"Go figure!"

The strangest thing was that beneath the planes' wings they could clearly see the long shape of air-to-ground missiles. The planes disappeared as suddenly as they had come, and Marc went back to staring at the road, where they were making slow headway.

"Whose zone are we in here?" asked Maud.

"The last checkpoint was Croatian, if I remember correctly."

"Will there be any more ahead of us?"

"I'd be surprised. On the other side of the mountain but not before. There's no one around here."

Marc was more relaxed now that they had left the main road. The mood in the cab was almost joyful. Maud fiddled with the radio dial, and eventually found a station playing traditional Balkan music, with the sound of drums and clarinet.

"Shall I make some sandwiches?"

"Good idea."

Rummaging in a crate behind the seat she found a last piece of ham and a stick of butter wrapped in wax paper. The peasant woman's bread was soft and fresh. They ate without pulling over.

"Delicious."

"You know what's missing? Tomatoes."

They both laughed. For the first time since the beginning of their solitary escapade, Maud felt her fear receding, making room for a sort of optimistic well-being that made her want to sing. A bit farther along she took the wheel. Next to her, Marc lapsed into a deep sleep, undisturbed by the bumps in the road.

She took the opportunity to remove her big glasses. To be honest, they were practically useless; she was only slightly nearsighted. As a teenager she had insisted on wearing glasses and deliberately chose frames that with each change were increasingly clunky, to make herself look ugly. Now she inspected herself in the rearview mirror. Marc would see her like that when he woke up; she hoped he would think she was beautiful.

From time to time she glanced over at him and studied his sleeping face. His features were relaxed, revealing another person. Gone was the tense warrior he played during the day; nor was he the man surrendered to desire she saw when they were making love. He seemed much younger and more vulnerable, almost frightened. His expression in sleep was that of a defenseless, unloved child who is hurt and sad. She was troubled by the feelings that came over her when she gazed at him like this. She had often imagined love but it was always as an absence, like a strength she felt inside but did not know how best to use. She would rather bury it where no one could see it—until she herself forgot about its existence most of the time. In their vacation chalet there was a room where no one stayed and which her parents referred to as the guest room. Her mother had gone to a lot of trouble with the decoration. But no one ever visited. That was what it was like, the compartment in her mind that Maud called love. Rather than see it empty, she would rather not open the door. And now a man had come in and everything in that secret space seemed ready to welcome him. Was it the same for him? She rather doubted it. What place did she occupy in his mind? Had he ever thought about it? He knew desire—but love? Was there a space inside him to welcome someone? She didn't think so. Oddly enough, this notion did not diminish her own feelings—on the contrary. She felt sorry for him, because of what he was missing. He had built his mind into a fortress, and mobilized everything in order to defend himself against the outside world. He must suffer from this cruel emptiness more than anyone. But the gentleness of his sleeping face showed he hadn't quite gotten over it. Basically, she concluded, they were not so different from each other, even if their lives seemed to have nothing in common.

"Do you really think they could have gotten away on that little road?"

A cold butt dangling from his lips, Lionel was staring at the road map.

"Where else?" muttered Vauthier. "I'm a real idiot not to have thought of it sooner."

Lionel looked crushed. He had thought there would be an easy end to the matter, and now everything was up in the air again. Marc had managed to get away and everything would be more complicated now, by the looks of it.

After their conversation with Vauthier, Arkan and his cutthroats continued on their gruesome way, looking for new prey.

"They got a good head start," said Lionel, his hands flat on the wheel, his shoulders sagging. "We'll never be able to catch up with them."

"On the road they've taken, no fear, they won't be able to go very fast. Or very far. Start the truck."

They set off again. A heavy silence reigned in the cab. Everyone was lost in thought.

Alex, still sitting on his bunk at the back, felt a wave of untimely anger. As long as Marc and Maud were in immediate danger, all he could think of was how to help them. Now that he knew they were safe, at least for the time being, he began to think of the double betrayal he had suffered. What angered him most of all was that they had left him behind. He had always been loyal to Marc: why hadn't he included him when they ran away? The other betrayal was that Marc had switched the explosives and not said anything. Because of this, the mine in Kakanj would not be saved and the region would be ruined by the time peace returned, someday. Strangely, it even affected his feelings for Bouba. Alex still wanted to go to her, but something was diminished now, perhaps even broken. He understood that she represented more than just herself to him. He had embarked on this adventure with the idea of saving not just one person but an entire country. Clearly, that was ridiculous, but at the same time it meant a lot to him. It was as if he wanted, through his dangerous act, to appropriate that patch of earth and make it his own. But now, going back there could only ever be yet another exile.

Alex mulled over his anger and gradually it faded. Deep down he understood Marc, even if he didn't share his commitment. They had two irreconcilable visions of war. There was no possible compromise. Marc had acted according to his convictions. Alex could not fault him for that. Similarly, from a practical point of view, given the urgency, it would have been impossible to organize an escape including all three of them. Not taking him along was also a way of leaving him out of something he did not support.

In the end, his mind was made up: he would continue with

the others. Because he had promised Bouba; because she was waiting for him. And because he could not let these swine exact their revenge on Marc and Maud, whatever grudge they might have against them. But to continue, he had to restore a semblance of trust, and prevent them at all costs from dumping him at the first opportunity.

"What are you going to do if you catch up with them?" he asked.

"You really do worry about your little pal!" snickered Vauthier. "How touching. Particularly since he didn't worry too much about you."

Alex sat farther back on his bunk and shrugged.

"I know. I don't care what you do to him. I've thought it over: he's a bastard."

Lionel glanced at him, astonished.

"Ah, but you see," said Vauthier, nudging Lionel in the ribs with his elbow. "From time to time there's some good news. You must never give up hope. Even soldiers . . . "

It was late afternoon by the time they reached the turnoff leading into the mountains. They got down from the truck at the start of the road. The snow had melted here, too. But after a careful search, they found the tracks of Marc's truck, still visible in the muddy ground.

"They want to cross the mountain on this road?" cried Lionel, observing the narrow track that disappeared into the hills. "No way, the trucks will never make it through there."

"That's just what I told you. They're toast," said Vauthier, with a wicked smile.

"Are we going there anyway?"

"You bet! But first of all, we're going to have a nice dinner here and pitch the tents."

"But they're over a day ahead of us."

"No matter. Sooner or later they'll get stuck. We might as well be in shape when we catch up with them."

While they were setting up camp, Alex went on thinking about how he ought to behave. He concluded that he shouldn't wait for the other two to hand him over to the UN. The best solution would be to abscond with the second truck himself. He wondered whether they were transporting any medication he could use to drug them, the way Marc had drugged him.

The first thing would be to get hold of the keys. As a rule they stayed in the ignition at night. They'd had trouble unblocking the steering one morning, and ever since they no longer ran the risk of removing the keys. But that evening Vauthier took them and kept them on his person. He walked past Alex, jangling the keys in his hand, shooting him an ironic look. Alex would have to come up with something else. He went to sleep right away after dinner, leaving the other two by the fire.

Lionel, too, since their encounter with Arkan, had been thinking things over. He had come around to the idea of letting the paramilitaries deal with the problem, but he was far more reticent to give chase himself. The whole idea of the chase was beginning to worry him. Up until now, as far as La Tête d'Or was concerned, his conduct had been irreproachable. Marc was to blame for everything, from the moment he altered the nature of the shipment to this flight, which was nothing but theft, pure and simple. But now, by sending his own truck down this hazardous route, by seeking a confrontation that could well turn violent, by going outside the perimeter within which his papers authorized him to travel, Lionel, as head of the mission, would have to answer for whatever happened, and he knew it would probably cost him his job. Vauthier let him smoke his joint to the end, not speaking.

"Don't you think," began Lionel, staring at the flames, "that we could just let them screw up all on their own?"

Vauthier was playing with his beer bottle, tilting it this way and that to vary the fluty sound the wind made in the bottle-neck.

"Don't you see where they're headed?" continued Lionel; his teammate's silence made him bold. "It's a farm track! You don't even know if it goes through. And anyway, it's outside the zone we have permission to drive in. We have no idea what they'll find there. They could even end up in the middle of a battle on a front line."

Vauthier still hadn't said anything, so he went on.

"I suggest we keep on the main road," concluded Lionel eagerly. "As soon as we can, we'll report them, and the UN will pick them up on the other side."

Vauthier still didn't speak, and Lionel eventually thought this meant he was willing to go along with it. At last he dared to look him in the eyes, wearing a broad smile. But what he read in the other man's beady stare chilled him instantly.

"That's right," said Vauthier calmly, with a grimacing smile. "You go and tell the UN that one of your drivers has run off with a truck full of explosives. So that the entire world will know that France sends dynamite in its aid convoys."

Lionel looked down. Vauthier patiently explained to him why they had no choice.

What Paris wanted was clear. Vauthier's correspondents had given him a quick rundown: that truck must not reach its destination. It was a political issue, one that surpassed them all in importance. French intervention in the Bosnian conflict must be limited to providing UN peacekeeping contingents; the government absolutely refused to be drawn into the war. These military explosives, however, were clearly destined for fighters in the Muslim-Croat coalition. They intended to blow up a road, some barracks, a bridge, God knows what—and France would be held responsible for an act of aggression. It risked being drawn into the war. That would be a catastrophe, and Lionel's association would be the first victim. If, on the other hand, they dealt with the problem in time, everyone would be satisfied, and Lionel would receive official congratulations, and so on and so forth.

"That's the gist of it. How we go about it, that's up to us, to choose our methods and means."

Vauthier let his words sink into Lionel's ever more tormented brain. Then he changed his tone. His broad face lit up with a malevolent joy.

"What could be better, in the end, since I have a score to settle with that gentleman, and you with his young companion."

Lionel gave a weak smile. Vauthier's tirade had convinced him that he had no choice but to engage in this manhunt, but his words had done nothing to assuage his fear. Even the thought of revenge no longer aroused in him the slightest enthusiasm.

Vauthier realized he was going to have to keep a close eye on Lionel.

The next morning they set off. The tire tracks were still visible and all they had to do was follow them. There were very few turnoffs, and hardly any risk of going wrong.

The air felt warmer: during the night the wind had veered to the south. It brought a breeze warmed by the Adriatic sun, not enough to heat up the ground, but the far-off hills were misty. High clouds scudded by overhead. If they burst, they might bring rain, but no more snow.

As night fell, Maud thought that Marc, who had rested during the day, would decide once again not to stop. So she was pleasantly surprised when he pulled over onto a flat space and turned off the ignition.

"We can't keep going on a road like this without headlights," he explained.

That was true, but she knew him well enough now to

understand that he had not resigned himself to it spontaneously; he found it hard to let go of his daytime persona, so concentrated and tough.

"Even if you don't need your glasses anymore!"

He looked at her with a smile and she saw he had understood. She burst out laughing, and pressed herself briefly against him.

They stayed for a long time in the silent truck, collecting their thoughts. Then, without knowing who had made the first move, they were in each other's arms, kissing feverishly. They struggled awkwardly out of their clothes, banging against the dashboard, then made love on the rough fabric of the seat.

Afterwards, they stayed wrapped around each other, not moving, exhausted by passion. The wind whistled around the truck, and the snow reflected a silken, voluptuous, blue glow into the night.

Only when they began to shiver in the unheated cab did they find the strength to get dressed again and go out. They heated up a snack and pitched their tent. Then they slid into the same sleeping bag and fell asleep.

5

Before the danger, before the struggle, there would be that peaceful morning: for both of them, it would remain the happiest of all those strange days.

Initially, the mountains welcomed them. When Marc drove the truck into the first hairpin turns, there were not yet any trees near the road. They could see out onto the open snow-covered plain they had just crossed. The road was narrow, really more of a track than an actual road, and it would be impossible to pass any oncoming vehicles. But there must not be much in the way of traffic in that region. Moreover, if the map had not indicated that the road went over the mountain, anyone would suppose it was just a forest track, reserved for timber workers.

The engine chugged but did not seem to be struggling, and the slope was gradual. The sky was enigmatic, and gave no sign of its intentions: there was a bit of everything, clusters of black clouds, pale blue patches, and to the west, a yellowish glow that augured rain.

Maud went on dozing, or it least that was how she made it look, because she wanted to daydream. Not for anything on earth would she have shared her thoughts with Marc. Because she was imagining things that she was sure he would not like. Life with him, not her whole life long, just another life, the one that might come after this mission. They were so well attuned, in this strange world of discomfort and danger, that she wondered how they would be together in a normal environment.

Did the word "normal" even have any meaning for Marc? Had his life ever been like other people's? And she herself, what would she have thought of him in a banal, everyday setting? It was only in this atmosphere of danger and fighting that she had opened herself to love, because here she could play her part, social and sexual roles were turned upside down, and she was free. But after this?

Everything they were going through was harsh and difficult, and even their love shared something of the violent nature of war. In a way, they had collided. Their union was stronger and more complete than if it had been preceded by a slow approach. Maud felt as if she knew this man in depth. But for all that, she still knew almost nothing about him.

She would have liked to question him about his love life; he hadn't said anything about it. Had he lived with other women? Did he have children, commitments, female friends? But she didn't dare ask him straight out. She felt more comfortable with more neutral subjects.

"What was it like moving to France and finding yourself in a military school?"

"Why do you ask?"

"No reason. I've been trying to imagine what it must be like joining the army at the age of five."

Marc didn't seem to like the question. Fortunately, the mountains put him in a good mood and for once he wasn't wearing his usual daytime impenetrable face.

"I was cold all the time," he said with a smile. "I had come from Beirut, so you can imagine Normandy . . . "

"Did you make friends?"

"Friends?"

He shrugged. Maud sensed the question must seem absurd to him, but he hesitated to explain why. In all likelihood he would have to give a long explanation to make himself understood, and he didn't like that sort of thing.

"When I got there," he began, hunting for his words, "I didn't speak French. I was shorter than the others, and my skin was darker because in Lebanon I was always out in the sun."

He paused and hunted in his pocket for a cigarette. It was always a sign of emotion, because he almost never smoked except when he was upset.

"They called me 'the Arab.'"

"Who did?"

"The other kids, and probably the teachers, too. Coming from them, it wasn't a compliment. A lot of our teachers had fought in Algeria, and the pupils' parents, too. Most of the boarders were military kids."

"Did you have any family in France?"

"No. My paternal grandparents stayed in Serbia, and my father was an only child. They could do what they wanted and no one would stick up for me. And kids can sense that."

"They beat you up?"

Marc made a dismissive gesture, as if to banish an insect or an unpleasant memory.

"It only lasted a year. By then I had figured it out. There was only one way to cope: be the strongest."

"Even when you're the littlest?"

"Strength isn't just physical. For a start you have to know how to suffer, and how not to be afraid. I trained for several months without telling anyone. They went on hitting me, and I would provoke them so they'd hit me even harder. After a while I managed to control the pain."

"How?"

"I put myself outside my own body. I saw myself suffering, but I didn't suffer. It's hard to explain. When you manage to do this, it's almost like pleasure. I don't know if you can understand what I mean. You close yourself off completely. Everything happens on the surface, but deep down you feel tough, and intact."

Maud was astonished to see how conscious Marc was of his own transformation. The metamorphosis he underwent when confronted by danger, and which she had witnessed: this was something she had assumed he possessed by nature, and she had thought it was involuntary. In fact, it was the result of a decision, a consequence of his will. If, over time, it had become natural to him, in the beginning he'd had to train it, like a muscle.

"Then you have to learn how to hit back. Just defending yourself is pointless. You're better off letting them do what they want with you if you can't hit back so hard it hurts."

They were driving through the woods now, and Marc's face was in shadow. He was smiling, never taking his eyes off the road.

"On the weekends, the others went home. I stayed at school. I found books in the library about combat sports. I learned which blows would hurt, which ones would do damage, and even which ones would kill. I got permission to use the gym on my own on Sunday afternoons. There were punching bags, dumbbells, everything I needed. During the week I went on getting pounded, and didn't react. I didn't want to strike back until I was really ready."

Maud had rarely heard Marc talk for this long. She thought he had probably never shared these memories with anyone. By suddenly releasing them, he was carried away by their strength.

"And then one day, it was May 20th, I can't remember the year but I remember the date, this big guy in my class came up to me at recess. It always started the same way. He asked me to do some humiliating thing, to tie his shoelaces or something like that. I never agreed, so they would all jump me. But that day I pretended to obey. I went closer to him. He was blond, with pimples on his cheeks, I still remember. He had some aristocratic name, with 'de' in it. The others respected him because he was strong and sturdy. Above all, his father was a colonel in the tank brigade, and he worked in Paris at staff headquarters. He let me go right up to him. I kept my eyes down as usual. But at the last minute, instead of doing what he asked, I sprang on him. I didn't waste any time shoving him around; right from the start I landed two well-aimed blows, one in the liver and the other, with the side of my hand, on his throat."

"Did you kill him?"

"Almost. He passed out. He was suffocating, because I'd ruptured his larynx. They took him to the infirmary and then the hospital and the doctors saved him just in time. He was out for five weeks."

"And they didn't expel you?"

"They wanted to. Everyone testified against me. The head-master wanted to expel me. But when they told my mother in Lebanon, she got I don't know whom to intervene and they kept me on."

"And the others didn't try to take revenge?"

"Far from it. From that day on, they left me alone. Even when the big guy I had hit came back, he watched his step. They were all afraid."

He tossed his cigarette butt out the window.

"I went on training, but I never used my strength. I didn't want to become a bully myself. Gradually, the kids got into the habit of coming to me whenever they had a problem, like when they had to get some rivals to agree, or when some little kid was getting picked on by the bigger ones. They knew I was capable of killing and of getting myself killed. No one wanted to cross me."

"Is that why you didn't have any friends?"

"There were some guys I liked and who came to me for help. But friends, real friends, no, I never had any. Ever. That was the price I paid, I guess. Like I said, physical strength is not all of it. What you need to protect yourself is mystery. You have to be impenetrable, unpredictable. Friendship is just the opposite: you open yourself up, you let someone in on your thoughts. At school, it was too dangerous. Later, by the time I was in the army, it had become a habit. I haven't changed."

"You're not friends with Alex?"

"Alex is a buddy. I like him a lot and I respect him. He's a good kid. But he doesn't know me. Know how I know? Right this minute he's behind us with the other two, and he'll be dragging my name through the mud."

"And women?"

"What about women?"

She got the impression that he had stiffened.

"Do you trust them?"

He let a long moment go by while he was thinking.

"No."

She burst out laughing, and after a short hesitation, he laughed, too. It was a nervous laugh, that let off some of the tension. At this point in their conversation, she sensed she ought to stop and leave him alone. He was ill at ease, on the defensive. But she wanted to know more, and after all, she did have the right to.

"Have you known a lot of women?"

"What a question!"

"A typical girl's question—is that what you think?"

By adopting that tone, she was making things easier for him. He could drop the heavy confessional mode he'd been in, relax and joke a little.

"Girls are like buddies. I let them come near but I don't let them in."

"Never?"

"Never."

"You've never been in love?"

"Not to the point where I'd let my guard down like—"

"Like with me."

They laughed again and at the end she leaned over to kiss him. He slammed on the brakes.

"Stop! You'll run us off the road!"

"I don't care. I want you."

The truck came to a halt in the middle of the narrow road. The engine was still idling, and they could hear the wind gusting down from the mountaintops, whistling, louder than the purr of the engine. They threw their clothes on the floor of the cab and kissed with a violence they had not known at night. The light on their bodies enhanced their desire and made them feel as if they were exploring each other for the first time. As he took her, Maud pushed Marc back by his shoulders so she could look at him and luxuriate in the twin sensations of distance and intimate proximity. As if she were trying to convince herself that he was really the same man she could see here in broad daylight, this man who was penetrating her. She looked right at him, and he looked back and did not blink. What she knew about him now gave her the sweet opportunity to believe that those black eyes trained on her would allow her to see into this impenetrable man's most deeply guarded secrets. He only closed his eyes when the moment came to let the pleasure in.

He collapsed against her and she stroked his thick hair, spreading her fingers to trace invisible, ephemeral furrows. Then as he leaned to one side, she began to study the tattoos that covered his shoulder. The India ink had spread into his skin and the lines were blurry. Seen this close up, there was nothing frightening about the drawings. The disgust Maud had initially felt on seeing them had vanished. The vaguely colored shapes were puzzles to start with, like the half-erased pictures beneath the enamel of an ancient ceramic. She touched them with her finger, then squinted to make the shapes appear, and like patterns in a carpet, once she had located them, that was all she could see. On his prominent shoulder muscle was some sort of mythological griffin, spreading two crenellated wings that looked like a bat's. Beneath it, running down his arm, was a double-edged sword with snakes winding around it, and in a cartouche coiling along either edge, there was an inscription she could not read.

"Are you looking at my tattoos?"

"Did you choose them?"

"Those two I got in Africa. I served in Chad for two years. There was a Chinese man who was pretty good at it."

"But why those two in particular?"

He sat up. They were both naked, sitting side by side. With her white, empty skin, she felt vulnerable, plain. But he looked as if he were clothed, perhaps because of his muscles, but above all because of the inky adornments covering his arms and chest, forming a kind of shell.

"This dragon, here," he said, looking at his shoulder, "is evil."

He seemed a bit embarrassed, and laughed.

"All the crap in the world, the violence suffered by innocent people, vice, treachery, abuse of power, all of that."

"The Devil, in a way. Are you a believer?"

"I never wanted to believe in any one god. But I had plenty to choose from. My mother was Muslim, my father was Protestant, and at school they took us to Catholic Mass. For me to believe in a god, he would have to be universal. All the ones they offered me were these limited gods who didn't extend their influence beyond their own followers. The only thing they all had in common was evil. That is the only universal belief. And that one I did not refuse."

"And the double-edged sword?"

"Is salvation. Against evil, there is only strength."

"Basically, you would like to be some sort of knight."

She was immediately sorry she'd said it, because it had been slightly ironic, and he might take it badly.

"Don't worry, I'm not one of those lunatics who thinks they're du Guesclin. But when I left secondary school and had to choose a profession, I couldn't see myself being anything other than a soldier. It's not that I liked the profession per se. But I figured I could bear arms not to serve a machine, a state, or a bunch of politicians, but simply to combat evil."

Maud listened gravely to what Marc was saying. She was impressed by his sincerity. But she could not help but smile at some of his declarations. Why did women have this gift that allowed them to see the little boy inside the adult man? Because that was precisely what she felt at that moment. The intimidating tattoos, the big muscles, Marc's fierce demeanor were no more than the derisory armor that a lonely, vulnerable child had put on to protect himself. His vision of the world stemmed from his childhood purpose of surviving humiliation and bullying with no other recourse than his own courage and the strength he had not yet acquired. The years had gone by and had eventually hardened him, armed him. But he still had the heart of a child.

They got dressed, digging cheerfully through the pile of clothes scattered on the floor. Then they set off again.

The sky was overcast now but it wasn't raining yet. There were fewer and fewer trees, and soon they were in a region of barren high mountain pastures. The wind twisted little shrubs the goats had ravaged. Enormous limestone boulders rose up out of the carpet of grasses and clustered in fortresslike circles. The road was starting to look like a country lane: two parallel chalk-white grooves on either side of a strip of dirty grass.

Maud offered to relieve Marc at the wheel. He stopped and they got out for a moment to stretch their legs. From the high vantage point on the mountainside, they overlooked the entire plain, and could see for miles. Marc took the binoculars from the glove compartment and peered into the distance. The little snake of road they had driven up was clearly visible. He adjusted the focus and suddenly let out a swear word.

"What did you see?"

He hesitated, lowered the binoculars and squinted, then looked again.

"They're after us."

6

Vauthier had the instincts of a hunter. From time to time he made them stop the truck while he got out to crouch down on the ground and study the tire tracks; depending on how clear they were, he could estimate how much time had passed since Marc's truck had gone by. They stopped off at farms along the road and asked the peasants, using sign language, whether they'd seen anything. As was to be expected in such a desolate region, any vehicle that went past was observed from behind the lace curtains in the kitchen. Vauthier confirmed his suspicions:

"They're not even a day ahead of us. We've got a good chance."

"Maybe, but their truck is faster than ours, especially going uphill."

Lionel was skeptical. He might have gone along with Vauthier's opinion, and agreed to take the track, but he was beginning to regret it.

"They don't know we're after them," said Vauthier. "I'm sure they think they've been safe ever since they turned off onto this road. They'll screw up. Mark my words, if we drive day and night, we'll catch up."

As he drove, Lionel had time to think over Vauthier's rationale, and his faith in what they were doing was dwindling. Surely they could have dealt with the matter by getting in touch with the UN, without triggering any major diplomatic incident. There was plenty of evidence against Marc proving that he had acted on his own. Above all, Lionel was beginning to have doubts about Vauthier himself. Some of the things he said did not add up. If he really was an intelligence agent, would the official organisms he worked for let him take this sort of initiative on his own? And above all, what did he intend to do if they did manage to catch up with the other truck?

He glanced behind and saw that Alex, who was on his rest shift, was asleep on the bunk. So, discreetly, amenably, because he was still afraid of him, he began to question Vauthier.

"How did you become a cop?"

"Me? But I'm not a cop. That would go against all my convictions."

"You're joking, aren't you?"

Vauthier turned to Lionel, his expression grave.

"I would like a bit more respect from you. I'll say it again, I'm not a cop."

"You told us yourself that you worked as an informer!"

"So? That's something else altogether."

Vauthier slumped on his seat, then leaned back, with his cowboy boots up on the dashboard.

"You want to know how I got into this work? Well, I'll tell you. But first let me tell you a story. When I was a kid, I used to see my old man come home from the factory, in Decazeville, where his bosses treated him like a dog. He was a militant in the Communist Party, my old man, and on Sundays I went with him to put up posters. And when I looked at those guys from the Party, I could see that they really didn't give a damn about him. What they wanted was for the workers to stay nice and quiet and let them, the Party big shots, fill all the good positions. And even as a little boy I told myself that no one would ever make me a slave. Ever! No bosses, no phony politicians, no cops. No one."

He sniffed noisily and wiped his nose on his sleeve. For a split second Lionel wondered whether he hadn't shed a tear.

But Vauthier was already continuing his story, his voice a touch too loud.

"When I was eighteen, there was the war in Vietnam. I was a conscientious objector. I hung out with guys who demonstrated against the Americans. The 'American imperialists,' as we called them. I was a rebel, excitable, always getting into fights and so on."

"And did you believe all that stuff?"

Vauthier went on as if he hadn't heard the question.

"But then I did something stupid and the cops got me."

"Stupid, how?"

"A break-in, to finance 'the cause.' I was living in Saint-Ouen in a squat with a particularly radical bunch of Trotskyists, real politicized. They were older than me and I wanted to show them how smart I was. With a pal we held up this bar with a betting shop, at opening time. What we didn't know was that they'd already been done three times the year before and the cops had their eye on the place. A patrol was waiting for us on the way out. My pal managed to run away but I was taken into custody."

"Did you go to jail?"

"No, that's the thing. I ended up with this strange guy, a sort of fat Commissaire Maigret, with the pipe and everything. His name was Meillac, and he was doing the rounds of the local police precincts to meet informers. We had a chat, and I liked him. He was a real clever guy, completely free, too, in his way. He's dead now, but we knew each other for years. He had studied philosophy, and he was a policeman by calling, so he could see, and understand."

"So he recruited you?"

Lionel was completely fascinated. He would have dreamt of a life like that, but he knew very well that he didn't have the guts.

"In a way. But he told me above all not to change anything.

212 · JEAN-CHRISTOPHE RUFIN

I went back to my squat and I made up some story to explain that the cops had let me go by mistake. And I went on being a militant. I was living two lives, in a way. When I organized demonstrations or even more violent stuff, I really threw myself into it. But then on the side, I was feeding information to Meillac, and I liked talking to him."

"Did he pay you?"

"Yeah, not bad. And that meant I could fulfill another dream I had. I was able to take up motorcycle racing. I entered competitions and I won a few. Until my accident, and then I had to stop."

"Didn't your leftist friends wonder where the money came from?"

"I didn't let on. I kept my two lives separate."

Vauthier laughed again, his jowls shaking.

"It went on for years. Then Meillac retired and he put me in touch with other departments where he had friends. I left the squat and hung around with new groups—extremists, ecologists, global justice types. You gotta live. I went where they told me to go."

"'They' who?"

"The people who were paying me. Police security, customs, internal and foreign intelligence."

Lionel was flattered that Vauthier was sharing these secrets with him; they were proof that Vauthier considered him worthy of the truth. Because there could be no doubt about it: it was the truth. Unlike Vauthier's other declarations, these ones rang true. However, there was something still nagging at Lionel. Since they were in the process of telling things straight, Lionel decided he could come out with what he really thought.

"You know what seems weird to me about your story?"

"No, what?"

"How can these top government services, all the ones you

just mentioned, how can they give you the order, just like that, to kill a guy?"

"Give me the order?"

Vauthier sat up straight and stared daggers at Lionel. He felt around in his pocket, pulled out an old piece of chewing gum, and tore off the paper, nervously. Then he rammed it into his mouth and began chewing noisily.

"Nobody gives me orders. I'm not some poor cop who follows orders and is taken advantage of. I'm an agent, an informer, a provocateur. By any name—they're all pejorative. Obviously, people don't like what I do. They wish they could enjoy the same privileges."

He turned the handle to open the window and spat his chewing gum out.

"That was the deal Meillac offered me. Maybe I wouldn't have found it all by myself. But over time I realized it suited me. And since then I've never done anything else."

Lionel thought it was strange that Vauthier was speaking so frankly. For a moment he wondered if he wasn't playing Meillac's role now, for him.

"I sent guys to jail because they thought they were so smart with their fancy language and pretty speeches. Ecologists, anarchists, all sorts of leftists, guys who thought I was on their side and one day they found themselves wondering who could have ratted on them. And sometimes I even screwed their women—hey, they needed consoling."

Vauthier burst out laughing, a deep, hoarse laugh. Lionel suddenly got the impression Vauthier had gone too far, wallowing in his own abjectness, as if he wanted everyone to share some self-scorn he might be feeling.

"But don't you ever get disgusted doing this job?"

Now Lionel thought he had touched a raw nerve. Vauthier turned to him and raised his chin.

"Disgusted?"

Lionel sensed he was going to get angry, that there was an insult ready to fly. Instead, Vauthier turned and stared out at the road.

"Imagine there's some guy who's a real pain in the ass, just looking at him makes you break out in a rash, you wish he would die: has that ever happened to you?"

"Sometimes."

"Well, suppose you decide to bump him off. One fine day you take a gun, a knife, any old thing, and you kill him. Can you imagine any greater pleasure? Well I'll tell you, there is a greater pleasure: it's when you can do it with a clean conscience. When you know that no one will ever blame you, that they'll even congratulate you."

Vauthier laughed, but Lionel sensed his words were meant to be a sort of conclusion. He became lost in his contemplation of the tracks left on the road by the truck they were chasing. At this point the tracks were disappearing under the fresh snow. For a long while they drove along a white carpet. With his head up against the windshield, Vauthier peered at the ground. Then came a sudden, slight descent, where there were trees on either side and less snow, and they could see the tire tracks again. Vauthier relaxed.

"In any case," he concluded, leaning back against the seat again, "it'll be the greatest damn pleasure of my entire life when I get to stand in front of that bastard again."

Lionel understood there was nothing to add.

Marc was at the wheel again, his expression suddenly impenetrable. This was his combat face. He was pushing the engine as hard as he could, but the slope was steeper and steeper; the truck wouldn't go much faster. It had started drizzling, and the wipers were worn: the windshield was covered with a mixture of dust and water and it was like looking through a dirty curtain.

"Are we still far from the top?"

"I don't know."

Maud sensed he was angry with her for having instigated their stop. All vestiges of sensual delight had left her. All that remained was a vague feeling of humiliation, as if the love she had shown him had been abruptly reduced to something secondary and futile, mere entertainment. She could understand the urgency of the situation, but she thought that didn't explain everything. For Marc, serious matters were elsewhere, never in feelings. That was what drew her to him but it was also the source of a pain she might not be able to bear for very long.

Marc hunted for a cigarette in his pocket but couldn't find one. She began looking for another packet among their belongings on the seat behind them. She found one and opened it. She lit a cigarette and handed it to him after moistening it with her lips. It was like a kiss, and she hoped he would notice. But he was completely aloof, as if to show he couldn't count on anyone anymore. Could she even hope that if things got really dicey he would remember she was there with him?

She turned her gaze to the road and, unseeing, let the irregular sweeping of the windshield wipers hypnotize her as they smeared their film of clay across the glass.

A bit later, Marc braked sharply and tore her from her reverie. The rain was coming down hard now, and it was getting dark. Marc flung open his door and jumped out. She watched him take a few steps from the truck then stop; he was streaming with water. He was looking at something she could not see through the curtain of rain on the windshield. She opened her door and got out. She was wearing nothing but a shirt and was instantly drenched. The rain was cold, and the wind, which had not let up, made her shiver. She went up to Marc.

Over the last few miles the terrain had gotten steeper.

Ridges of rock towered above the road as it grew narrower and ran alongside a cliff. The mountains were furrowed with gorges, where water streamed down rocky funnels then flowed across the road. There were no bridges, no underground pipes, just embankments here and there in the places where the streams wore away at the road. They had to be reinforced every year in the spring. Now, just ahead of them, one of these little torrents came rushing down, and the surface of the road had been washed away by the flow.

Over a dozen yards or so, the way was nothing more than a narrow ledge of rock. On one side, the cliff; on the other, the precipice.

In the pouring rain, Marc was measuring the width of the ledge. Initially he estimated it by taking long strides, but as it would be down to the very centimeter, he had taken off his belt and was using it to make more precise measurements. Not saying a word, he went back to the truck to evaluate the distance between the wheels.

"It's worth a try," he said. "You'll guide me."

Maud went to get a windbreaker in the cab. She put it on over her damp clothes. She wasn't much warmer but at least she didn't feel the wind. She went and stood on the far side of the landslide.

Marc climbed behind the wheel and started the truck. From a distance, it seemed he could never make it across. And yet as he drew closer, Maud saw that the width of the truck and that of the narrow passage were indeed more or less the same. Very slowly, Marc drove the front wheels onto the eroded section. He had folded back the outside rearview mirror, and the truck was scraping the side of the cliff. On the side of the void, the tire was clinging to the bedrock. Marc kept going. The transmission was stiff and in spite of his efforts, his progress was jerky. With every forward lurch, pebbles sprayed from the right front wheel, the one that was on the side of the void; this gave Maud the uneasy impression that the edge of the road was crumbling away. But the truck continued to move forward, and she soon focused on the rear of the truck as it entered the narrow stretch. The rear axle consisted of four wheels, and was wider than the front. On the side of the precipice, while one of the two wheels still clung to the ground, the other one was directly above the void. The truck kept going, and now the front wheels had reached the far end of the landslide, where the road returned to its usual width. But suddenly Maud heard the engine roar, the vehicle stopped moving, and the rear wheels began to spin. Marc stepped on the gas and tried again, three or four times, but the truck would not move. Finally he pulled on the handbrake, slid across the cab, and got out on the passenger side, because the other door was blocked by the cliff face. Peering under the truck, he tried to figure out what was wrong, but he couldn't see anything out of the ordinary. In order to inspect the rear, he had to climb over the roof of the cab.

"What do you see?"

"It's the top of the load that's catching."

There was a slight overhang to the cliff face. The cab was lower and had made it past without difficulty, but the rear of the truck was bumping up against the overhang. They would have had to plane down the rock to widen the passage, but they had neither the time nor the means. Marc assessed the situation without answering Maud's questions, then climbed back on board.

"Don't stay there in front," he shouted. "Back up ten meters or so."

She was annoyed he wouldn't give her any explanation but this was not the time to make a scene. She backed away down the road.

Marc revved the engine, flooring the gas pedal, then shot it into first. The truck lurched forward, instantly halted by the overhang, but at full rev it moved all the same. Two things happened, given the thrust of the engine, to shake the massive vehicle. Most visibly, the rear axle slipped toward the outside: rebuffed by the rocky overhang, the truck pivoted slightly and the second outer wheel was now approaching the void. At the same time, the tarp covering the load was wrenched out of shape by the abrupt motion, and there came a tearing sound from the side of the cliff. The entire maneuver took only a moment but Maud was petrified with fear. She was certain the truck was going to tip into the void. She let out a cry. She waved to Marc to stop. Forgetting what he had told her, she started hurrying toward the truck. At the same time, he revved the engine as high as he could and let the gear pedal out. The truck lurched forward again. For a split second the two rear wheels hovered over the void, but didn't have time to sink down, because at the same time the tarpaulin bows restraining the load gave way. At full power, the truck, now freed from what was holding it back, hurtled forward.

Maud saw it all in a flash: the enormous hood bearing down on her and, behind the windshield smeared with dust and water, Marc's inscrutable, almost cruel face, determined to get past the obstacle, even if it meant running her down. She felt the fender hit her and knock her over. The truck was still moving forward. When at last it stopped, she was lying beneath the engine. She didn't think she had lost consciousness. And yet when Marc pulled her by the shoulders to get her out of there, she felt something burning on her cheek, although she had no memory of having touched anything hot. Apparently she had banged against the exhaust system when the truck ran over her, but she hadn't felt it. As she stood up, she realized that her skin from cheekbone to ear was shriveled and very painful. And she must have fallen flat onto a stone, because there was a sharp pain between her shoulder blades.

Marc was calm again, even tender. He laid her down on the

seat, took some compresses out of the first aid kit, and dabbed her burn with a cool lotion that brought some relief.

"Did we get to the other side?" she asked.

"We did."

He kissed her, and did not reproach her for coming too near the truck; he even made a vague apology. She was torn by contradictory feelings, all equally powerful, and she didn't know whether to laugh or cry. They were safe. Again she saw the wheels spinning over the void, and she remembered thinking the entire truck was going to tumble over the edge. But at the same time the image of Marc coldly bearing down on her would not go away.

"We mustn't stay here," she said.

She was again aware of the situation. The thought of action helped her suppress her emotions. She sat up straight, and it was almost a pleasure to test the pain she could still feel in her back.

"Are you okay?"

"Yes, don't worry about me. Let's get going."

"First we have to fix the load. The tarp came off and the bows at the back, too. There's nothing left to support the boxes on the left-hand side."

"Let's have a look."

She got out, gritting her teeth to control the pain. The cold air on her burn was stinging. She must have hit something else when she fell, because her right arm hurt when she moved it, and she could feel a heavy ache in her lower back. It was surely nothing serious, but she must be covered in bruises.

Walking around the truck, they saw the extent of the damage. The entire left-hand side of the load was exposed now, and a few boxes had already fallen off. The pouring rain was swelling the cardboard, and the boxes were getting soggy. They couldn't drive off like that. With every bump in the road they would lose more boxes from the load.

"We have to get rid of as many crates as possible. We'll push the ones we keep toward the front, and we'll try to cover them so they don't get wet."

"Do you remember where the explosives are?"

"Yes, fortunately, I hid them all the way in, close to the cab, and I put some red tape next to the label."

Marc climbed up onto the bed and began throwing boxes onto the ground.

"What shall we do with them?"

"We'll just leave them on the road. So much the better for whoever finds them."

Some of the boxes were marked with a green cross: they contained medicines. Other, heavier boxes were full of dietary supplements. There were also big bundles of tightly packed clothing, and Marc grabbed these by the plastic straps that bound them. Maud tried to move the boxes out of the way, but she couldn't lift anything. So she moved the lightest ones, shoving them with her feet.

The load was a lot bigger than it looked from the outside. Marc got rid of almost half. What was left was sheltered, because the tarp was intact from the middle to the back. He pulled tight the torn pieces of canvas and lashed everything down with the help of the straps holding the rear tarpaulin bows. The end result did not look very good but at least the remaining cargo would stay dry. He jumped to the ground and wiped his hands on the corner of a bale of clothing.

It was a strange sight. There on that desolate mountainside lay dozens of bundles, splattered with mud. Oddly, Maud viewed it as a kind of litmus test. The idealism that had brought her here to begin with was now revealing its derisory, almost ridiculous nature. These crushed boxes scattered across the road portrayed all too tragically the futility of the humanitarian endeavor. In the face of the complexity and horror of war, these bundles of clothes, packages of food, and boxes of medication were grotesque. And now this lighter truck, with its shipment of weapons, seemed to have been liberated from that hypocrisy. They were finally getting down to basics. In that moment Maud felt proud to be leaving behind her ambiguous role as rescuer, a role in which she had never felt completely comfortable. The only thing that made her sad, made her almost want to cry, was that this initiation into warfare brought her closer to Marc, whereas he, driven by the call to action, paid her no more attention. She could not forget that look of his behind the windshield. To reach the goal he had set himself, he was prepared to break down every obstacle, even if it meant crushing her beneath his wheels to attain it.

The wind had dropped and a fine rain was falling, on the verge of snow. They were cloaked in the mountain's silence. Maud let it soak in, as if it were a remedy that could restore some peace, after these moments of fear and violence. Marc, too, was straining his ears, but it was not to hear the silence. He raised a finger. Still far away, almost imperceptible, a hoarse sound, like the buzzing of an insect, came through the damp air. A regular sound, with louder spurts. Maud stared at the leaden sky. She thought it must be an airplane or a helicopter. But as she concentrated, she understood. The noise was coming from the road, from behind them.

"It's them," whispered Marc.

"Already."

They rushed over to the cab and climbed in. Marc turned the ignition and they drove off.

7

W hat the hell is that?"

Lionel, who was at the wheel, saw the indistinct shapes scattered across the road in the distance. He thought it must be rocks that had rolled down from the cliff, and he braked.

"Go check it out."

Alex opened the door and got out. He recognized the boxes and thought they must have fallen off the other truck. But as he walked further, he saw the road made an elbow-like turn, and that in the turn, where the road crossed the gorge, a landslide had eroded the road. He gestured to Lionel to drive up to him. Vauthier jumped out of the truck and walked over to the landslide. He was beside himself.

"Christ almighty! And they made it over, on top of it . . . "

"Why did they abandon the load?" said Lionel, who had come up to them.

"Not the entire load," said Alex.

"Of course not, not everything. He's not going to let go of his dynamite, now, is he."

Vauthier assessed the problem right from the start.

"They must have smashed in the tarp. You can see they scraped the side of the cliff."

A scrap of canvas was hanging from a small outcropping of rock above their heads. And on the ground, on the side of the precipice, they could also see clearly where the rear wheels had slipped, loosening a clump of earth and making the passage even narrower.

"If they made it across, then so can we . . . "

But Vauthier shrugged, and Lionel did not insist. They had already noticed, when driving over a bridge a few days earlier, that their truck was slightly wider than the other one, by twenty centimeters or so.

"We could put a log across," Lionel suggested.

"And do you see any trees around here?"

The mountain was completely bare. Only a few dwarf spruce trees clung to the rocks, their trunks no wider than a hand.

"Right, well," Alex concluded, sitting on the fender.

He wouldn't have been sorry, ultimately, if the chase had ended there. It was even the best conclusion. No one would lose face, and the worst would be avoided.

"Right, well, what?" Vauthier spat.

He would not admit defeat. While the other two watched him, he got busy on the road, tapping his foot to check how solid it was on the side of the precipice, carefully examining the cliff face and its overhang, measuring the width of the passage and that of the axles. He was turning it all over in his mind. They let him get on with it and Alex set about cooking some food. He took out the cooking stove and placed it under a canopy he fashioned by lifting up the back of the tarp. They took the time for a leisurely meal. Lionel did his best to hide his relief. Alex didn't even try. He was whistling. Vauthier, off to one side, was still thinking. Several hours went idly by. Lionel smoked a joint to calm his nerves, and looked as if he were sleeping. Alex was clipping his fingernails.

Then Vauthier gave a sudden start.

"I've got it! Get up, you two. We have no time to lose."

But as far as Lionel and Alex were concerned, a page had been turned. In their minds, the case was closed: something beyond their control had forced them to give up the chase. End of story. They had moved on to something else.

"Listen, Vauthier, you have to know when to call it quits," said Lionel. "If it's no good, it's just no good. It's nobody's fault."

"Get up! I'm not asking you your opinion."

"Well, we're giving it to you."

Alex looked calmly at Vauthier. As he hadn't been able to shave the last few days, his face was covered with a black beard as curly as his hair. All the childishness of his clean-shaven face was gone. Vauthier, by contrast, who was no better groomed, looked older and somehow weaker for the gray hair sprouting irregularly on his cheeks. They were obviously not on an equal footing. All the more so in that this time Lionel had clearly chosen sides. He stood next to Alex and didn't move.

Vauthier looked at them, one after the other. Then he pursed his lips.

"Have it your way," he muttered, scarcely unclenching his teeth.

He turned on his heels and walked calmly over to the truck. They saw him climb into the cab and rummage around inside.

When he got back he planted his feet before them.

"So you've been thinking?" said Alex, not looking up.

Lionel was lying down, his head against a rock. Groggy from his joint, his eyes were half closed.

"I've had a right good think."

"So, what's the deal?"

"You do what I say."

It was only then that Alex turned and looked at Vauthier and saw he was pointing the barrel of a 9-mm gun at him.

"What's the matter with you? What do you want?"

"They gave me a mission. I am going to carry it out, right to the end."

"But it's impossible now!"

"We'll know that once we've tried everything."

Lionel and Alex got slowly to their feet, not taking their eyes off the gun.

"I want you to do exactly as I tell you."

There was nothing to say. Vauthier let a moment ago by, as if to let the new balance of power sink into their minds. Then he focused his gaze on Alex.

"When you were telling us about construction explosives the other day, you showed us a bunch, if I remember correctly. Where are they?"

Alex could lie. It would be easy, all he had to do was say that Marc had them. But Vauthier had a sharp gaze, he would miss any hesitation. And Alex had already hesitated.

"They're in my backpack."

"Go get them."

Alex got up, dragging his feet. He came back with a parcel.

"I warn you. They won't work if they're wet."

"That's what we'll find out."

In any case, the rain had almost stopped. Vauthier opened the packet and took out the little bars of explosives. There were five of them.

"They come in boxes of six. Where's the last one?"

Alex reluctantly got back up, rummaged in his bag again and returned with the sixth explosive.

"It's meant for coal. I doubt it will work on anything else."

Vauthier didn't bother to reply.

"Lionel, get with it. Take the truck and back up as far as that spot, there."

Lionel sat behind the wheel and reversed the truck to place it in the shelter of a fold of land.

"You, mister tough guy, get me one of the bundles of clothes those morons threw out."

Alex got up, crossed the landslide, and seized hold of one of the bundles. It weighed at least a hundred pounds, and it was a struggle to bring it back. Vauthier had him place it against the cliff just under the spot where the overhang blocked their way.

"Now, move off over there to the other side."

Alex walked a dozen yards in the opposite direction from where Lionel had parked the truck.

"Okay, that's enough."

Vauthier put the gun in his belt and climbed on top of the bundle. From there, with his arm outstretched he could reach some cracks running along the overhang. Keeping one eye on Alex, he scraped at the earth in the cracks. He managed to make several holes into which he rammed the explosives. He jumped off the bale and put the last two explosives at eye level, just beneath the overhang. Then he took his gun back in his hand and removed the safety catch.

"You got a lighter?"

Alex came over and handed him his lighter.

"No, keep it, I've got matches. Okay, now it's your turn to get up there."

"What for?"

"When I tell you, you light the explosives up on top. I'll take care of the two on the bottom. But I warn you: we don't have one fuse for all of them, so we'll have to get a move on. The minute they take, we make a run for it."

Alex climbed on top of the bale.

"When I'm ready, I'll start counting," said Vauthier.

He began hunting in his pockets for the matches.

Alex, perched on his bale, put his hands on the cliff face and leaned his forehead against the cold stone. After all these days of tension, of poor sleep, of betrayals, the group falling apart, all this madness and absurdity, he felt overwhelmed. He was on the verge of tears. He looked at the little sticks of explosives and thought about Bouba. He had done all this for her and now here he was, teetering on a bale of old clothes, in the rain, doing something that no longer made any sense. Would he ever see her again? And how would they live? As he evoked her memory, he realized he almost couldn't conjure up her features. Basically, he had loved the idea of her as much as the person, and now he no longer believed in that idea. Marc was right. You couldn't play smart with war. It was a filthy, evil thing. You had to end it once and for all and—

"Three. Did you hear me? For Christ's sake, I said three!"

Alex came to. Vauthier had already lit his fuses and was running for shelter. Alex clicked the lighter and lit the first fuse. The flame flickered in the cold air. The second fuse. The flame went out. He flicked nervously on the striker wheel. The wind wasn't very strong but it was blowing against the cliff face and stopped the gas from lighting. A third fuse, his hand was trembling, from the fear and cold. His thumb was slipping off the damp wheel. Below him he could hear the other fuses crackling.

"What the hell're you doing?"

Vauthier was screaming. He'd hidden behind the side of the gorge and was peering around the corner, a wild expression on his face. He thought there was something funny going on: was Alex trying to sabotage his plan in order to save his buddy?

The fourth fuse caught. Alex jumped, but the bundle rolled beneath his feet and he tripped. Just as he was getting back up, there came the blast of the first explosion. As he'd thought, it wasn't very powerful. It shook the rock and Alex stood up. But just when he was on his feet, the other sticks exploded one right after the other, in a shower of little stones. Until all of a sudden the rocky overhang collapsed, hurtling sharp fragments straight at Alex. They flew into him, then onto the road before continuing on their way down the precipice.

The sound of stones crashing down the slope beneath the road eventually grew fainter, then stopped. A deep silence enveloped the mountain. Lionel, next to the truck, and Vauthier, hiding behind a rock, stood motionless for a long time. Then they ran to the site of the explosion. Lionel rushed over to Alex, but Vauthier wanted first and foremost to see the results of his operation.

228 · JEAN-CHRISTOPHE RUFIN

"He's dead," cried Lionel, turning Alex over on his back.

Vauthier walked over, halfheartedly. He crouched down next to Alex and took his pulse.

"He's not dead. He's just knocked out."

They could see injuries in several places. The most serious was a deep gash on his left shoulder. Another rock had struck his skull from behind, and Lionel had to remove a big piece of rubble from on top of one of his legs.

"What should we do?"

"Just wait. It's not bleeding too badly. He'll come around. We'll count his limbs afterwards."

Having delivered his verdict, Vauthier went back to look at the cliff face. He was very pleased. Once they removed the rubble that had come down, the space would be wider. Above all, there would be nothing blocking the truck at the top, since the overhang had collapsed, shattered by the explosives.

Alex was moaning, beginning to regain consciousness. When Lionel tried to sit him up, he cried out, holding his shoulder. It must be worse than it looked. One arm was hanging limply, as if dislocated. Then with his good hand he rubbed his head. He was dazed and didn't seem to know where he was. He was beginning to feel numb from lying on the cold ground, and he was shivering.

"Okay, just what is wrong with him?"

Vauthier, heartened by his inspection of the cliff, leaned over the injured man. He prodded the various spots that seemed affected and several times Alex cried out, with a start.

"Well, that's a good sign, he's reacting."

"Do you think he's in danger?"

"If we leave him lying here, I'm sure he will be. Let's go lay him down on the bunk. Bring the truck closer, and get a fly sheet from one of the tents."

Lionel ran off to do what Vauthier told him. He put the fly sheet on the ground and they began to slide Alex onto it. They did not know which end to lift him from without making him scream. When at last he was lying on the makeshift stretcher, they each took one end and lifted him up. It took them a good ten minutes to get him into the truck and settle him in the back.

"I'll give him something for the pain at least," said Lionel.

"Don't waste your time, the other guys have the first aid kit."

Lionel dug all the same in his own toilet bag, and found a box of Paracetamol. He gave Alex two tablets to take.

Vauthier was getting impatient. All these maneuvers had slowed them down, and the light was beginning to fade. He had vague hopes of being able to get past the obstacle that same day, and he set about moving the stones that were still blocking the road. But some of them were too heavy to be moved by one man alone, and he had to wait for Lionel to finish looking after the injured man before he could get him to do some work. Once they had cleared the area, they saw that it was wide enough now for the truck to go through. But it would be a very tight squeeze all the same, and it was out of the question to attempt it right away, with the fading daylight. They had to resign themselves to camping on the spot and waiting until morning to continue.

For Vauthier, the only encouraging thing was that Alex's accident put him temporarily out of action. Only one man left to keep his eye on . . .

"Do you think they managed to get through?"

Maud was lying on the seat, her head against the door. The burn on her cheek was stinging and her back was very painful. She must have fallen harder than she realized, and she could barely sit up.

"I don't think so. But with that bastard Vauthier, you can't be sure of anything."

Marc had been driving since morning. Maud was in too much pain to replace him at the wheel. She could see he was at the end of his rope. His eyelids were heavy, and from time to time his eyes closed. She had tried to put on the radio, but in these mountains there was no reception. At one point they heard a faint buzzing sound, getting louder. They thought they'd managed to get a radio station. But then the sound was suddenly very loud and they recognized a jet engine. Two fighter jets flew high above them, then disappeared beyond the ridge.

The road was wider now. There was no longer a precipice on one side, which meant the driving was not as dangerous. They were heading across a gentler slope, the landscape less rugged. The wind was driving a continuous fall of fine snow straight at them. It was taking a while for the snow to stick, because the ground was not yet very cold. But before long it formed a visible layer, painting everything white, even the road.

When night fell, Marc turned on the headlights but it was just as difficult to see. Fatigue, poor visibility, and the fact that they could no longer tell the road from the shoulder compelled them to stop. Marc took out a sleeping bag and covered Maud with it. He wrapped himself up in blanket and wedged himself behind the wheel. In less than five minutes he was asleep.

Maud could not sleep. In the dark her injuries seemed even more painful. From time to time she managed to doze off, but then she was awoken by nightmares. She dreamt she was falling off a precipice, or that she was crushed by a boulder hurtling from the top of the mountain. Worst of all, she imagined Vauthier suddenly standing there with a gun in his hand. She saw herself cutting his throat.

It was strange how much she had changed by growing closer to Marc. Before this, for as long as she could remember, her rebelliousness had been an abstract thing: she hated the injustice of the world, but she had no grudges against anyone in particular. Aid work had given her the means to act on her diffuse indignation. It was not satisfactory, and gradually she had been compelled to commit herself more directly, to leave behind the sacrosanct principle of neutrality. In the end she had followed Marc into his idealism of combat. Now the world, for her, was no longer a magma where the invisible forces of evil were laboring. It was a battlefield, where friends and enemies clashed. She had never had an enemy before now. At the most, she'd had to deal with adversaries. It wasn't the same thing. When confronted with an adversary, you fight. An enemy, you eliminate. She was discovering a new feeling: hatred. She hated Vauthier and everyone like him. And when she surrendered to her daydreaming, thoughts of murder came to her. To her complete surprise, she was not disgusted. She even felt a deep pleasure imagining a knife sinking into that man's throat, seeing the gush of blood, hearing the death rattle. And she was terrified by her own transformation. Wasn't she becoming just like all those ruthless paramilitaries, those men who were guilty of the worst atrocities? Because she sensed that the nature of hatred meant knowing no bounds. If Vauthier were handed over to her, unarmed, in chains, at her mercy, would she not be capable of killing him all the same? And would she not feel an even greater pleasure in watching him suffer?

One thought chased another. She could not unravel them. All she knew, hounded by pain in this silent darkness, was that she felt lost.

Just before dawn she fell asleep, and when she woke again it was broad daylight. A strange daylight, as it happened, because the light seemed to come from the snowy ground more than from the gray sky, where the snow was still falling. Marc must have begun driving again very early. There were dark shadows around his eyes and his black stubble, so carefully shaven every other morning as was his habit, darkened his features and made him look harder than ever. Driving through snow and mud required great concentration. He was visibly exhausted.

Maud tried to move, to see if she could drive, but it was even worse than yesterday. Sleeping in the cold had exacerbated the pain. Never taking his eyes from the road, Marc reached behind him for a packet of cookies, and handed it to Maud. She smiled at him but he didn't look at her.

"So how are we doing? Is it still far?"

"We're driving along the side of the mountain, now. It won't go up anymore."

"That's good."

"Yes and no. If they're following us, they've got a better chance of catching up with us than if we were going uphill."

She peered out at the landscape. These old mountains, like the Vosges or the Jura, had rounded summits, and they had come to a sort of high plateau which they had to cross to reach the other slope. From time to time they saw farms and sheepfolds again.

"You're not going to drive all day, are you?"

"I'm okay for now."

The high plateau of central Bosnia undulated interminably. Sometimes they went down into hollows, sometimes they regained altitude. When they reached the top of one of these high points, Marc stopped the truck, with no explanation.

"Give me the binoculars."

Maud took them out of the glove compartment and handed them over. He got out and stood at the edge of the road. She watched as he stared for a long time at the horizon.

Suppressing her pain, she managed to sit up and wipe the condensation from the windshield. From where they had stopped you could see a vast panorama, and if the weather had been better, they might have been able to see all the way to the Adriatic. With the falling snow they could still see most of the high plateau they had crossed. Without binoculars Maud could make out only a white expanse for miles around. Sometimes the road dipped into a hollow, and then it rose up again. They were stopped on a high point. To the south, the ruined towers of a medieval castle stood out against a leaden cloud filled with snow. Marc came back and tossed the binoculars onto the dashboard. More tense than ever, he turned the ignition.

"What did you see?"

"They've been through here."

Maud didn't say anything. She could hear the spite in his voice. She was angry with herself for being injured and unable to drive. If their pursuers were able to take turns driving, Marc on his own would not be able to keep up the pace. He was certainly aware of this and must be evaluating the consequences of their failure: the inevitable confrontation, the discovery of the cargo, perhaps even death.

Maud tried to move but it was hopeless. As soon as she held out her arms, she felt the pain in her back, so sharp she wanted to cry out.

"How far ahead are we, do you reckon?"

"Barely six hours."

"What can we do?"

He didn't answer and this angered her. As if she didn't matter. He seemed so hostile she could not help but recall what she had thought during the night. When it came to action, he was alone. It was the hidden side of his strength, the rules of the game in his world.

Maud felt like crying, and was annoyed with herself.

They drove in silence for almost an hour. Suddenly Marc stopped the truck again. He gave no explanation and without a word he went back out onto the road. First she saw him squat down in front of the cab and touch the frozen ground. Then he went out of sight, around the back. When he returned, he was covered in snow. It was coming down hard now, and in the space of a few minutes the windshield was covered in a white film.

Marc switched on the wipers and the landscape reappeared. It was then that Maud then saw the narrow track leading off to the left. It was covered in snow and she had not seen it initially. It was surely because of this track that Marc had stopped the truck at that particular place.

"Do you want to go up that way?"

He didn't need to answer. He had already turned the wheels to the left and was heading that way. The track was fairly steep for a few yards and the truck struggled. Then it rose more evenly. It was certainly a dead end, leading to a field or a barn.

"Do you think the snow will cover our tracks? Is that what you went to check?"

He merely nodded.

Then suddenly the track seemed to fade away. They were surrounded by whiteness and there was no indication of where they should go. Unfortunately they had not gone far enough from the main road to stop. Marc got back out and walked through the snow to try to determine whether it was possible to drive farther up. Maud saw him disappear behind a hedge that the snowflakes were covering in white pom-poms.

She was at her wits' end, filled with a sort of rage, and she did not know whether it stemmed from despair, anger, or shame. She felt as if she had been making the wrong choices for a long time; perhaps she had always been making the wrong choices. She should never have followed this man, should never have made an exception for him to the caution that had always protected her from humiliation and suffering. And now she was here, injured, betrayed, cast adrift. She screamed.

Her long cry, initially shrill, then fading to a deeper note, gave her some relief. She tried again, but it wasn't natural anymore. She felt self-conscious. Her determination was coming back, if not her strength. She would not give in so easily.

Not long thereafter, Marc reappeared. At first he was only a shadow in the white shadow of whirling snow. Then she saw him, covered in snow, and he opened the door.

"Did you find a way through?"

As he did not answer, she ignored the pain that was searing through her back, and slapped him.

IV
DESTINIES

1

Marc didn't move. Maud's hand had hardly shifted his head. There was just that very particular sound of skin slapping against skin. It was the last thing he would have expected. He'd had his fill of smacks when he was a child, and he'd delivered plenty of his own since then. His primary reaction was astonishment. Perhaps that was what she wanted. Moreover, she seemed surprised by her own gesture.

They stared at each other for a long time. She realized that, unwittingly, she had obtained what she wanted: for him to look at her.

"I'm here," she said, "even if I'm completely useless to you now. I exist. Do you know that?"

That was when she understood. He really looked as if he were emerging from a dream. Danger, action, combat had held him in such a tight grip that everything else around him disappeared. He wasn't treating her like an enemy; he simply did not see her. She was rather ashamed of her gesture, although she was pleased with the result.

"I'm sorry," she said.

He leaned over and kissed her. His rough stubble felt sore against her lips. It was a minor pain, and she liked it, and for a moment it made her forget the others. She was angry when she felt her eyes filling with tears. Why was she crying? Such stupid feminine weakness! Unless, on the contrary, it was the sign of a more subtle sensibility, one that enabled her to gauge the tragic dimension of their situation, the impending doom. She turned her head away.

"Let's not waste time. Have you figured out how to get out of here?"

"It's up there, through the undergrowth. There's a little hut three hundred yards from here."

While he was starting the truck and focusing on the road she quickly wiped her eyes with the back of her hand.

Under the trees the snow was not as thick, and when they left the field they were back on a forest track covered with pine needles. They drove up to the little house. It was made of stone, all lopsided, with a thatched roof held together by wire mesh. The place would have looked abandoned but for the thin column of bluish smoke rising from the chimney.

Marc switched off the engine. No one came out of the house. The silence was thick in the snow-covered clearing.

"Do you have any idea who lives there?"

"Not yet."

Leaning down to the floor of the cab, Marc opened a trap-door Maud had never noticed. It was a little compartment for the battery. He slipped his hand inside and took out a big black pistol. He checked the magazine and cocked it. Then he opened the door, got out, and walked over to the hovel.

There was only one window, and it was closed from inside with wooden shutters. The door was made of poorly joined planks, rotted at the bottom by rainfall. Marc could easily have knocked it down with one kick but he knocked softly several times, like an ordinary visitor who wants to show he has come in peace. He heard voices whispering inside. He put his face up to a gap between two planks and said a few words in Russian. A few more moments went by, without any apparent reaction.

Then suddenly the door opened a crack. A child's face appeared, hardly any higher than the lock. It was a little girl wearing a green kerchief. Marc hid the gun behind his back so as not to frighten her.

"Hello," he said.

"Hello, sir," answered the child.

"Are you all alone?"

He tried to adjust his Russian words with what he knew of Serbo-Croatian.

The little girl seemed to hesitate. She looked over at the truck and saw Maud.

"No."

"Are your parents here?"

"My brother and sister."

She had opened the door a bit wider. In the darkness Marc could make out an adult figure in the background.

"Can we come in? My friend is hurt."

The girl didn't understand the word "hurt" and Marc pointed to Maud, mimicking pain.

The little girl turned around, probably to see what her brother would say. He must have gestured to her because now she opened the door wide. Marc called to Maud and went inside the house.

The interior was plunged in darkness but streaks of light came in through the poorly joined shutters. The room smelled of burning wood and rural poverty, with sour odors of junket and dried herbs. The little girl's brother must have been around thirteen. He had already lost the round cheeks of childhood, and his bony face was framed by curly black hair. Once Marc's eyes got used to the darkness he noticed that the boy was holding a sort of wooden club, something they must have used for stunning animals. It was probably the only weapon he had. Marc discreetly put the safety back on his gun and slipped it in his belt behind his back. Something moved in the darkest corner. He could just make out a very young child hiding behind a wooden chest. This must be the sister the little girl had mentioned.

Maud had managed to get out of the cab, wincing with pain. Standing was actually less painful and she walked to the door. When she opened it, Marc noticed the boy tightening his hand around his club. When he saw Maud, he relaxed.

Marc suggested he open the shutters to make a bit more light, and the boy did not object. A rough-hewn wooden table took up most of the room, with two benches on either side. Marc sat down on one of them, not to relax, but to put himself level with the children and seem less threatening. The three of them looked famished, and were pale with cold. The thin log smoking in the fireplace gave off almost no heat.

"Where are your parents?"

The children didn't answer. Had they understood? They seemed above all fascinated by Maud, who was smiling at the little girl.

"Papa? Mama? Where are they?" said Marc.

"Zenica," said the boy.

"Father soldier? War?"

Marc mimed shooting with a rifle. The boy nodded.

"And your mother?"

The boy looked at his sister and murmured something Marc did not understand.

"I get the impression she's dead, but maybe the little girl doesn't know," suggested Maud.

Suddenly muffled sounds came from somewhere deep inside the hut, as if someone was banging on the ground. Marc stiffened and slipped his hand behind his back, ready to pull out his gun.

"Is there someone back there?"

The sound started again and this time they knew it for what it was: a large animal stamping its hooves on the ground.

"You have animals?"

The boy didn't understand the question but he guessed what might be puzzling the visitors.

"Cow," he said. "And horse."

Looking around the room and at the children, Marc had quickly grasped the situation. A soldier must have brought his children to the sheepfold for shelter while he was fighting in town. The mother had been killed in the war, or had died from some disease. The eldest was looking after the younger children, and he had nothing but his club to defend himself.

There was no telling from their appearance what community they belonged to. Then Marc noticed a little frame on the wall near the door at the back that contained some Arabic script. There was every reason to believe they were Muslim, unless they were staying in a house that didn't belong to them.

Having made these observations, Marc stood up and went out. A few minutes later he came back carrying two boxes he had taken from the load. He put them on the ground and opened them beneath the boy's watchful gaze; he was still holding his club. Marc took chocolate bars and packets of cookies from the first box. The children looked at the colored packages, not daring to touch them. Marc tore them open and spread a pile of cookies and candies across the table. The little girl's eyes were shining but she hesitated to take any. She waited until her big brother had cautiously picked up a cookie and begun to eat it. Then there was a mad scramble; the little girl helped herself greedily and stood her little sister on the bench so she could have some, too.

In the meanwhile, Marc had sprung the straps on the second box. It contained a little bundle of clothing. Coats and jackets spilled out of the box the moment he opened it. Maud helped him find clothes in the children's sizes. Taking a closer look at them, she realized how scantily and poorly dressed they were. She helped the little girl to put on a bright red fleece that went well with her kerchief. The little girl stroked the soft fabric, her eyes full of wonder. The boy had put down his club and was now hunting shamelessly through the box. He found a parka lined with synthetic fur. It was a khaki green, with a very military look: that was probably what he liked about it.

Marc and Maud had gained the children's trust. All they had to do was let them rummage through the boxes, laughing and eating their fill of sweet things. Maud was having fun with them, clapping her hands when one of the kids tried on a new outfit, and helping the younger ones learn to use the zippers.

Marc stood in the light of the window. He had brought the road map in along with the boxes. Now he was studying it, trying to figure out where they were. Maud came over to him and stood behind his shoulder. He pointed at the dotted line on the geological survey map which must indicate the track leading to the sheepfold.

"Are we going to stay here?"

"Yes."

"Are you sure, what about the tire tracks . . . "

He shrugged, as if to say that was the risk they would take. The snow was falling steadily, and they had to hope it would cover the road. It was obvious he had made up his mind. Something else was worrying him now. He unfolded the map to study the opposite slope of the mountain, the one that went back down to the north, to Zenica. By road, the city was still quite a distance, because the road was winding. But the map indicated a sort of path that went straight down to the city. He measured the distance on the map, parting his thumb and index finger like a compass.

He called to the boy. He came nearer, still glowing in his new jacket.

"Zenica: twenty kilometers?"

The boy spread his hands: he didn't understand. Marc counted to twenty on his fingers.

"Zenica. Kilometers."

"Zenica," said the boy.

"Horse?"

"Yes, horse."

The boy gestured to Marc to follow him. He pushed open a door and they went out into a little yard. The stable was a simple awning protecting the animals from the weather. There was one very thin red-brown cow. It was her milk that fed the children. On the other side of a partition made of planks stood a workhorse; its sturdy pasterns were thick with dirt, but it still looked young and sturdy.

"You, drive horse?"

Marc illustrated his words, mimicking straddling the animal. The boy proudly confirmed that he knew how to ride. They went back in the house, and the boy stuffed a rag along the foot of the door.

Maud had taken the youngest child on her lap and was playing with her. Marc and the boy went closer and sat around the table. It was obvious that the boy did not understand what Marc wanted.

"You, go on horse, Zenica, now."

The boy shook his head. His father must have ordered him not to leave the house, and to keep watch over his sisters. Marc insisted, and as the boy still refused, he reached for his gun. The boy jumped. There was a moment of panicked misunderstanding. The young Bosniak thought that Marc was threatening him, but in fact his intention was to show him that he would protect the house and its occupants during his absence. Finally Marc managed to get his point across, and the boy calmed down. But he did not seem altogether convinced for all that.

"Show him what is in the truck," said Maud. "There are still quite a few boxes of food and clothes. Tell him he can have it all, if he does what you ask him to do."

Marc led the boy outside. Maud saw them next to the truck, talking continuously. When they came back, the boy had winter hats for his sisters and he was wearing sturdy Gore-Tex hiking boots.

"Got it. He'll do it."

The boy called his sisters over to him and explained something in their language. The two girls did not look particularly worried.

In the meantime, Marc took a paper and pen from his pocket. He wrote a message and folded it in four. Then he called to the boy.

"Before Zenica," he explained in Russian, "road to the right. Village of Lašva."

The boy nodded that he knew the place.

"In Lašva, checkpoint."

The word was all too familiar in the region, and he did not need to explain.

"At the checkpoint, you ask for Dr. Filipović."

"Do you think he'll find him?"

"He's the head of the Croatian enclave. Everyone knows him."

"*Doktor* Filipović," said the boy.

Now he was filled with the importance of his mission. With his new parka and sturdy boots, he must have felt he looked the proper fighter. His own father probably wasn't as lucky. He took the message and put it in the inside pocket of his jacket, which he closed again carefully with a Velcro strap.

"Your name, Comrade," said Marc.

"Alija."

He shook his hand and the boy stood up straight, as if to attention. Then they opened the door leading to the stable, and Maud heard them saddling the horse. They went around the house. The boy was already in the saddle, his legs spread wide across the horse's ample back. She watched him ride off, gradually covered by the snow that was still coming down steadily.

Marc stamped his feet on the threshold and came back in.

"How long will it take him?"

"He knows these mountains. He shouldn't get lost. He'll get there before night."

"What did you write in your message?"

"I said we're here but we can't go any farther."

The little girls were playing at piling up the cookies to make castles, laughing when they tumbled down.

"Do you think the others will go by without finding us?"

"We'll find out soon enough."

Marc, too, had searched in the boxes of clothes and found what he wanted: a sort of long green raincoat that went down to his feet. He put it on over his fleece jacket, pulled a black beanie onto his head, and put the pistol in his pocket. He went out, took the binoculars from the dashboard, and set off into the woods to find an open spot with a view onto the road below. While he was settling in, several military planes flew overhead. He had no better luck than the previous times trying to determine where they came from.

2

The snow that had fallen during the night made it hard to see the passage clearly. It was not as narrow now, but even to make it across the section they had blasted the day before, it was still a matter of inches.

"I'll drive," said Vauthier.

"But you've never driven this truck."

"Don't you bother about that. Go ahead and guide me."

Lionel reluctantly agreed. But in the end the truck made it across the landslide without a hitch, even more easily than Vauthier had anticipated.

Two problems remained: there was the time they had lost, and which had to be made up. And there was Alex, still lying on the bunk in the back, slowly recovering. Once he had driven over the tricky section, Vauthier let Lionel in, then went on driving.

"It's not really such a good idea," said Lionel. "You don't have a license for driving trucks."

Vauthier looked scornfully at his neighbor.

"You are unbelievable! You really think the police are checking licenses around here?"

"No, but still, there is the insurance . . . "

Lionel was clinging to details to not confront the terrifying reality: they had left all legality behind. As far as the association was concerned, this convoy had gone mad. The vehicles were no longer following each other, but in the middle of a chase on a mountain road; half of the load had been thrown out; they had an injured man; there were weapons within reach; and in one of the trucks was a load of dynamite. There was no possible justification for any of this, not to mention what would happen if they managed to catch up with Marc. And now he didn't even have anything left to smoke to calm himself down! He'd underestimated his supply of weed because he hadn't planned on such a long journey. The joints he had smoked the day before had depleted the last of his stock. He was completely disoriented, with no energy to stand up to Vauthier about anything—to stand up to anybody, for that matter. He curled up in the corner of the seat and kept his eyes fixed on the snow that was coming down thicker than ever.

He didn't realize he had fallen asleep. When Vauthier woke him up, he had no idea of the time.

"Take the wheel. I've been driving for three hours."

Lionel got out, shivering, walked around, and drove on. Beside him, Vauthier fell asleep almost immediately.

The road was monotonous and the thick blanket of snow made it impossible to focus on anything precise. Lionel drove in a half-sleep. He daydreamed, and every thought that came to him was unpleasant. He wondered what he had done to deserve this—he was a man who had always respected procedure, who was known at headquarters for his punctiliousness. It had to be the fault of that bitch Maud. What had gotten into him, to go and get infatuated with her? For two years in Lyon he'd had the same girlfriend; they'd split up when he left on his mission to Africa. If he hadn't been so stupid, he could have gotten back together with her on his return. But instead, he began to enjoy his freedom. He enjoyed the position of strength that his status as head of mission gave him. Several girls had demonstrated they liked it. It was as if he were getting his revenge on life by charming young women who were fascinated by relief work. And he thought it would be the same thing with Maud. Instead, she had humiliated him, and look where he'd ended up . . .

Here and there on the white carpet of road he caught glimpses of the other truck's tire tracks. They were getting harder and harder to see in the thick snow, and then they disappeared altogether over long stretches. In the beginning he paid attention, but before long he stopped thinking about it. He even avoided thinking about it. The prospect of catching up with the others was so terrifying that it was better to banish it from his mind altogether.

At one point he thought he saw tracks leading off to the left, and vaguely wondered if it wasn't the entrance to a side road. Only several minutes later did it occur to him that Marc's truck might have headed that way. But he didn't stop. His muddled thoughts were not up to making deductions, and the routine of driving was stronger than anything.

The road had started to go gradually downhill, and was narrower again. Lionel was concentrating all his attention on steering the truck along the difficult, dangerous route. Once again there was a threatening precipice to the right, and the slightest slip could be fatal.

Vauthier was snoring. From time to time when he was jarred by a bump in the road he opened his eyes, then went back to sleep. At one point he let out a long groan and the noise must have woken him up, because he sat up straight and rubbed his face.

"Where are we?"

"Nowhere new. But now we're going downhill."

They had lost quite a bit of altitude, and here and there between the clouds they could see a valley coming closer.

"There's bound to be a checkpoint when we come down off the mountain," said Vauthier. "Watch out."

But for the time being they still couldn't see anything, just the road, deeper and deeper under the snow.

"There are no tire tracks."

"It's been a while now."

Vauthier raised his eyebrows.

"Did the tracks disappear all of a sudden?"

Lionel didn't dare mention the turnoff he had noticed. And besides, had he really seen it? It was all so muddled. He wondered if he hadn't dreamt it. What was the point of risking another argument with Vauthier?

"The snow is thicker and thicker," was all he said.

Vauthier looked preoccupied but didn't say anything.

They drove for two more hours, and saw nothing but whiteness everywhere, on the ground and in the air, heavy with snowflakes.

Until at last, thanks to a sudden patch of clear sky, in the distance at the entrance to a pine forest they could make out the humped mass of a checkpoint.

"There's the checkpoint. We'll find out what time they went through."

They drove slowly up to the guard posts. Dark figures came out and stood across the road.

When the paramilitaries came over they could see the Croatian coat of arms stitched on their caps.

"*Pomoć*," said Lionel, per usual.

He was forcing himself to smile but something inside him rebelled against his own introduction. He was increasingly unsure that he belonged to the humanitarian world. A convoy wrenched apart by hatred, and completely altered by its dangerous load, then this chase that could only end badly: it all made him feel that now the reassuring word *pomoć* was nothing but a falsehood. But the paramilitaries didn't seem to notice or care. They calmly checked their documents, and went round the back to inspect the load. They didn't even seem surprised to find an aid convoy using that mountain road. Their minds were numbed by the cold, and it slowed their gestures. Clearly they wanted to wind up the procedure as quickly as possible, so that they could go nice and easy back to their place by the brazier inside the guard post.

"Ask them when the others went through," whispered Vauthier.

"I don't speak their language!"

"Use signs."

Lionel questioned one of the paramilitaries, but he merely looked at him, not understanding.

"We'll only get them worried, that's all."

"Wait."

Vauthier got out of the truck and Lionel saw him gesticulating in the middle of a group of paramilitaries over by the guard post. He was rotating his arms round and round, imitating driving a truck, then he drew female curves in the air, no doubt to describe Maud. The soldiers laughed. As he wouldn't give up, they spoke among themselves and in the end, they shook their heads. Vauthier repeated his gestures but still got the same negative answer. He came back to the truck, looking furious.

"They didn't see them," he said, climbing back in the cab.

"That's impossible!"

"Go ask them yourself."

The paramilitaries had lowered the rope blocking the road and were waiting for the truck to start up again. But Lionel didn't move. He could sense Vauthier looking daggers at him.

"You really didn't notice anything abnormal, with the tire tracks?"

"No."

His "no" was so faint it could not possibly convince Vauthier. In a toneless voice he added, "There might have been one spot, with a track leading off to the left . . . "

Alija was proud to be going down the mountain on his horse. He had really taken his mission to heart. It was a real mission, the way he imagined. Which meant that even if he didn't understand the order, he was prepared to get himself killed to carry that mission out. His father had often talked to him about the war. He had been a soldier under Tito, because for him it was a perfectly natural destiny. The father of his father had also been a soldier. The land on which they lived had been forged with blood. Not recently, either, and the stories the father told his son often contained descriptions of battles he seemed to have taken part in himself, even though they had been fought . . . in the Middle Ages.

They were Muslim, and the religion itself was the result of a combat. Alija's father was a follower of the history of the Bogomils, a persecuted sect who, when the Ottomans arrived, thought they would seize their chance to escape the vicious cycle of oppression and poverty. And since that time, it had never been a bed of roses.

Alija, with his strong horse and his khaki jacket, felt just like a warrior. The only thing he didn't have was a weapon. But it was not the weapon that made the warrior, his father had often told him as much. It was danger. And he had all the danger he could hope for.

The mountain itself was rife with danger: cold and snow, landslides, precipices. Alija knew these dangers well. But as he drew nearer to the valley, he knew he would encounter other far less predictable forms of danger. There were armed gangs rampaging through the region; he might stumble on a local conflict; and above all, there was the unpredictability of the checkpoints. If he came upon fellow Bosniaks, everything would be fine. But how would the Croats treat him? And what would he do if, worse luck, he happened upon a checkpoint of Serbian Chetniks?

But for now, the snow blowing into his face, the rolling motion of the strong horse, and above all the military jacket keeping him warm made him feel both invisible and invincible.

The whiteness all around him made it hard to tell exactly, but Alija now got the impression that the light was beginning to fade. He kicked the horse's sides impatiently, to make it move faster. Finally, after more than three hours, he could see the main road. As far as he knew—but everything could change so quickly in this war—the checkpoint for the mountain was higher up. Which meant he had gone by it without any trouble. Now he had to find the village, Lašva, where the foreigner had told him to go. Alija had told him he knew where it was. A soldier always has to obey orders. He wasn't lying when he said he knew Lašva. It was a name he'd heard his father say, in his presence. But he'd never been there and he wasn't altogether sure where it was. He would have to ask the way. Unfortunately, there was no one on the road. With this awful weather, it was unlikely any of the peasants would leave their houses. He was going to have to knock on someone's door, if he found a house.

And he did find one, set all alone in a bend in the road. He'd already come very far down and the snow at this altitude had turned into a cold, heavy rain, streaming down his parka. Alija dismounted and knocked at the door. No one answered. Yet he could see a column of smoke coming from the chimney. He knocked again and spoke through the door. He didn't want to give his name, which would indicate his ethnicity. He merely shouted that he was on his way to see his father, and was looking for the village of Lašva.

Several minutes went by. He was soaked, and beginning to lose patience. He was about to get back on his horse when a window cracked open. The face of a very old woman appeared in the space between the wooden shutters.

"Good day to you, grandmother," he said, forcing a smile. "Can you tell me if I still have far to go to Lašva?"

The old woman's head shook uncontrollably. Alija wondered if she was in her right mind. He repeated his question more slowly, more loudly. The woman turned to look at him but it seemed as if she still hadn't seen him. Suddenly he realized she must be blind, and he would have to explain a bit more. He tried to make his voice sound confident, and he understood she must have taken him for an adult. He gave a more detailed explanation.

"I'm thirteen years old, grandmother, and I'm going to see my father there, because my little sisters are sick."

The old lady blinked her wrinkled eyelids.

"You're almost there," she said at last, her voice weak and quavering. "Keep going for two kilometers and turn right. You'll see Lašva if you walk a little farther. There's a big barn at the entrance to the village."

Alija thanked her and continued on his way.

He found the turnoff the old woman had described and went right. Daylight was ebbing and with the low cloud cover it was quickly getting dark. He urged his horse on but it refused to trot, swinging its neck and merely walking a bit faster.

Alija had no light, no way to signal his presence in the night. And he still could not see Lašva.

At one point he thought it might be better to stop and wait for dawn before approaching the checkpoint. But he couldn't see where to take shelter. He was soaked and it was getting colder. If he had to he would burrow inside a ditch and wait. After all, it was also a soldier's lot to submit to discomfort and deprivation. He was lost in these thoughts when in the ever-deepening obscurity he saw the dark mass of a building up ahead. It must be the big barn the old woman had mentioned. He kicked the horse's sides with all his might. Every step of the animal's hooves in the crepuscular silence thudded with a dull, damp sound. Alija saw the entrance to the village. He thought he could make out the shapes of vehicles parked on the side of the road, but there was no light. The curtain of rain, still falling steadily, obscured the landscape even more.

Suddenly, when he thought he had almost reached the entrance to the village, Alija saw a figure emerge from the shadows and seize the horse's bit. And then five or six men surrounded him, with a gun pointed at him.

After night fell, Marc came back into the hut. He was gray with cold, his shoes were soaked, and his long coat had offered little protection against the damp, in the end, so as it melted the snow had penetrated his clothing. He went into a corner of the room to dry off and put on fresh clothes.

Maud had spent the day making the house more pleasant. She had brought in gas lamps from the truck; their light accentuated the dirt and disorder. She put away everything that was lying around, washed the floor and the table, and fed the fire in the chimney until the temperature in the room was almost warm. Then she began making a good supper with the food still left in the load. At first the children looked at her, amazed, then began to help out with varying degrees of efficiency. The older girl even entrusted her with her most treasured possession: a little transistor radio on which they managed to get a faraway station playing a steady stream of what sounded like Greek music.

When Marc sat down at the table with them, the little girls, intimidated, did their best to serve the dishes that were bubbling on the stove. Maud even found a bottle of wine that had been hidden away in the truck. She poured Marc a full glass to warm him up.

It was a strange family atmosphere. Initially it had made Maud feel better, when she was still alone with the children. But Marc's sudden and unexpected arrival made her uncomfortable. While she worked she had been thinking about him, doing it for him, yet once he was there, his presence destroyed her dream and, oddly, took away all her enthusiasm.

He had brought in with him his preoccupied, inscrutable air. The warmth, the music, the little girls' cheerfulness seemed to have the opposite effect on him from what Maud had hoped. His hard gaze, his tense, almost aggressive expression were proof that he viewed all her efforts as useless, and any comfort as incongruous. His attitude was a brutal reminder of where they were, and of the critical situation they were in. And for Maud to feel a little moment of pride and happiness in transforming this house and restoring a little sweetness and joy into their lives suddenly seemed perfectly laughable, even ridiculous.

They ate in silence because the children, although they did not understand what was going on, could feel the tension, and did not speak. Marc answered Maud's questions even more laconically than usual, monosyllabically. Did he see anything on the road? No. Did he think Alija had reached his destination? Maybe. What would they do the next day? Dunno.

She soon stopped questioning him, and a heavy silence fell. From time to time the cow in the stable next door stamped her hooves, making the glasses tremble. Once supper was over, Marc got up, took out a cigarette, and put his chair over by the window.

Maud cleared the table and washed the dishes in cold water in the hollowed-out stone that served as a sink. She bluntly refused help from the older girl, who ran to her sister on the far side of the room, in a dark corner.

Maud was sorry to be so hard but she was desperate to hide her emotion and the tears she felt welling inside. It was not disappointment in Marc's behavior she felt. In a way she understood it. Her distress was deeper, more irremediable. More complex, too, full of contradictory feelings she was trying to untangle.

Everything she had always fled from she found now in this hut.

All day long she had turned herself into a homemaker, or, worse, a devoted servant. She could not stop thinking about

Marc, taking every opportunity to be thoughtful and attentive, forgetting her fatigue and her own desires. But she could see that this show of submission had inspired neither pleasure no surprise. Not a single word of thanks, not a single tender gaze. She had sworn long ago she would never fall into such a trap.

What she had not foreseen was the irrepressible desire, the love that both appalled her and took over her life, like a pushy visitor who plunks down his suitcases in a house where he's not welcome. And when she dried her calloused hands on the rough rag, and turned around and saw this man seated with his back to her, and those shoulders where she could picture, beneath the folds of his shirt, the inky blue arabesques, while she thought she could feel the texture of his black hair in her fingertips, it was all she could do not rush over to him and offer her lips and her entire body.

The little girls had gotten ready for bed: they had taken out and unrolled a mat stuffed in a chest. They lay down next to each other beneath a red blanket full of holes. Maud felt a rush of pity, and went to kiss them good night.

The children were exhausted by their busy day. They fell asleep quickly, the little one almost immediately, the older girl after a brief struggle against sleep, probably because she was curious to go on watching these strangers who had moved into her house.

When she was sure the girls were sound asleep, Maud got to her feet. To be honest, she was in no hurry to be alone with Marc. He was still sitting by the window with his back to her. She could tell the evening was going to be very long and tense.

She went back to the big table that she had cleared and wiped with the rag. The wood around the candle shimmered with a tawny glow. She took two glasses from the sink and filled them with wine. Then she pulled up a chair next to Marc and sat down. She was at a slight angle to him and could see his profile. He took the glass without saying anything. Maud let the silence continue. She drank her wine slowly, taking little sips. Somehow the bitter taste of the cheap wine was what she needed. She wouldn't have wanted a rounded, smooth wine. Anything that was an irritant to her body strengthened her self-awareness and self-preservation.

They had to get out of there. Then she would be able to get away. Not see him anymore. Make him suffer. But was he even capable of suffering for someone?

The silence was absolute, a genuine silence of snow and countryside. The cow must have fallen asleep on her bedding as well. Time had come to a standstill and yet, it was time that they were actively letting pass, like a fisherman watching his line spool out in the wake of his boat.

Marc seemed attentive only to the silence. His vigilance was focused on the slightest cracking sound, the slightest whistling of the wind through the windows.

A bit later, Maud got up and went to unroll the other mat on which Alija usually slept. She lay down without removing her clothes. An icy draft snaked along the floor between the front door and the one leading to the stable. It was a sign of discomfort but also of life, an invitation to freedom and movement. Instead of letting herself go to sadness or even tears, she began daydreaming about this puff of air that had come from the Adriatic. It had been laden with snow and now it was seeking warmth, like some prowler stealing through the tepid air of the hut before it would rush down the mountain and slip renewed and livelier than ever all the way to Italy. Riding on this wintry will-o'-the-wisp, she fell asleep.

Alija wasn't afraid. The cell where they put him was completely empty. He would have felt more disoriented if the paramilitaries had put him somewhere very different from the hovel where he lived with his sisters.

It wasn't exactly a prison, but in this war nothing retained its usual function. Houses became shelters for snipers, post offices were staff headquarters, schools were hospitals. So it was no surprise that this cellar was a dungeon.

The Croatian soldiers didn't believe a word of his story. The only thing they understood was that a Muslim child had suddenly appeared in the night, on his horse: that was suspicious. And as they couldn't consult anyone about it before daybreak, they had put him here in the meantime, once they'd made sure he wasn't carrying a weapon.

A big lad with round cheeks, scarcely any older than Alija, wearing a baseball cap, brought him a piece of bread and some shriveled yet juicy apples. They had talked for a while and they realized that they used to live in the same town before the war. They even found some mutual friends. The boy's name was Franko and he was very proud to announce that he was personally responsible for this makeshift prison. He had to confess they didn't have many prisoners. It was more usual now, in these parts, not to take any prisoners . . .

Alija told him, as he had told the paramilitaries, about the message he had to deliver to Colonel Filipović.

"Filipović? He's not a colonel! He's a general!"

The fat kid spoke with particular respect. Alija asked him if he knew him.

"Of course I know him! He's my uncle."

He wouldn't say whether the general was in town just then. No one must know where Filipović was, since he was the commander for the entire region. However, it increased his own importance if he implied that he had the means to get in touch with him at any time. And when he went away again, he promised to speak of it personally to his parents.

Alija fell peacefully asleep. In the early morning, another jailer brought him some barley porridge.

Several hours went by. Alija was particularly worried about

what they had done with his horse. But no one came to see him, and he had to keep his worries to himself.

It was almost noon when the door to the cellar opened abruptly. Franko came in, with a solemn air, and ordered Alija curtly to his feet.

"Fix yourself up a bit. The general is coming."

Before long a man came into the cell and stood in front of the prisoner. He was wearing a gray uniform streaked with black, and a military beret cocked slightly to one side. The man was as thin as the boy was chubby. To be honest, they didn't look at all alike, and Alija shot a questioning glance at his young warder.

"General Filipović," trumpeted Franko.

The former doctor, now general, had retained from his former profession pleasing manners and a certain gentle way. As if he might suddenly ask, "Where does it hurt?" He inspired trust.

"Well then, young man," he said tranquilly, "apparently you have a message for me?"

"Yes, General."

"Yes, sir," corrected Franko.

"Yes, sir."

Alija hunted in his pocket and pulled out the paper the paramilitaries had ignored. Filipović turned toward the bare light bulb hanging above the door and read the note Marc had written. Then he turned back to Alija. His eyes were narrowed, and his gaze, all of a sudden, was hard and wary.

"What does he look like, the man who wrote this?"

Alija didn't really know how to go about describing a stranger. He was a stranger, that was all. The doctor helped him. Was he tall? What color were his eyes, his skin, his hair? Did he have any tattoos on his body? The boy replied as best he could.

"There are two of them, are there?"

"Yes, two."

"What is the other one like? Is his name Alex?"

"I don't know her name. But she's kind of small."

"What do you mean, 'she?' He's not with another man?"

Alija was pretty sure that Maud was a woman, but given the general's self-confidence, he was beginning to wonder.

"I think she's a woman but . . . "

Filipović was getting impatient.

"You think, or you're sure?"

"I think . . . "

"Is her skin black?"

This time the boy protested. He might have his doubts about the person's sex, but he was categorical regarding her skin.

"Not black at all. On the contrary, this person has very white skin. She is blonde with very blue eyes."

Filipović reread the note attentively.

"Did you see what kind of car they came in?"

"It's not a car. It's a big truck, and the back is all torn up."

"All torn up?"

"The side of the truck was kind of smashed in, torn off."

"Did you see the load?"

"Yes, there's still a lot of stuff. This jacket, for example, they gave it to me. I think they must have lost about half of what they were transporting. But toward the front there are still plenty of boxes."

Franko turned to his uncle to check his expression and decide whether he ought to believe what this so-called messenger was saying. But the general wasn't giving anything away, so he looked sternly at Alija.

There was a long moment of uncertainty, while Filipović went on thinking without speaking.

"Where is the farm?"

"In the mountains."

"Far from here?"

"On horseback, I could take shortcuts and it didn't take

long. But by road, with this weather, it will take longer. When my father drove us there, it took four hours, roughly."

"There's no I address, I suppose."

"Not that I know of."

"Can you see the house from the road?"

"No."

"Then you'll have to come with us."

"And my horse?"

"Leave him here. We'll bring him back to you."

3

I t hadn't been all that easy. Once they were through the checkpoint, Vauthier had to fight with his teammates to convince them to go back.

This time, Lionel felt he was in a position of strength. After all, they had managed to make it over the mountain, and whatever the damage to the convoy, they were nearly home safe. Down in the valley they could see the lights of the first villages. Kakanj was one of them. It was out of the question to go back up the mountain just to seek a confrontation with Marc.

Alex, too, was relieved. He was feeling better, and for some miles now, he couldn't stop thinking about what he would do if Vauthier found himself face-to-face with his former comrade. He had seen Vauthier's weapon but he knew that in the other truck Marc also had a pistol and ammunition enough to defend himself.

Earlier on, neither Alex, weakened by his injury, nor Lionel, in particular, would have had the strength to stand up to Vauthier. But now they had gone through the roadblock and the paramilitaries would not make it easy for them to go back again. This eventuality reinforced their own determination.

In any case, by the time they got to the checkpoint, it was too dark for them to imagine any immediate return. They stopped for the night a bit farther along, in the shelter of a shed made of sheet metal where there was still a bit of fodder. A dozen or so yards away stood a few farms scattered along the road. Without saying anything to his two teammates, Vauthier disappeared in that direction. Good riddance! They were glad he was gone and they had a relaxing dinner with what remained of the food in the truck. They talked and gave each other courage. If they had to, they would ask the soldiers at the roadblock for protection. Then they got out their sleeping bags and dozed off on a bed of hay, sheltered from the snow that was still falling silently on the roof.

By dawn it had stopped snowing. They could see luminous patches of clear sky. Lionel got up first and lit the camp stove to make some coffee. Alex was still in his sleeping bag. The warmth brought some comfort to the pain he still felt here and there. It was not even seven o'clock when a mountain tractor stopped outside the shed. It was a sort of miniature truck that had been painted red until the rust, over time, fringed it with brown spots. The rear was a sort of wagon that could transport an animal or bales of fodder. The tiny cab in front could fit only one person. An old peasant was driving the vehicle. At the last minute Lionel and Alex saw Vauthier sitting in the back, in the empty wagon.

"It's all settled," he said, jumping down and walking over to them. "Officially, I'm going to go and repair the truck that stayed behind. Are you coming with me, yes or no?"

"No," said Lionel, without even waiting to hear what Alex had to say.

"In that case, happy trails, guys."

He went back to the tractor, climbed into the wagon, and knocked on the cab to tell the old man he could get going.

They heard the wheezing sound of the engine heading away down the road.

Alex got out of his sleeping bag, wincing with pain.

"He's going to kill him!"

"And?"

"What do you mean, and? You're going to let him?"

"What can we do?"

It wasn't mere resignation in Lionel's tone. Alex could also perceive the hint of a certain satisfaction. After all, wasn't this the best outcome for Lionel? He wouldn't have to get involved, the truck was safe, the mission, or what was left of it, would be intact. By fleeing, Marc had chosen to be an outlaw; he would get what he deserved and, in any case, Vauthier would take the rap for it on his own. But Lionel's old jealousy would be vindicated, too. Basically, he'd be glad to see Maud pay the price for what he still saw as a betrayal: she would witness her lover's death at Vauthier's hands.

"Well, I don't agree."

"Then you go get a hay wagon, too, and go catch up with them," grumbled Lionel.

Once again he had the self-confidence of the weak man who knows he is protected.

"No. We're going together, with the truck."

Lionel snickered.

"You think it's funny?"

"Kind of."

Alex was not in any physical shape to threaten him and he knew it. Lionel went on calmly sipping his lukewarm coffee. There was a long silence. Alex sat down, painfully, in the hay, to think. Finally he got back up and went to stand in front of his companion.

"You think you'll get away with it, just like that?"

Lionel gave him a nasty smile.

"You're mistaken."

"Oh, yeah?"

"Listen carefully. If Marc gets killed, I swear there will be consequences."

"Such as?"

There was an expression on Alex's face Lionel had never seen. The look in his eyes was earnest, grave, and frightening.

"When we get back, I'll need a few days to recover. But then . . ."

"Then?"

"I will kill you."

Lionel let out a little laugh, but Alex was implacable, gazing fixedly at him.

"You want to spend the rest of your life in jail?"

Alex didn't answer. Lionel studied the black eyes staring at him. There was something indefinable about them, a wild yet rational strength, and he was shaken. His only hope was that it would all be over with quickly. And he had just one wish: to get back to France, to the peace and safety he cherished more than anything. Now here was this imbecile delivering threats he was perfectly capable of carrying out someday. Lionel understood that, even after his return, he would never be completely safe. He would always be in thrall to this mad verdict, which was all the more dangerous for its very madness.

"Come on," he said, trying to sound as friendly and rational as possible. "Be reasonable. What could you possibly gain?"

But his words rang hollow, betraying his fear. Alex still said nothing.

So Lionel got up and decided to voice his anger, although this was hardly any more convincing.

"What the hell is the matter with you all? You really are a bunch of loonies! Why did I have to get stuck with your filthy business? I've never seen anything like it in a humanitarian organization."

His last words sounded particularly ridiculous and as he said them, Lionel could see for himself how inept they were now to describe their tragic undertaking. They had not been on the side of peace or charity for a very long time. They had all succumbed to hatred and infighting. Remembering the reasons why they had come to Bosnia merely emphasized how far, how irremediably they had drifted from those reasons. Lionel had hoped that on reaching Kakanj things would go back to normal—to neutrality, to simple aid work. Now he could see that such hope was utterly in vain.

He sat back down.

"Well, what do you want?"

"We're going to take the truck and catch up with that bastard before it's too late."

"The paramilitaries will never let us back through," said Lionel absently.

"Let me deal with them."

Sure enough, half an hour later, they were driving along the road toward the mountain. It had been fairly easy to persuade the soldiers that they had to go to repair the other truck, probably because Vauthier had already prepared the terrain, by giving them the same excuse.

The snow was beginning to melt, and the tracks from Vauthier's vehicle had left two furrows of dirty mud; that was just like him.

The little girls woke up first and when she heard them starting the fire and boiling the water, Maud opened her eyes.

Marc wasn't there. She looked for the raincoat he'd left to dry on the back of the chair and didn't see it. He must have gone back to his lookout post above the road.

Maud drank the coffee the elder girl had made. It was much too strong but the child was waiting proudly for Maud's reaction. She forced herself to drink it with a smile.

But she had no desire to go back to the games they had played the day before. She gestured to the little girls to leave her alone.

She sensed things were coming to a head. She was waiting for resolution, not knowing whether to hope for it or dread it. The Croatian soldiers would come for their cargo. She didn't care whether it changed the war or not. As far as she was concerned it was over. As soon as she could she would get out of there, as quickly and as far away as possible.

The night had banished her uneasy feelings from the day before. She could see things more clearly now. Never until this morning had she been so acutely aware of being fiercely on the side of life. In this cold, dark hovel, wasn't it life she had put all her energy into restoring the day before? All she had to do was see the love in the eyes of the two little girls when they looked at her.

As she thought about them she realized she must have hurt them, getting up in such a bad mood. They were hiding on the other side of the room, looking at her, not understanding. She gave them an affectionate little wave. They instantly rushed over to her, full of joy. The little one climbed on her lap and shyly touched the burn on her cheek, her eyes full of pity.

"Dolly?" asked Maud.

The two little girls looked at each other blankly. Maud made signs to try to explain to them.

"Do you have dollies?" she said again.

The older girl nodded and went to rummage in the chest where they put their mat in the morning. In the meantime Maud rocked the little one in her arms and followed her thoughts once again.

She had no grudge against Marc; she was even grateful to him. Without knowing it, without meaning to, he had freed her from fear.

The little girl came back to her, proud to show her what she had found in the chest.

"Dol-ly," she said, trying to pronounce the word correctly.

Maud burst out laughing. In her arms the little girl was holding an entire collection of hats, among them an old beret, a moth-eaten sheepskin cap, and a felt hat faded from years of rain and snow.

Maud gently conveyed to her that these were not dolls. The

child seemed somewhat disappointed, but did not lose heart. She went over to the sink and began searching underneath it. From a distance she showed Maud a horsehair broom, a chipped enamel pot, a plastic basin. Every time, Maud shook her head with a smile. Then the little girl seemed to have another idea. She hesitated, looked over toward the window as if to make sure no one could see her, then began pushing the big table to one side. Maud doubted that she would find dolls underneath it but she let her go ahead. The table was on an old coarse flax carpet which with the years had begun to look like a huge floor cloth. When she had moved the table far enough, the child rolled up the carpet and a trapdoor with a wooden shutter appeared in the floor. She raised the shutter, grimacing, and reached in to pull something out of the hiding place. It was long and rigid, wrapped in rags. She brought it over to Maud, holding it in both hands like a precious offering. It was clearly not a doll. Maud, out of curiosity, nevertheless took the bundle and began unwrapping it. The shining butt of a rifle appeared, then a well-oiled barrel. It was an old Mauser that must have dated from the Second World War. She wondered why Alija, to protect his sisters, had resorted to a club rather than this considerably more powerful weapon, which seemed to be in good condition. Probably their father, when he left them on their own, had instructed them not to go around with such a weapon, which might suggest the boy was a combatant.

Maud maneuvered the breech, careful to aim the barrel at the wall. The mechanism was in perfect working order, but there were no bullets in the chamber. The space for the cartridge was empty. She showed the hole to the little girl, who immediately went back to the trapdoor. She brought out another bundle. It was a supply of ammunition, carefully stored in a waterproof box.

Maud thanked the little girl, who seemed pleased to have

figured out at last what the word "dolly" meant. Then she motioned to her to put everything back where it belonged.

She would have to find something else to amuse the children because it was clear they didn't have any toys. Maud looked around for a piece of paper and started drawing to distract her two protégées.

She was just finishing up the outlines of a house, with the door, windows, and a smoking chimney, when Marc burst into the room.

"There's a tractor coming up the road," he said. "Get ready."

"Is it your Croatian friends?"

"I have no idea. It doesn't look like it."

"What are you going to do?"

"Wait for them lower down."

He had his gun in his hand and the children stared at the weapon, fear in their eyes. They were not afraid of the rifle hidden under the table, because it was a familiar object, and they knew they mustn't use it. But Marc's huge Manurhin, with its black metal and short barrel, evoked danger and death to them.

"Is the tractor still far?"

"It's not going quickly but in ten minutes it will be here."

"Have a coffee in the meantime."

"No," said Marc, "I'm going back."

He opened the door and an icy gust blew into the hut. It was snowing again. Maud stood on the threshold and watched him disappear into the mist with the strange impression that it was her duty to imprint this moment on her memory.

4

M arc had spent so much time watching the place that he had eventually acquired a fairly precise knowledge of that patch of forest and mountain pasture. He had noticed a sort of track that wound down through the trees, probably an old trail that was used in summer for rolling bales of hay. He followed it and reached another bluff located just above the road. From there he could observe the clearing, and the track they had come up on arrival. The only disadvantage was that he could not see the actual turnoff from the main road. And that was just where the tractor had stopped. Marc could clearly make out the regular sound of the engine idling. Less distinct was the sound of voices. Someone must have gotten down from the tractor to study the tire tracks. Then the engine began to run more quickly. The vehicle made a maneuver and finally drove away in the direction it had come.

Once again the silence was heavy, shot through with resonant flurries of wind whirling a light snow. Marc tensed his entire body, listening to this silence he had come to know so well, but which seemed different now somehow. He couldn't hear any particular sound. However, he sensed a human presence. He went down flat on his stomach on the icy ground and crawled to the edge of the bluff. It was there that he suddenly saw Vauthier.

He was at the edge of the fir trees, moving forward without a sound, not twenty yards away from Marc. His little eyes were studying the ground and the woods all around. But he didn't think of looking up at the rocky ledge where Marc was hiding. He was careful not to make any noise, lifting his feet to avoid stepping on a branch or stumbling in a hole. Clearly he wanted to take the hut by surprise. He had his right hand deep in the pocket of his jacket, and Marc was sure he was holding a gun in his fist.

Marc had the advantage of location, which he knew in detail. Very quickly he decided to head for another point in the forest, still high up but not as steep, where he could easily creep up on Vauthier with his gun aimed at him. He withdrew and moved soundlessly up to the new bluff. When he got there, Vauthier the intruder had also climbed and was only ten yards away. Marc decided to call out.

"Get your hands out of your pockets, Vauthier, and above your head!"

Vauthier hardly seemed surprised. He did as he was told, pretending to smile.

"I didn't think I'd find you out in this weather," Vauthier said calmly. "You'll catch cold."

"What are you doing here?"

"We are part of the same convoy, aren't we? Didn't you want us to come and find you?"

"What have you done with the others?"

"They're waiting for me a bit farther along. I guess they're not as eager to see you as I am."

The situation was increasingly absurd. The snow was gently falling, covering their hair and eyelashes with white flakes. Marc's pistol looked like a marzipan figurine covered with icing sugar. For a moment he felt like lowering his guard, and holding his hand out to Vauthier. After all, nothing had destined them to be enemies, nothing justified Vauthier's violence. But he immediately regained his self-control. Since childhood, he had known that things are not like that, that nothing explains hatred, that weakness merely exacerbates it, that there can be no forgiveness without force or without victory. This brief moment where Marc was lost in troubling reflection sufficed for Vauthier to leap behind a trunk, and a moment later he fired. The shot raised dust from a tree's bark just next to Marc but didn't hit him. He barely had time to hide in turn behind a fir tree.

Maud, in the hut, heard the shots. She put the little girl down and went out, not taking the time to put a coat on. She could not see more than ten yards ahead through the curtain of snow; the shots must have come from higher up the slope. Two more rang out. She went back into the hut.

Vauthier was extremely agile, in spite of the snow. He jumped from one tree to the next and Marc couldn't get him. At one point he saw him spring between two fir trees and he fired. But the bullet landed in wood, with a dull thud. A moment later, as he was heading toward the place he thought his aggressor was hiding, a shot rang out behind him and barely missed him. Vauthier had managed to go around and must now be somewhere behind him.

It was as if everything was in suspense, ominous. The inert whiteness of the landscape seemed to be waiting for blood to come alive. Two lives on borrowed time, stalking beneath the shroud of snow and fog.

Marc took off the long coat: it was making it hard for him to run, and the dark color was too visible. Underneath he was wearing a light gray fleece which blended better with the landscape. He hung the coat on a tree before springing to the next one. From there he heard another shot and saw the coat swing. A bullet had gone through it, fired from higher up.

The two duelists circled around the woods, each one trying to surprise the other by taking him from the rear. It looked as if neither would win at that game: Marc's training and Vauthier's cunning canceled each other out. In the beginning, Marc fired in self-defense: he wanted to neutralize his adversary, to shoot him in the arms or legs but spare his life. But it didn't take him long to realize that Vauthier was shooting to kill. When his bullets lodged in the bark of the fir trees, it was at eye level. A rage to kill came over Marc.

There could be no truce, only victor and vanquished.

The silent duel unfolded to the rhythm of the danger, at times rushed, when one of them thought he'd nabbed the other and fired; extremely slowly in the interludes when the threat was once again invisible and they moved silently to change position.

Until there came the sound of an engine on the road. This was yet another danger, because it distracted them from their vigilance and directed their hearing elsewhere. In comparison with the almost imperceptible rustling as they brushed against branches, or the snow crunching as they leapt from one tree to the next, the chug of the diesel seemed like a vulgar din, crushing every other sensation.

Marc did not know what to make of the sound. Was it his Croatian friends, and if so, should he be pleased? Or was it Lionel and Alex coming to lend Vauthier a hand? Should he wait, play for time and count on some help from outside? Or should he precipitate the outcome, to avoid having to confront any new adversaries?

Vauthier had been following the same line of thought, and he decided to intensify his craftiness and aggression. He fired more frequently, more precisely. Marc escaped one of his bullets only because of an involuntary move he made while preparing his next leap. The bullet landed in the tree trunk he thought he was hiding behind, and missed him by only an inch or so.

The truck on the road was drawing nearer, and before long it stopped. A door slammed. Then the silence returned.

Just then Marc saw Vauthier from behind, crouching on the ground. He hadn't even realized that his adversary had circled around him. He was at some distance, and Marc had the time to take precise aim. He held the 9 mm with both hands, and lined up his foresight on the target, like during practice.

It all happened very quickly. A voice rang out, lower down, on the path leading to the hut. It was Alex. Vauthier turned around, pivoting on himself. Marc was distracted by the voice, and his aim was off. The shot went wide. As he got to his feet, Vauthier fired blind, with one hand.

Alex heard the shots and headed straight for them, up the slope. Branches tore at him; clumps of snow fell on his face.

When he reached Marc he found him lying facedown. He turned him over. A bullet had gone into his shoulder. There was a clean little hole in his gray fleece. The blood must be flowing on the inside because on the surface all you could see was the cloth with its clean cookie-cutter mark.

In the same instant, another shot rang out. It came from much higher up and it wasn't the sound of a pistol. A few yards away Alex saw Vauthier's head where he was lying on the ground, behind a tree, inert.

Lionel arrived in turn, after struggling up the steep slope. He looked at the scene, failing to understand.

"Go see to Vauthier, I'll take care of Marc," shouted Alex.

He had opened his friend's jacket and was trying to see how serious the wound was. As he had thought, there was blood all over his chest, his scarlet, warm, living blood. The shock had winded him momentarily. His breathing was uneven. Alex slapped him on both cheeks and he opened his eyes.

Lionel had reached Vauthier. He turned him over: Vauthier had collapsed facedown in the snow.

"Jesus Christ," shouted Lionel, "he killed him!"

But when he opened his blood-soaked jacket, he saw that Vauthier was still breathing. He had a bloody wound just above his belly.

From the road came the sound of vehicles. Doors slammed.

Before long an entire group began climbing up the track leading to the hut. Alex called out for help. Two Croatian soldiers
in uniform appeared beyond the fir trees. Several others followed, officers among them. Alex didn't take the time to find
out who they were. The most urgent thing was to get the
wounded men to shelter.

He grabbed hold of Marc, who was moaning, and the soldiers lifted his legs. Others went over to Lionel and helped him
carry Vauthier, who was still unconscious. The two groups
went back to the track and slowly up to the hut.

"They've killed each other," said Lionel, pale and distraught.

"I don't think so. Marc was already hit when someone fired
on Vauthier."

"Are you sure?"

"Absolutely, I saw him fall. He was lying on the ground
when the other shot was fired. It couldn't be him."

"But who, then?"

As they continued up the track they found the truck parked
under the low-hanging branches of a larch tree, protected from
the snow. Lionel was dismayed to see how damaged it was. A
futile thought, given the general catastrophe, but he could not
help but think of what his bosses would say: after all, they had
entrusted him with this materiel.

Alex was staring at the door to the hut, which had not been
closed properly and was creaking with every gust of wind. He
motioned to the Croatian soldiers who were helping him carry
Marc to put him on the ground for a moment. Marc had
regained consciousness and was moaning. Behind them, Lionel
also stopped and lowered Vauthier to the ground.

There were footprints in the slush outside the hut but there
was no one in sight. Off to one side a long object lay in the
snow. Alex approached it cautiously and bent down to pick it
up. It was an old Mauser rifle. Droplets were forming along its

well-oiled barrel from the humidity. He handed it to Lionel, who took it awkwardly, aghast.

Then he kept walking. He'd had the presence of mind to retrieve Marc's pistol and he held it out in front of him. His military reflexes had come back to him, and he wedged himself against the door frame and kicked the door open. The room was dark; holding his weapon out toward the interior he stood for a long moment in the door, the time it took for his eyes to get used to the dark.

The room was silent, but with his senses on the alert Alex perceived a soft, intermittent sound, a sort of irregular breathing, not even a whimper. The first thing he could make out in the darkness was the eyes of a little girl. She was standing in the middle of the room, staring sternly at him. He went in.

There was someone he could see only from behind, who seemed to be sleeping, their upper body slumped on the table. As his eyes adjusted, he recognized Maud's hair. At first he thought that she was dead, too. But gradually he made the connection with the faint sound he could hear and he saw that beneath her fleece she was breathing. She was not asleep. Her breathing was jerky, irregular, and with each exhalation there was a sort of hiccup. He went closer and realized she was sobbing. When the little girl saw him approach Maud, she pressed herself against her and put her thin arm around her.

Alex realized he still had the gun held out in front of him and he lowered it.

Lionel had followed him inside, and when he spoke his voice shattered the thick silence enveloping the scene.

"What's wrong with her?"

Alex motioned to him to be quiet. He squatted next to the table and the child, reassured by his gentle movements, stepped back.

"Marc is here, outside."

Her initial reflex was to push him away with her hand, so

he would leave her alone. She even shot him a brief, indignant look, as if his desire to show her Marc's body was sickening and cruel. But when she met his gaze she saw nothing there but gentleness and surprise. She sat up, slowly, and stared at him:

"You mean?"

"He's alive, yes. We need to make some room to bring him in here."

But she was already on her feet, rushing out the door.

"Where is he?"

5

When she saw Marc fall, after Vauthier's bullet hit him, Maud was instantly convinced he'd been killed. It was a strange reflex, but one that made sense to her, given the atmosphere of these last days. The violence, vengeance, and danger meant that death hounded the fugitives and filled all their thoughts.

Now when she saw Marc there outside, alive and even conscious, sitting on the ground holding one hand to his wounded shoulder, Maud succumbed to a flood of nervous tears mingled with joyful laughter. She fell on her knees in the snow and kissed him, she caressed his face, which was covered with dried sweat and a scattering of pine needles.

She got up and shoved the soldiers to get them to carry Marc into the hut at once. But he insisted on walking and she helped him stand. He put his good arm around her shoulder. It was a joy for her to feel his weight, which she almost could not bear, and to watch the warm vapor rising into the air before her face as she breathed with the effort. Marc staggered the last few feet and went into the hut. The terrified little girls were cowering by the door to the stable, their eyes huge with fright.

In the meantime Lionel and two soldiers struggled up the track carrying Vauthier. Unconscious, he was heavier than ever, and they had to put him down in the snow several times to catch their breath. When they were finally inside the hut, there was a crush; the room was small and there were many of them now, encumbered by the inert body in their midst. The Croats were shouting something in their language but no one seemed to understand. Initially they laid Vauthier down on the threshold, with his head outside. Then Lionel shoved the big table against the wall and they lifted him up to put him on it.

Marc sat in the only armchair in the room, his legs stretched out on the stool. The soldiers didn't know whether they should stay there or go out, so they stood clustered by the door. Maud came and went, fetching water by the sink, taking sugar and alcohol from the cupboard.

Suddenly more men in uniform arrived. There were five or six of them, but there was no more room, so several of them stayed outside. All the soldiers stood at attention, because one of the newcomers was wearing an officer's stripes.

Alex thought he had seen him somewhere before. Then he recognized him: it was Filipović, the "general" commanding the Croatian forces in the sector. He'd known him in Kakanj, although he had never been on such a friendly basis with him as Marc had. He went up to him and embraced him.

But this was no time for effusiveness. There were urgent decisions to be made. As the military leader, Filipović was the key to the situation. But above all, he was a doctor. He could examine the wounded men, give them first aid, and a prognosis.

Alex instinctively led the physician over to Marc, even though his case was less urgent.

Filipović hadn't noticed him in the gloom. When he saw him, he went over and warmly shook his good hand.

"You came!"

"Yes," said Marc, "and I kept my promise."

On hearing their words and seeing the air of complicity between the two men, Alex frowned. Filipović must have known about Marc's plans; perhaps he was even the one who had organized and financed this whole business with the explosives.

And yet Marc had always pretended to Alex that he believed they were construction explosives. In short, he had lied. And maybe he was the one to blame for this whole sad affair.

Maud had been looking after the patient all the while. Not without difficulty, she had removed his fleece and now she was trying to cut away his shirt, which was clinging to the wound, sticky with blood. Filipović helped her and examined the wound.

"The bullet went out the back," he concluded, standing up. "It went through the soft tissue in your shoulder. The only damage is to the muscles. Nothing serious. It was the shock that knocked you out."

He took Marc's blood-soaked shirt and tore off a strip of cloth.

"This will give you some relief," he said, once he'd tied the knot on the makeshift splint. "When we get to a hospital, we'll see what needs to be done."

"Thanks," said Marc, then pointing to Vauthier, unconscious on the table: "He's the one you should see to, urgently."

Before Filipović headed over to the table Marc held him back for a moment with his good hand.

"I brought what I promised," he whispered.

The Croat gave him a knowing smile, but his expression was quizzical, almost pitying. He put his palm on Marc's cheek.

"Don't you worry about that," he said.

He got up and went over to the table. With the help of one of the soldiers, Lionel had uncovered Vauthier's stomach. He was dabbing at the wound; the cloth was already soaked with blood. Vauthier had regained consciousness but seemed to be drifting in a state of confusion and delirium. He was moaning, his skin drained of color.

After examining Vauthier for a long time, the doctor took Lionel to one side.

"The bullet didn't touch any vital organs. But it's still

inside, and he's losing a lot of blood. If he stops bleeding, he may survive, but it can start again at any time. We have to get him out of here urgently."

"Isn't there anything to give him for the pain? It must be terrible."

"We don't have any medications on us. We have to take him to town."

"Okay, then, go ahead. Take him right away."

"We can't take him in any of our trucks. They're for troop transport, the wagon at the back is open to the elements, and the springs are gone in the front seat, it's no good. Are there bunks in your trucks?"

"In one of them, yes."

"All right, then we can lay him down on it. Marc, can you sit up? We won't be able to go very fast. The road is in poor condition. It will take us at least three hours."

"I'll be all right."

Maud had given him something to drink and his color was slowly returning.

"Where is the truck with the bunk?"

"Down below, on the road."

"Go get it and park it here, behind the other one."

Lionel was preparing to leave when Filipović motioned to him. He took him aside again.

"How did this happen?"

"They shot each other, I think."

"With what weapons?"

"Vauthier had a 9 mm, and Marc, too, I think."

"Pistols? For Marc's wound, that seems right. But the other guy had a bullet from a weapon of war . . . Anyway, it doesn't matter. We have to get them out of here first."

He waved to Lionel to go ahead and told two soldiers to go with him.

The departures left some space in the room. Alija had been

waiting outside, and now he seized the moment to dash in. His sister rushed to him with a cry of joy.

The convoy was together again, almost like when it first set off, but that was the only joyful thing about it. They drove one behind the other, Maud's truck in the lead with Marc by her side. Lionel followed, alone at the wheel, while Vauthier moaned on the bunk behind.

The sky had cleared as if to celebrate their reunion. A bright sun shone on the snow-covered fields. The dark summits filled the horizon to the north, and to the south, beyond the barren slopes, they could see the distant misty trace of the Dalmatian coast.

But this new convoy wasn't anything like the one that had left Lyon a few weeks earlier. For a start, the trucks had suffered, particularly the one in the lead, where the tarp had been torn off and the load half emptied; it had been patched up as well as possible. Above all, they were no longer alone. In front of them was the general's command car. Alex had asked to ride with him, because back at the hut he hadn't been able to ask Filipović all the questions he was dying to ask. Behind them came two troop transports. Men in arms, muffled up in their long capes, stood clinging to the slatted sides.

In the first truck Marc sat sideways to avoid absorbing the bumps from the road in his injured shoulder. He had to turn his back to Maud as she drove.

She couldn't see his face. she wondered if, as the pain ebbed, he would once again put on his tight, inscrutable daytime expression, or whether she would recognize his nighttime features, when the tension receded and he was open to tenderness. As there was no way of knowing, she remained cautiously silent and felt somewhat awkward. Once the time for anxiety and urgent gestures was behind them, she wondered how all this would affect Marc, what state of mind he would be in. She didn't know whether he was grateful to her for her attentiveness or whether, on the contrary, he would resent her for having witnessed his weakness. She did not want to be the first one to speak.

Initially, Marc closed his eyes, drowsy. Then he looked out the window. Against the white screen of snowy landscape he was reliving the moments of the hunt in the forest. The images that came to his mind roused him.

"It happened so fast . . . "

Maud wasn't sure he was talking to her.

"He was right there in front of me. And then I heard Alex's voice."

Maud tightened her hands on the steering wheel. The road was full of potholes and she had to hold the truck steady so that it would not tip into the precipice. She gritted her teeth. She, too, saw the scene of the shooting again. She was outside the house. She heard the first shot. Marc fell, his face in the snow. And then she saw Vauthier . . .

"I would never have thought Alex would do such a thing for me."

Marc went on talking to himself. Maud felt tears welling. She clung even tighter to the steering wheel, to stop the tears from coming.

"I thought he was mad at me. Actually, I'm sure he was mad at me. And yet, he did that."

"What did he do?"

Maud had shuddered. Could it be that . . . On hearing her, Marc tried to turn to her but the pain stopped him midway.

"Kill Vauthier! Otherwise, I'd be dead already."

Maud almost let go of the wheel from the emotion. All at once she realized the extent of the misunderstanding. She felt like laughing, and as her face lit up, a single tear slipped out, no longer warranted. She gave herself a moment to be sure her voice would not tremble with emotion, then she said at last, "It wasn't Alex who shot Vauthier."

It took Marc a moment to understand what her words implied.

"Who was it, then?"

He turned abruptly, and he winced with pain when his shoulder touched the hard seat.

Maud had never felt such a tangle of feelings inside her all at the same time.

She turned to him with a smile. They looked deeply into each other's eyes. For the first time, she was certain he could see her. And that he was taking the full measure of what her love was capable of.

The general's command car was an old Soviet model. The steering was loose. The soldier who was driving constantly swung his arms to the right then to the left, and his passengers were on the verge of feeling carsick.

Filipović was sitting in front. The dashboard and the door on his side were littered with empty beer cans and cigarette packs used as ashtrays. Alex was squeezed in behind, in a tight space among khaki backpacks and piles of old newspapers.

Filipović had not stopped asking him about their trip, the incidents that had happened along the way, and the reasons for the shoot-out between Vauthier and Marc.

Alex had to tell him everything and explain who was who in the group. As he summed up the events, he was struck by how absurd it all was. Why they had behaved the way they did remained a mystery, in more ways than one. The only thing that stood out in the midst of so much futile destruction was the encounter between Marc and Maud. It was the only edifice to rise from the ruins. As he thought about this, he returned to his own uncertainties and found the courage to interrupt Filipović and question him in turn.

"And Bouba?" he said.

The general looked down. He knew about Alex's hopes.

"She's fine."

Alex waited. Filipović was silent for a long while. Then the doctor in him prevailed. Adopting the cheerful tone of the physician delivering an unfavorable prognosis, who does what he can to attenuate his patient's despair, he decided to come straight out with it.

"She waited for you, Alex. The months went by and she waited for you, believe me. But you know how impatient young women can be."

"I tried to write to her but it's hard, with the war . . . "

"I know, I know. I'm just trying to explain what she might have felt."

Alex had leaned forward and was clinging to the general's seat, unaware that under the pressure of his nails he was tearing the worn brown cloth.

"The main thing, for girls like Bouba, is to get out of this war, you understand, to go and live somewhere else. They know, perhaps better than we do, that time is passing . . . "

"And?"

"And there was a team of German journalists who came to do a report on Kakanj."

He broke off and looked furtively at the young man, and decided that it would hurt less if he delivered one clean, sharp blow.

"She left with a photographer. A very decent fellow, very serious. He arranged everything to get her out of Bosnia with her refugee papers. I think they got married as soon as they got to Leipzig."

Alex was staring straight ahead of him. He had gone pale. Filipović, not turning around, laid a fatherly hand on Alex's where it still gripped the seat back.

"Take heart," he said. "It's surely for the best."

The winter sun, level with the mountaintops, flooded into the cab and dazzled them with its unbearably white light.

6

In the other truck the atmosphere was morose. On his bunk Vauthier was no longer moaning, and had fallen asleep.

Lionel was somewhat reassured to see the convoy back together again. It gave a semblance of normality to the mission. He hoped that from here on he'd be able to get everyone home safe and sound. To be sure, the materiel was damaged, and a good part of the load was missing. But none of that really mattered.

The two wounded men were more of a problem. However, their regrettable condition was the result of a purely private quarrel. If he analyzed the situation one element·after the other, Lionel concluded that his case was less desperate than he had feared. Anyone who did not know what had really happened during the trip would think, when all was said and done, that the result was almost positive. The problem for Lionel was that he did know what had happened. He could not forget that he had completely lost control of events. As head of mission he had turned out to be a complete failure. He need not admit this to others; but confronted with himself, he could not hide it.

And yet, what troubled him the most, the source of his greatest anguish, was the realization of his utter solitude. In this regard, the most painful failure was Maud's betrayal. All things considered, he had undertaken the trip for her sake or, at least, with an eye to winning her over. He had to admit that, in fact, he had neither the inclination nor the talent for working in the field, particularly in a position of responsibility. He had been at his happiest during his stint in Lyon, at the headquarters of La Tête d'Or. Were it not for his stupid plan to gain even greater influence over Maud, to win her once and for all, he would never have set out on this wild venture.

In their close quarters in the trucks, he had also come to realize that he was not at all popular with the others. In the end, the only one he felt close to, whom he might actually have befriended, was Vauthier. Of course he knew that Vauthier was using him. He had even gone so far as to threaten him. And yet Lionel went on feeling inexplicably drawn to him, more out of admiration than affection.

And now the only one he felt close to was lying on his bunk between life and death. Lionel felt that solitude and failure were leaving their mark on him. In the silence of the cab, he surrendered willingly to his brooding thoughts.

Suddenly he give a start: just behind his ear a deep voice had spoken. He glanced behind him and saw that Vauthier had turned slightly onto his side. His head was just behind the driver's seat, so in spite of the engine noise Lionel could distinctly hear his words.

"Say, are you feeling better?" he asked. "You're awake."

"No point driving fast," said Vauthier again.

"Why?"

"'Cause I'm going to die."

Vauthier gave a weary wave of his hand. Lionel turned his head for an instant. He could see the purple shadows under Vauthier's eyes, his waxy skin, his pinched nostrils searching for breath.

"What do you mean? You're doing better."

"I'd like something to drink."

"Filipović said you mustn't. Because of the wound in your stomach, you understand?"

"I'm fucked either way."

Lionel protested again, but he noticed Vauthier's parted lips, how terribly dry they were, his teeth covered with a sticky white coating. He reached for a plastic water bottle in the door and handed it to Vauthier.

"Thanks."

He drank, stopping to breathe between each sip. There was a long silence.

"Tell me something."

Vauthier's voice was clearer now that he had drunk something.

"What?"

"Is he dead?"

"Who? Marc?"

"Who else?"

Lionel adjusted the inside rearview mirror to look at Vauthier. He could see his sharp gaze.

"No, he didn't die. He's just hurt."

"Is he going to make it?"

"Sure. It doesn't look too bad."

"Shit."

In the rearview mirror, Lionel saw Vauthier close his eyes. And suddenly he was afraid he might drift off and not wake up again, like an exhausted mountain climber in a blizzard. He had to keep talking to him, to keep him awake, provoke him even, so that he would mobilize all his strength and not let death come any nearer.

"There's something I don't get, Vauthier. Why do you hate Marc so much?"

Vauthier opened his eyes and stared at the gray canvas ceiling splattered with spots of dirty grease.

"Hatred . . . " he said thoughtfully. "How can you explain hatred?"

He was still holding the open water bottle in his outstretched hand. Now he raised it to his lips, but spilled some water on his face. He shook his jowls like a dog shaking itself. His eyes were shining with something like joy.

"Hatred is happiness. You don't know that yet, do you? It's a passion, a reason for living. It's a real luxury. Maybe the only luxury."

Lionel observed this monologue out of the corner of his eye. He was glad he'd attained his goal: Vauthier was no longer drifting off. But now he mustn't get too excited.

"Hatred is as strong as love. Except you don't need to ask the other person for their opinion."

He took another swallow of water and moved his dry lips to soften them.

"Okay," said Lionel, "but why Marc?"

It was actually a question he'd been wanting to ask for a long time, a question he could also ask himself, because he'd disliked Marc, too, even long before Maud went off with him.

"It's like love, I told you. There's nothing to understand. You can never understand. You can always find reasons, but they're false."

Lionel suddenly got the impression that Vauthier was having more difficulty breathing.

"There's just one condition," he added, his voice hoarser and not as loud, but forced, as if he wanted to get his message across. "To hate, you need someone who's like you."

"You think that you and Marc are alike?"

"Not identical. Not equal. But similar. Look at the people around here. Look at their hatred. They're different. But similar."

Vauthier let out a long, loud moan, almost a stifled cry. Lionel saw he was holding his stomach.

"Are you all right?"

Vauthier's entire body was taut, writhing with a searing pain. It was taking his breath away, as if he'd received a violent punch in the stomach. The spasm lasted a few seconds, then he

292 · JEAN-CHRISTOPHE RUFIN

relaxed. Lionel wondered if he should stop or, rather, wave to the others to go faster, in hopes of reaching the hospital sooner.

"In any case, tell him something for me," continued Vauthier, his voice scarcely audible. "Tell him, you swear?"

"Tell who? Marc?"

"Yes."

"I swear. What is it?"

"He'll find out anyway but I want it to come from me."

"What will he find out?"

There was another spasm. Vauthier was holding his stomach with both hands. Blood was oozing out through his fingers clenched against his wound.

"His explosives . . . "

"Well?"

"In town, you remember when we stopped for the night?"

"At UN headquarters?"

"Yes."

"Well?"

"We took them out. We couldn't take the risk."

"You mean . . . "

"There's nothing left in his truck. Nothing."

The road had just passed below a fortress, one of those castles that had been the glory of Bosnia in the Middle Ages. For centuries its parapets and crenellated towers had been keeping watch over the place where two valleys opened out. Once a front line, now the place was deserted, and no invader would dream of going by there. In winter the old walls served as a refuge for jackdaws and raptors.

Oddly enough, instead of being reassuring, this human vestige made the stony landscape even more desolate and gloomy. An image of strength vanquished by time, the fortress clinging to its rock made all human endeavor to conquer death seem derisory. These surroundings left an overwhelming impression of fragility, cold, and extreme solitude. A heavy silence reigned in each of the vehicles.

In the silence Filipović heard the faint sound of a car horn far behind him. He opened his window and leaned out. The convoy had stopped and he was a hundred yards ahead. He motioned to his driver to halt and he got out.

"Stay here," he said to Alex, still sitting behind. "I'll find out what's going on."

The snow was melting in the sun and the general's military boots sank in, leaving deep footprints on the road. When he reached the convoy he saw that Lionel had gotten out of his truck and walked over to the one Maud was driving; he was leaning against the door.

Filipović went over to Marc's side; Marc rolled down the window.

"What's going on?"

All three of them were silent, their faces haggard. Lionel had one arm on Maud's window and was staring into space. A Croatian soldier had sold him some weed back at the hut. Now he'd made a huge joint and was taking long, deep puffs.

"Vauthier's dead," said Marc.

This was sad news, of course. But no surprise to Filipović, who knew how bad his wound was. He thought the others knew, too; it shouldn't have come as a surprise to them. He could not understand why they looked so downcast, particularly as he knew their story, and knew that they had any number of reasons to despise Vauthier.

"It's tragic, of course," he said. "But you knew it might happen, didn't you?"

They didn't answer, so he followed another line of thought. Maybe they were worried about the legal consequences of his death.

"You cannot be accused of anything. It was legitimate defense."

Still the silence, and Lionel noisily inhaling his smoke. Maud held her face in her hands. Finally Marc spoke, eyes lowered.

"That's not it."

"What is it then?"

"The explosives . . . "

"Well?"

"You know I came back because of that."

"Yes, I understood," said the general somewhat formally. "You implied as much. Thank you. Our poor people will be truly grateful. And all of you—"

Marc was getting impatient. Shaking his good arm, he moved his torso, and this hurt his shoulder. He made a face.

"No, no. Don't say that. When you find out . . . "

"Find out what?"

"That bastard Vauthier and his cop buddies removed the explosives from the truck."

"What do you mean?"

"We stopped for one night in town, at a UN building. Apparently, they took the opportunity to search the load. We did all that for nothing."

Marc did not have the outlet of tears. For him, sorrow took the form of a rush of dry-eyed rage. He thought about the bridge they would not destroy, the war that would go on, the helplessness of the world, with which he could not reconcile himself. Filipović held out his hand and squeezed his arm.

"Listen, Marc, it's normal for you to be disappointed. Only a few days ago if you had told me this I would have been desperate. But now everything has changed."

"I don't see why."

It was only then that Filipović understood. The convoy had been on the road and they must not have heard. Everything had fallen into place so quickly.

"Of course, how could you know . . . There was a massacre

in Sarajevo, at a market. The international community was unanimous in its condemnation, and at last they decided to do something. NATO has entered the war. Their planes have been bombing every day."

Maud lifted her head and Marc looked at Filipović, stunned.

"And guess what one of their first targets was . . . the bridge over the Drina!"

"The one we wanted to blow up with our explosives?"

"The very one. There's nothing left. You should see it."

Maud and Marc looked at each other, incredulous. But Filipović, more and more excited, continued his story.

"They've been striking barracks as well. You should see them run, those bastards. They don't know where to hide now. Planes are attacking tanks, troop convoys, artillery posts. And in the meantime our own forces have been advancing. We're winning, do you understand?"

"There will be peace soon," said Maud, thinking suddenly of the little girls in the hut.

"And it's victory they need, first and foremost!" exclaimed Filipović.

Marc's very words. She looked at him. He had closed his eyes. His features had softened and for the first time, in the pale light of the snowy day, she saw his nighttime face.

Then everyone suddenly relaxed and they all burst out laughing. Even Lionel, still leaning on the window, roused himself.

Filipović reached into his pocket for a flask, and they all drank to this happiness that had returned, by way of defeat.

Alex, all the while, was still waiting for the general. He climbed out of the old jeep to stretch his legs. The news of Bouba's marriage was beginning to sink in, and he felt less pain, less trouble. It had been a blow, and now it left him feeling as if he were recovering from a bad hangover. He realized he had spent all these weeks in a trance.

He walked a few steps ahead of the command car, looking off into the distance. It was twilight, and invisible veils in the sky were tinted orange and green. The mountaintops were already dark. Suddenly, from the snowy north, he saw a flock of wading birds heading due south. They were in perfect formation, powerful and serene as they flew off into the distance.

Alex thought that he, too, ought to be looking for a new place of exile, but this time he would go far away from the cold climate, from these mountains he'd thought were his own, under love's illusion.

With a smile he decided he, too, would leave and head for the sun.

AFTERWORD

S ome readers might be surprised that I decided to use the English word "checkpoint" as the title for this book. It is true that unlike "checklist" or "checkup," the word "checkpoint" does not yet have an entry in French language dictionaries. And yet to me it seems the word has no real equivalent, and that it has acquired an almost universal use, including in our language. The official translation, "point de contrôle" (or "poste de contrôle"), is not really satisfactory. It only covers one of the word's meanings: that which refers to a classic military use, for example the famous checkpoint between West and East Berlin, Checkpoint Charlie.

The checkpoints to be found in many places on the globe are not nearly as well-ordered. They reflect the chaos, violence, and fragmentation endemic to countries in the midst of civil war—in the Middle East, in Africa, or in Eastern Europe. In these extreme situations, the border is everywhere. Every man becomes the guardian of his own territory. A rope strung across a road, a few shacks made of leaves, often rudimentary weapons, and there you are, at a checkpoint.

From a metaphorical point of view, the checkpoint has also become the symbol of the passage from one world to another, from one established ensemble of values to its converse, a door onto the unknown, perhaps danger.

Today, in particular since the bloody attacks upon France in January and November 2015, we are experiencing a radical shift. We feel we are standing at a mental border now. The need for *security tends to prevail over all other considerations. It would be an illusion to think that humanitarian work will be left out of this transformation of mentalities.*

For half a century we dreamt of ourselves as kindly, generous, and charitable. Humanitarian, in other words. Conflicts unfolded elsewhere, far away, and those citizens who wanted, here, to get involved did so according to the ideals of Henri Dunant: humanity, impartiality, neutrality.

Over recent years, this peace-loving face of humanitarian work has yielded several times to military involvement. To assist the populations of Libya, Syria, and Ukraine, the international community finally resolves to arm them. First it was supplies that were parachuted, then before long it was weapons. The United States, with a head start of fifteen years in its confrontation with terrorism, has long been converted to offensive intervention: in Kosovo, Afghanistan, and Iraq, they bombed in the name of human rights. Once again, they were pointing the way to the future, and now everyone in the West is ready to imitate them. Because the victims are no longer far away, now, but close at hand. It is no longer just the Other who is made to suffer; it is we ourselves.

This evolution does not only concern states and their armies; it reflects a debate that concerns each of us.

This novel dramatizes these contradictions, questions, and heartbreak. It has been constructed like a sort of in camera road movie. Through their own personal drama, the five characters confined in the cabs of the two trucks experience in real time a radical change of their world, a change in which all convictions are overturned. They have embarked on a "classic" humanitarian mission—to deliver food and medicine to civilian victims of the war; they will go through real checkpoints but also confront a more essential mental border. What do the "victims" need—to survive or to win? Where must aid go: to their animal side, demanding sustenance and shelter, or to their strictly human side, demanding the wherewithal to fight, even at the risk of self-sacrifice?

To illustrate these dilemmas I decided to drive the trucks across the territory of another war, in Bosnia. This choice allowed me to divest this book of anything that might have seemed too preoccupied with the details of an unstable present, where ephemeral adventures occult essential issues. The war in the former Yugoslavia happened long enough ago to seem almost forgotten. One does not need to know it in detail to understand what the characters in this book are going through. Everything one needs to know can be found in the course of the book. This war is simply one example of chaos, without the exoticism of Africa or Asia necessarily setting it at a greater emotional distance. This is Europe tearing itself apart, a Europe where everyone has decided to take up arms for protection against the threat they are afraid of. There is a bit of our present day in this long-ago past and, I fear, a great deal of our future.

But Bosnia also brings to the story the splendor of its landscape, the cold beauty of winter: monotonous and subtle, it only unveils itself gradually, through slow observation. Above all, Bosnia enabled me to fill this book with images that are also personal memories, buried deep in my mind, memories I thought I'd forgotten.

One episode in particular affected me deeply. In the middle of one winter during the war, after a long journey in an uncomfortable armored vehicle, I went into the power plant in Kakanj, and I got a shock. All the machinery fallen silent, crows croaking as they flew over the site, the dirty snow clinging to the black mass of the plant's huge corrugated iron sheds: it all came together to make the site into a representation of the end of the world. A detachment of peacekeepers, from the French Engineers, were guarding that desolate place to prevent any further massacres. When a young sapper opened one of the huge coal ovens for me and in the dim light I saw a family of refugees huddling against the metal for its faint warmth, I felt that here was the stage set of a tragedy. But at the same time the young French soldier, as he spoke to one of the daughters of the family, looked at her in a way that clearly showed the two of them were in love. So at the very heart of what was so inhuman, a sort of hope went on living. All sorts of reversals were possible: those who had come to offer their protection, instead of fighting, were making love. But one could sense that in the name of that love, those soldiers might come back again someday, alone, and really fight. I promised myself I would make that scene into a novel one day. And then I forgot about it.

In the meantime, the world has changed, and very quickly. Now from the Eastern Christians to the cartoonists of *Charlie Hebdo*, from the kidnapped girls of Nigeria to the beheaded hostages in Syria, there are new victims everywhere, and in them I see the face I glimpsed that day in Kakanj, the fiancée of the coal ovens.

One would like to love these victims with a special kind of love: the love that is a call to arms.